CALLING BACK THE DEAD

A NORTHERN MICHIGAN ASYLUM NOVEL

J.R. ERICKSON

DEDICATION

For my lifelong ladies: Cherie, Bufe, Audra, Hannah, and Carrie

AUTHOR'S NOTE

Thanks so much for picking up a Northern Michigan Asylum Novel. I want to offer a disclaimer before you dive into the story. This is an entirely fictional novel. Although there was once a real place known as The Northern Michigan Asylum - which inspired me to write these books - it is in no way depicted within them. Although my story takes place there, the characters in this story are not based on any real people who worked at this asylum or were patients; any resemblance to individuals, living or dead, is entirely coincidental. Likewise, the events which take place in the novel are not based on real events, and any resemblance to real events is also coincidental.

In truth, nearly every book I have read about the asylum, later known as the Traverse City State Hospital, was positive. This holds true for the stories of many of the staff who worked there as well. I live in the Traverse City area and regularly visit the grounds of the former asylum. It's now known as The Village at Grand Traverse Commons. It was purchased in 2000 by Ray Minervini and the Minervini Group who have been restoring it since that time.

Today, it's a mixed-use space of boutiques, restaurants and condominiums. If you ever visit the area, I encourage you to visit

The Village at Grand Traverse Commons. You can experience first-hand the asylums - both old and new - and walk the sprawling grounds.

PROLOGUE

he Northern Michigan Asylum for the Insane

1900
Ethel

"I DON'T WANT TO GO," Ethel begged, grabbing at her mother's dress. Her mother pursed her lips and pried Ethel's hands away.

"You've no choice, young lady. Now take your filthy hands from my skirt."

Ethel's father pulled her away from her mother and squatted to face her.

"It will be okay, Ethel. This is just for a little while. They'll get you sorted, and you'll be home in no time at all."

Ethel looked at the towering buildings in the distance, the huge brick structures topped with pointed spires like something from a fairy story, but not a good one. This was an evil castle where a wicked witch lived.

"Please, Father," she whispered, squeezing his hands until it hurt.

1

He stood and kissed her head, turning her toward the door. He nudged her forward, and she wanted to break away, run for the woods. If she escaped, they'd have to look for her, and then they'd be even angrier. Maybe they'd leave her at the hospital forever.

Finally, begrudgingly, she willed her feet forward. The tiny stones rolled beneath her flat shoes.

She studied the windows and saw faces peering down at her. They were dark and long.

"I'm scared," she murmured, and her father squeezed her shoulder.

"You're strong, Ethel, maybe too strong for your own good. There are other children here and doctors, wonderful doctors. You'll see."

They walked through double doors into a bright lobby with yellow walls.

Her father talked to a tall, slim nurse with curly red hair. She smiled kindly at Ethel, and a bit of Ethel's fear slipped away. She heard children laughing. One of them screamed, but not from fear - from delight.

Ethel peeked around the corner into a large room. Kids of all ages ran back and forth. Some sat at tables, drawing and reading, while others huddled in groups on the floor playing with toys. They were strangers, these kids, but they wouldn't be for long. Ethel knew how to make friends. In school, a group of children always followed her wondering what on earth Ethel would do next.

THE ORDERLY UNLOCKED the door and Ethel hurried into the bathroom, skidding to a stop on the icy tiles. She stared in horror at the toilet. Two dead rats floated in the water, their tails entwined. She backed up, shaking her head, and the orderly pressed a firm hand into her back.

"Just flush it, you silly child," she snapped.

"But..." Ethel pointed a shaky finger at the toilet.

"They're just rats, trapped in the night." The orderly pushed her aside and strode to the toilet, pulling the chain hanging above it. The rats swirled and disappeared.

"Go," the orderly barked.

Ethel sat on the cold toilet, legs trembling, squeezing her knees together to keep from looking into the watery bowl.

After she finished, she walked on wobbly legs back to the kids' room. Another patient, a little girl called Eleanor, asked her to play, but Ethel shook her head no. She feared at any moment she might begin to cry and never stop.

ETHEL WOKE in her little room and clenched her blanket close. She had to pee, and stood before realizing she was not in her room at Kerry Manor, but in this square, cold room. Another little girl slept in a bed along the opposite wall. Ethel started toward the door, but something dark and oozy stood there blocking it. She saw glowing red eyes in its black, shapeless face. She crawled beneath her covers. She heard it drag across the floor and pause at her bedside. Its sour breath poured hot through her thin blanket. She tried not to move a muscle, but fear loosened her bladder and warm pee spread into the mattress beneath her.

"TAKE OFF YOUR NIGHTDRESS," the orderly snapped.

She was a large woman with a face made severe by hair pulled so tightly in a bun it stretched the skin of her forehead and cheekbones.

Ethel glanced down the hall where other kids stood - some watching, others adrift in their own thoughts.

"I'll be naked," she whispered.

"And that's what happens when you wet the bed," the orderly said, pointing an accusing finger at a pile of linen with a visible yellow stain.

Ethel's face grew warm.

"Take off your nightdress, now!" the woman snarled.

"I won't," Ethel said, gritting her teeth.

Before she could react, the orderly shoved Ethel's head down, grabbed the bottom of her nightgown, and wrenched it over her head.

Ethel crossed her arms over her chest, turning away from the hall of kids.

"Those too," the woman hissed, pointing at her underpants.

Ethel shook her head and when the woman grabbed her arm, Ethel leaned down and bit her as hard as she could.

The orderly howled and shoved Ethel to the ground.

Another woman ran into the corridor, and together they lifted Ethel, kicking and screaming, and carried her down the hall to the seclusion room.

"Noooo," Ethel raged, kicking hard at the other woman, who was smaller with blonde hair tucked under a white cap. Her heel connected with the woman's jaw, and she cried out but held on to Ethel's wriggling legs.

They left her on the bed, naked and shivering. She wanted to go home, but when she thought of home and her parents sitting warm by the fire, she hated them. She hated them for sending her away.

"HELLO, ETHEL. HOW ARE YOU TODAY?" The doctor squatted down and smiled at her, revealing two rows of overly large teeth.

He reminded Ethel of her cousin's horse, Patriot, and she tried not to laugh.

"Nurse Jenson told me you wet the bed again last night?"

Ethel frowned and bit her lip.

"I'm scared to walk to the bathroom," she whispered.

"There's always an orderly in the hall, you know? They'd be happy to take you."

Ethel blinked at him. The night orderly's name was Gertrude. She was big and red-faced, and the other kids said she'd pinch you if you were bad.

"Yes, sir. I will next time."

"That's a good girl." The doctor patted her on the head. The doctor glanced down the hall, and Ethel followed his gaze. They were alone.

"Tonight's a full moon, Ethel. Did you know that?"

Ethel nodded.

"Nurse Jenson told Paula that this place is busy on the full moon."

The doctor smiled and nodded.

"Yes, exactly. Many people believe the full moon affects people, especially people of a certain disposition."

"Crazy people?" Ethel asked, shivering. She wasn't crazy, but she knew the big hospital contained lots of crazy people. "Will they try to escape?" she asked.

"Oh, no. We're very secure here. But the full moon is special for many reasons. Some of us doctors have a special meeting on the full moon. Would you like to come to the meeting? If you do, it has to be our secret. You can't tell anyone."

Ethel stared at the doctor's small brown eyes. They seemed too close in his face, but still she had to look at one, and then the other, which felt silly.

"Like a party?" she asked, knowing the other kids would be terribly jealous if Ethel were chosen for a special party.

"Sort of," the doctor said.

IT WAS WELL after lights-out when the doctor slipped quietly into Ethel's room. He helped her into her shoes and coat, and put a finger to his lips.

Once on the grounds, Ethel walked between two doctors. Neither held her hand. She searched the dark shapes of the trees. What if a beast jumped out and grabbed her? They would never catch it in time.

She wanted to reach for one of their hands, but they were deep in conversation, as if they'd forgotten she was there. She suddenly didn't want the attention of being the sole child at the party. She wanted to go back to her plain little room and listen to Mary snoring. Most of all, she wanted to be back at Kerry Manor, dozing beneath the lace canopy suspended above her bed. She would never defy her mother again or fight with the other kids at school.

After an endless walk, one of the doctors put a hand on her shoulder.

"Down this hill," he said, guiding her down a steep hill into a valley of odd white trees crawling over the ground. A huge weeping willow stood in their center.

Ethel wondered what might lie hidden beneath its tentacle-like branches.

"Over here," the doctor said, and they stopped at a wall of brush. Ethel looked up at him, wondering if he was joking, but then the second doctor reached into the brambles and she heard a loud click. A darkness opened before them, and before she could protest, the doctor had pulled her inside.

They were in a damp tunnel lit with torches. The flames cast strange shadows on the floor, and Ethel did not realize she'd stopped until the doctor pulled her roughly forward.

She shook as they walked into the darkness, more like a mouth than a hallway.

"Please," she whispered, but neither man responded.

Forward through the damp, dank tunnel they moved. Ethel had never been so scared in her life, and suddenly feared she would pee her pants and the doctors would be angry. She bit her lip and stuffed her hand between her legs.

More light lay ahead in the tunnel, and soon they left the darkness for a vaulted stone room ablaze with torches. Wooden benches sat in little rows.

In the center of the room, Ethel gazed at a raised stone platform. Two beds stood side by side, and one of them was occupied. The man within it was thin. Her mother would call him *thin as a garden stem*. Ethel stared at his big, sunken eyes like black holes and his teeth with no lips she could see.

"Is he dead?" she whispered, tugging on the doctor's coat.

He seemed finally to register her and carefully removed her hand, tucking it at her side.

"Not at all. He's suffering, to be sure, and that is why you are here tonight, Ethel. We hope you might help him."

"Me?" Ethel put a hand to her chest, surprised.

She noticed other men in the room, some of them talking, others gazing at her curiously. They wore dark suits, and several smoked pipes. One man sat on a wooden bench with a stack of books in his lap and a little silver instrument perched on top. Silver water rose up and down in a glass tube suspended within the little machine.

"I can't help him," Ethel stated. "I'm only ten, and you're the doctor."

She stepped away and stared at the doctor as if he might be the crazy one.

He laughed and patted her shoulder.

"Ten is the perfect age, Ethel. Did you know that numbers can be very powerful? Take today, for instance. Today is June 6th. Or if we consider the numbers, today is 6-6. And that number carries a bit of magic."

"Magic?" Ethel asked, glancing again at the funny little instrument. She knew magic only through storybooks. "Magic isn't real," she added.

The doctor offered her a half-smile and stood.

"You may not always believe that," he told her.

"A LITTLE SOMETHING TO help you sleep," the doctor murmured.

Ethel lay on the bed, watching the ceiling through tears. The man beside her mumbled and groaned, his breath sounding like a pig rooting in the mud. She wanted to clamp her hands over her ears, but they had strapped her down.

She pulled up on the restraints and lifted her head.

"I want to go home," she said.

"Not yet," the doctor murmured.

"I want to go home," she screamed, and the sound reverberated off the walls. The men turned to stare.

She didn't care. She thrashed in the bed, trying to pull away from the needle he held near her arm.

"If I miss, I'll have to poke you a second time. We don't want that, do we?" he asked, fastening a steely grip on her arm.

She shook anyway, screaming and trying to kick her legs. She screamed for her mother and father, for the nice nurse in the ward, Miss Davis, she screamed until her throat grew sore and her eyes heavy. When she finally stopped, she turned and saw the skinny man staring at her.

A man spoke, one of the doctors from earlier in the evening. She tried to listen and understand what was happening.

"Francis," the doctor said. "Is the demon here now?"

The man on the bed beside her nodded his head and laughed.

"Oh, yes, Master is here, Doctor. He is here." The man howled and shook.

Ethel's bladder released and soaked the bed beneath her.

The warmth spread down the backs of her legs and she felt embarrassed. Soon the doctor would notice, and he would announce it to the room. They would all laugh at her.

"Can we speak with the demon?" the doctor asked.

Ethel turned and gazed at the man beside her. He closed his eyes and his body shook. His mouth pulled back from his teeth until she could see his pale pink gums. The eye in her view rolled back into his skeletal head. The man seemed to change, grow more solid, stronger. He lifted his head from the bed and turned to gaze at the men on the benches.

"Yesss," the man hissed, and his voice had changed. It was deeper, like a growl.

"What is your name, Demon?" the doctor asked, stepping away from the man.

"Is this for me?" the man murmured in his gravelly voice, and Ethel realized he was referring to her. He watched her with a wolfish face and glassy, feverish eyes.

She tried to shrink away, but could do no more than turn her head and stare at the brick wall.

He terrified her. She didn't want to help him. But her head lay heavy, and when she closed her eyes, she found she could not open them again.

≈

ONE YEAR Later

ETHEL WATCHED her father carry his pipe into the study and close the door. Her mother was already inside, reading a book to Jared. Her sister would be knitting in the corner. Ethel lifted a milk crate from the butler's pantry and set it near the study door. She retrieved the hammer and nails she'd hidden in her room the day before. She climbed onto the crate and pressed a nail diagonally into the door, so that it would drive through the wood of the door into the frame. She paused, listening.

Her father brought up the new capitol building in Lansing, as she knew he would. His talk of politics always grew boisterous and angry. Each time his voice rose, Ethel tapped the nail lightly. Around the frame she moved, until the door was surrounded by nails. She had nailed the windows shut early that morning.

In the kitchen, she took a pile of rags and dipped each in kerosene, returning to the door and shoving them beneath. Had they smelled the kerosene she'd poured onto the curtains? Unlikely.

The match lit with a tiny scrape, and the flame engulfed the rag. She threw the match away and watched the fire consume the rags snaking beneath the door.

"What in God's name?" her father suddenly bellowed.

Ethel backed away, her hands balled into fists.

Her mother called out, and then her sister. Her brother began to cry.

Ethel went to the great room and retrieved her father's pistol. She walked trance-like back to the door and lifted the heavy gun, pointing the barrel. Her hand shook, dipped and rose as her scrawny arms wielded the weighted revolver.

The fire raged, consuming the door and beginning to blacken the surrounding walls. Smoke poured fourth and Ethel's eyes watered so she could barely see.

After the screams died, Ethel walked upstairs. She stood for a long time in her parents' bedroom, and then climbed into the dumbwaiter and pressed her hands over her ears. The screams had ended, and yet they echoed on in her mind. She closed her eyes and waited.

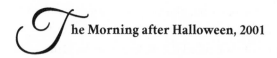he Morning after Halloween, 2001

Now
  Corrie

MY HEAD ACHED and my mouth tasted metallic, like pennies. I sat up, noticing the first trickle of early pre-sunrise light creeping in from the windows.

When had I moved to the couch? I patted the velvet sofa and tried to remember. Halloween night flitted by in fragments, images of the party, people laughing. I may have had a few too many Grave Digger cocktails.

Kerry Manor loomed around me, dark and soaring. The carved wooden face over the fireplace held me in its frozen gaze.

My last memory was Sammy draping his arm across my shoulder and handing me a shot of something sweet and vodka-laden.

"It's All Hallows Eve, my dawling," he'd whispered, sucking my earlobe. "Have another shot."

I stood, and the room rolled. Hunched over, I braced my hands on the armrest of the couch and noticed my white Bride of Frankenstein dress was streaked and damp with red. I touched the lace. It was still wet. Had I spilled a drink on myself or gotten sprayed by someone's fake blood during the night?

I sniffed the air and wrinkled my nose at the dank, metallic smell of blood. I pulled the fabric close to my nose. There was no mistaking the scent.

"Sammy?" I called my husband's name, my voice wavering. A tiny seed of panic took root in my stomach.

I left the room, glancing in the empty kitchen. At the sink, I saw a pile of bloody rags heaped on the counter. My feet dragged along the wood floor, my dress heavy. The stink of blood grew heady in the kitchen, the fragrance making me dizzy. I braced a hand against the counter's edge and looked out the window, somehow already knowing what I would see there.

Beneath the oak tree that flanked the water's edge lay Sammy.

I shrieked and pushed away from the counter, nearly tripping on my long dress as I burst through the back door and plummeted down the stairs.

I didn't have to touch him to know he was dead.

His eyes stared, unseeing, red veins snaking through white. His mouth hung open and a dark, gelatinous mass pooled inside and dripped onto his chin. I clutched his head and pulled him into my lap, screaming, howling. His body was stiff, cool to the touch, and less like a body than a mannequin. He looked like one of his lifelike wax figures, his realness merely an illusion, a talented artist's creation.

"No, no, no, please, no."

Hours passed, or maybe only minutes. Did I fall asleep beneath his body?

"You're not dead, Sammy," I murmured. I pinched his firm face and slapped his cheek hard. It would be just like Sammy to pull a prank on Halloween night. "It's not real," I told him, wiping the thick blood from his chin, smearing it across his cheek and my palm.

He had grown heavier, stiffer, and when I rolled him off me, I nearly threw up. The previous night's spirits swam in my head, churned in my belly. I crawled toward the water's edge, the sharp stones of the beach hard beneath my knees and cutting into my palms.

I waded into the lake, my dress a lead weight pulling me down. If I pushed out far enough, the water would swallow me whole.

I could join my husband. He couldn't have gone far.

"CORRIE!" The sound found me, a woman screaming, a sad confirmation that I was not dead. Slick hands took hold of my shoulders and forced me into shallow water.

I blinked and found Sarah, Sammy's twin sister, staring down at me, her face melted in grief and fear. She had thought I was dead, floating out there in the lake. I wanted to be.

"Sammy's-" she sputtered and stopped, glancing toward the tree where he laid.

She lifted me, soaked dress and all, and struggled up the rocky beach into the yard. She fumbled the glass door open and heaved me into Kerry Manor, depositing me near the fire that burned in the hearth, though I didn't remember seeing it when I woke earlier in the room.

"Here, let's get this off." Sarah undressed me as if I were a child. I stood, shivering, icy and hard. My legs trembled so violently that the moment the sodden dress pooled at my feet, I sank to the floor and pressed my face to my knees. I cried loud, gurgling wails, wishing I could reach deep enough to pluck out the despair and set it free.

wo Months Earlier

Then
Corrie

"This place is outta sight!" Sammy exclaimed.

I nodded, staring through the windshield at Kerry Manor, the Gothic monstrosity we'd be living in for the next eight months.

"Our Halloween Party will be awe-some," he continued, jumping from the car and pulling me after him. He spun me around and then left me teetering as he jogged to the porch.

I gazed at the steep gabled roof that ended in elaborately carved trim. Two brick chimneys sprouted from the roof, and a pointed iron railing ran the length of one of several rooftops.

I had to admit, it was a neat place to write a book.

"This guy's a genius," Sammy announced, producing a skeleton key from the small black box by the door. "He's restored this house to near-original condition. Can you imagine this place in its prime?"

I looked at the long black key and then at the tall, windowless door before us.

I couldn't believe that only a few years earlier the house stood condemned, a burned shell waiting for the forest and the lake to reclaim it. I knew little of Kerry Manor, though Sam had filled me in on the basics. A century before a fire claimed the lives of the entire Kerry Family. A handful of urban myths surrounded the creepy mansion - but having grown up in Cadillac, more than an hour drive from here, I knew few of the stories.

"Forget about the next great American novel, Corrie. This house is for writing horror. Mua-ah-ah," he cackled, jumping onto the porch rail with his teeth bared and hands raised like claws.

I laughed and shuddered at the same time. I did not share Sammy's fascination with the darker side of life. A therapist once told me that children of addicts tended to the extremes, and I veered toward the warm and fuzzy. I liked Disney movies and romance novels. Sammy often laughed at my insatiable appetite for happy endings, which he found unrealistic and downright boring. My love for Sammy had me endlessly dabbling in horror, but I would happily never watch Jason staking young blondes in his hockey mask, ever again.

"I thought it would be more... homey," I admitted.

"Homely?" he called, pushing open the door. "It is kind of homely, right? A house only a mother could love."

"A house only a monster could love," I grumbled. "And I said *homey.*"

The foyer yawned. I strained upward to see the shadowy ceiling. A sharp, medieval chandelier hung above us, illuminating the dark interior, but only barely.

A broad wooden staircase curved toward a landing with a tall stained glass window. Oil paintings hung along the stairwell. Images of families, their faces grim, stared out from drab maroon and brown backdrops.

"Are we looking at the Kerry family?" I asked, gesturing at the paintings.

"No." Sammy shook his head. "Dane bought most of the paintings in Paris. He considered recreating images of the family, but thought that might be macabre."

"Because they all died here?"

"Mmm-hmmm." Sammy wandered away, and I paused to look at a black wall sconce with spear-like arms pointing in several directions.

"Looks like a toddler death trap," I mumbled, making sure Sammy did not hear me.

I didn't want to ruin Sammy's excitement over our winter rental, and in all honesty, I felt it too. What a wild experience to spend a winter in a restored Gothic mansion. And yet... I rubbed my arms and smoothed over goosebumps beneath my fingers.

"Look at this fireplace, Gorey," Sammy called, using his preferred pet name for me.

I walked into the great room to more soaring ceilings and dark wood-paneled walls.

The fireplace mantel stood as tall as me, thick and ornate. In its center a pagan figurehead stared out, its face a whorl of groves, a sadistic smile stretched on its voluptuous lips.

I grimaced and touched my fingers to its partially open mouth.

"Is this in line with the original house?"

Sammy shrugged.

"Who knows? Though I'd imagine not. I'm guessing the Kerry family was Protestant. That was the prevailing religion of the time in these parts. A heathen mantel would not have pleased visitors."

"Are you a heathen?" I asked the wooden face.

"I'm not sure about him, but I'm experiencing some heathen tendencies right about now." Sammy picked me up and growled in my ear. "Let's go christen our room."

I laughed and shook my head, kissing his mouth and struggling out of his arms.

"After the tour."

High arched doorways and floor-length windows made each room appear impossibly tall.

A long, rectangular dining room was lit by a chandelier illuminating richly textured black wallpaper.

"Are those actual candles?" I asked, standing on tiptoe to peer into the fixture.

"No, but they sure look the part." Sammy ran his hands over the gleaming wood table. "Imagine all the laundry we can pile on this thing."

I laughed and slipped through another doorway, into an alcove with inset shelves filled with antique dishes.

"Does the owner realize we have a two-year-old?" I asked Sammy, admiring the silver-flecked china and wondering how I would keep Isis from turning the room into a pile of porcelain rubble.

We explored the study, home to another cavernous fireplace. Sammy pulled open the drapes and let light filter into the room, washing the gleaming wood floor and garish furniture in gold.

Leather-bound classics lined the shelves, black iron lions butting the books together.

"I may have to claim this room," Sammy announced, settling into a high-backed chair, surely hand-carved, with intricate whorls and spirals. He rested his hands on the desk, palms down. "In this room, you shall call me Lord Samuel of Kerry Manor."

I half-smiled, distracted by a mural of mossy trees and lush foliage that covered one wall. The image looked too real; as if I could step through and feel the spongy earth beneath me, smell the dank plants, overripe and sagging.

"Excuse me," Sammy cleared his voice loudly. "Lord Samuel of Kerry Manor is displeased with your lack of ardor."

I looked at him and grinned.

"Lord Samuel will have to take his complaints to the Queen. Oh, wait, that's me. Complaints are dismissed."

I laughed and danced from the room.

Down another hallway, I found a bathroom with a black claw-footed tub set in a deep arch. Above the black sink, a long medieval-looking gold and black mirror reflected my face. I stared at the woman in the mirror: freckled nose, creamy brown curls brushing the turned-up collar of my white coat.

I remembered a game one of my girlfriends insisted we play as children.

Stare into the glass and say Bloody Mary, Bloody Mary, Bloody Mary, and then turn off the lights and wait.

According to my friend, the ghost of a woman who wandered the streets searching for her dead child would appear behind me.

I tried it one time when I was ten years old. When the lights went out, panic seized me as if a monster had slithered from the bathtub drain and caught me around the throat.

I shuddered at the memory, glimpsing Sammy slipping into the bathroom behind me.

"Don't even think about scaring me," I told him, turning around.

"What, babe?" Sammy called from somewhere deeper in the house, maybe even walking up the stairs.

I blinked into the room. There were no windows, so it could not have been a trick of the light. I pulled the door back - nothing. I turned back to the mirror and stared into it a second time, entertaining a brief fantasy of a magic portal. What existed within the mirror was separate from my world. On the opposite side of the mirror, the Corrie of another dimension stood.

I studied the dark wallpaper, the bureau stacked with colorful bottles of perfumes and cologne - even those reminiscent of a time long passed.

Nothing moved in the mirror.

I ENDED my tour on the back porch and surveyed the endless gray water of Lake Michigan. The house stood at the tip of the Leelanau Peninsula in an isolated stretch of forest and stony beach. Our closest neighbors were a half-mile away. The Upper Peninsula lay across the watery divide, Beaver Island nestled somewhere between. You'd drown long before you ever caught a glimpse of either.

"What do you think?" Sammy asked, stepping behind me and

snaking his strong arms beneath my own. He pressed his forearms into my ribs and rested his chin on top of my head.

I reached a hand up and brushed it through his shaggy auburn hair.

"I'm wondering if this is crazy? Subleasing our house, uprooting our lives to spend a winter out here in the middle of nowhere."

"Crazy? No." He kissed the hollow beneath my ear. "Adventurous, exciting? Yes. And our life comes with us. Our home in Traverse City will be there in May when we're ready to go back but for now, for today, we can be Mr. and Mrs. Flynn of Kerry Manor," he said in a high English accent. "Really, though, what do you think of the house?"

"It's beautiful," I murmured. "And isolated."

"And…"

"A little eerie."

"And…?" he asked, eager but sincere.

He wanted me to say I loved it, I could write here, I could live here for the winter.

"And I like it," I offered.

"Yes! I knew you would. Wait until Isis sees it."

I imagined our little girl with her red cheeks and dreamy brown eyes trying to capture the house in a single glimpse. What would her memories of the house be when she grew older? The year we lived in the spooky Kerry Manor, or would she remember the house as a fairy-tale castle of sorts?

I thought of my childhood home, a small ranch ever in disrepair sitting on the outskirts of Cadillac. A rusted car stood on cement blocks in the backyard, left by a prior tenant. My mother worked various odd jobs cleaning houses and waiting tables. After my sister Amy turned sixteen and got a job, followed by me two years later, our mother stopped working. We paid the rent, the utilities, and used the bridge card to get groceries each week. My mother stayed home, drank gin and played sad music. I still hated Bonnie Raitt's *I Can't Make You Love Me*.

Like most parents, I wanted a better life for my daughter. Sometimes I lay in bed terrified that I was failing her. We watched too much TV, Sammy and I worked too much; she ate white bread when it should have been whole grain. When I aired my fears to Sammy, he would laugh and remind me that we had both grown up on sugar cereal and Wiley the Coyote and lived to tell the tale. Most days I agreed with him; others I merely powered through, hoping the rigid sense of doing it all wrong would soften at nightfall and I'd wake the next day renewed. I often did.

But in that moment, with Kerry Manor looming behind us, a flutter of apprehension, of foreboding even, stole into my thoughts. I wondered if we were making a terrible mistake.

ow
Corrie

"MRS. FLYNN? MRS. FLYNN?" I heard the detective talking and realized he spoke to me. Of course, he spoke to me. We were alone in
the room.

"Hmm," I asked, barely able to peek an eye up from where my
head rested on my hands. My face felt huge, like one of those
bloated fish in saltwater aquariums. I tried to focus on his face, but
everything had the blur that arose after hours of tears.

"Was there anyone at the party you didn't invite? Any
strangers?"

I looked at him, and a burst of hysterical laughter poured forth.
I closed my mouth and my eyes.

"I don't know," I mumbled. "Sammy had friends from the comic
book business. I had friends that brought friends. Sarah's friends
brought friends. It was a big party."

I smiled, remembering the look on Sammy's face halfway
through the night when people packed the house and lawn -
monsters and ghouls and skimpy angels everywhere. Paper ghosts

hung in doorways, skeletons danced near strings of orange lights, laughter and little periodic screams of fright echoed in the night. Our friends gushed about the towering old mansion, some shared stories they'd heard of Kerry Manor, a few insisted it was haunted.

"I understand this is hard, Mrs. Flynn, but..."

"Do you?" I asked, dragging my head away from my hands and fixing him with red, blurry eyes. "Really? Or is that just something you say?"

He blinked at me and set his large hands on the table. He wore a wedding ring, and Sammy's ring flashed in my mind, a smear of blood on the glimmering gold.

"Without sharing too much personal detail, yes, I do. I entered law enforcement because I lost a loved one to violence. For many years I was angry and wanted vengeance. Later, I found a way to make those feelings more productive. Here I am."

"Corrie?" Sarah spoke from the doorway and her voice trembled.

She'd pulled me from the lake but I'd hardly seen her since she peeled off my soaking clothes and left me in a heap near the fire. She still wore her construction woman costume. Black mascara rimmed her puffy red eyes, and she'd pulled her hank of blonde hair into a messy ponytail.

I swallowed and forced my legs to work as I stood and opened my arms for Sarah, for Sammy's twin. She rushed into me and burst into tears. My own tears returned with a force that threatened to pull us both under, sweep us into the great big lake beyond the window.

"He's dead," she murmured, as if it took the police and the paramedics and this troupe of experts to confirm what she'd known the instant she saw him.

I couldn't say it out loud. I nodded into her shoulder, grumbled a muffled affirmation, and then sank from her arms onto the floor. I could not be strong for Sarah. I had no strength left, no bones either, nothing of substance. I was a puddle of nothing and wished to dissolve into the cracks beneath me.

"What happened?" Sarah demanded, and I knew she'd turned

her gaze to the detective now.

I laid my head on the floor and closed my eyes.

"That's what I'm trying to figure out. I didn't get your name..."

"I'm Sarah Flynn, Sammy's twin sister. I called the police."

Twin - they always said twin - never 'this is my sister or brother,' but always my twin. I asked Sammy why one time, and he said, 'How could I leave out the most important part?'

"I'm genuinely sorry for your loss, Sarah. I'm Detective Collins. Were you at the party tonight?"

"Yes."

"Can you sit with me and answer a few questions?"

"Yes but..." She trailed off, and I imagined her staring down at me - strong Sarah. She could not sit and answer questions as I lay on the floor. I wanted to reassure her it didn't matter where I was. Nothing mattered now. In fact, the floor was preferable to some comfortable place that would make Sammy's absence more stark, more true.

"Let's get you onto the couch," Sarah said, crouching beside me.

"Here, let me," the detective urged. "Corrie, do you mind if I lift you?" he asked.

I shook my head.

Strong hands slipped behind by back and beneath my knees, scooping me from the floor. He deposited me on the couch. Sarah tucked a blanket around me, but I could not look at her. I rolled to face the sofa and stuffed the blanket into my mouth, biting down, suppressing the screams and sobs battling for release.

"Can we give her something?" Sarah asked. "I have a sedative in my bag."

The detective paused for a long time, and then finally said yes.

She slipped the pill into my mouth and I didn't bother swallowing it. I let it dissolve, bitter on my tongue, grainy when it slid down my throat.

Sarah

. . .

SARAH PACED AWAY from the detective. Her heart hurt and her mind felt foggy from the shots of tequila she'd been drinking only hours before.

"Tell me what happened when you found Sammy and Corrie," the detective started.

Sarah put an unconscious hand to her heart. It was still beating. Sammy's was not, but somehow hers was.

"I came back around four-thirty in the morning. I'd forgotten my phone here at the house. We were all drinking last night, and I forgot it."

"At four-thirty in the morning, you drove all the way back to Kerry Manor for your phone?"

Sarah frowned and nodded.

"Yes, I - the morning after Halloween we always have an early breakfast. It's a tradition. I met someone last night, and I was excited. I never went to bed. After she left, I decided to come back."

"She?" the detective asked.

Sarah felt a familiar flair of aggravation at his question.

"Yes, she, I'm gay. Is that relevant?"

The detective did not blush, the typical reaction when she announced her sexual preference.

"Everything is relevant," he said. "You drove home with a date and returned at four-thirty a.m. to have breakfast. What time did you leave here?"

"A little after one in the morning."

"Were there still a lot of people at the party?"

Sarah shook her head.

"No, maybe ten people still milling about, but I figured everyone would leave soon."

"And you returned at four-thirty. Did you call first?"

"No, I didn't call first. I realized when I got home, I forgot my phone. I tried to sleep for an hour, but I was wired so I got up. I..." Sarah paused.

"Leave nothing out. It's impossible to say what might be helpful at this point."

"I had a weird feeling while I was trying to sleep. I might have dozed for a minute and then, I don't know. I sat bolt upright in bed and needed to come back to Kerry Manor."

"You had a weird feeling?"

Sarah rubbed her temples. Exhaustion seeped in, blurring the edges of her vision.

"Sammy and I were connected. We were twins. As children, we shared feelings sometimes. I can't explain it to you, but I think that's what it was. I think I sensed something had happened to Sammy."

"So, you came back to check on Sammy?"

"No. I mean, I had a weird feeling, but it wasn't like I realized something bad had happened to him. I was coming back anyway, and I knew I'd never fall back asleep. When I got here, there were lights on, but everyone had gone home. I ran upstairs to wake them up."

"You intended to wake them up at four-thirty in the morning after you guys had been partying all night?"

Sarah rolled her eyes.

"Yes. He's my twin brother, my best friend, and Corrie comes in a close second. They're my best friends. It's not unusual for me to do that."

"Okay, and then what happened?"

"Their bed was empty. I figured they passed out in the great room in front of the fireplace. But that room was empty too. In the kitchen there were rags by the sink, bloody rags."

The detective nodded.

"Did you touch them?"

Sarah squinted, trying to remember. Had she touched them?

"I don't think so. I looked at them and then looked through the kitchen window. The moon illuminated something in the lake, something big and white. I walked onto the porch trying to see it, and then I realized I was looking at Corrie."

"Corrie was floating in the lake?"

"Yes."

"Face down?"

"Yes. I ran to the water, but before I got there, I saw..." She saw him again. Sammy, lying beneath the oak tree, his face gray, his clothes a puzzle of dark splotches. Blood - she hadn't quite known it in that moment, but yes, it was blood.

"Sammy," she breathed, clutching her shirt and twisting it in her hand as if that might ease the tightness in her chest.

"Did you go to him?"

"I started to and then stopped, because I knew." She paused and forced the words out in a burst. "I knew he was dead."

"How?"

She blinked at the detective, angry that he'd forced her to relive a moment she wanted to forget.

"His eyes. They were cloudy, and his body looked contorted, like he was frozen in place."

"Rigor mortis had already set in at four-thirty a.m.," the detective murmured, writing in his notebook.

"I walked into the lake and turned Corrie over. I thought she was dead too. The lake was freezing. Her body was so cold and heavy in her dress. I turned her over and dragged her to the beach. She spit up some water, and I carried her back into the house."

"Did you notice any injuries on Corrie?"

Sarah shook her head.

"She was half-drowned. I didn't exactly inspect her, but I helped her out of her dress. She just laid there shivering, her teeth chattering. I wrapped her in a blanket and called the police."

"Did she say that someone attacked them? Her and Sammy?"

"No. I think I asked her, or I asked what happened. She didn't know. She woke up and found Sammy dead."

"She went into the lake on her own, then?"

Sarah nodded.

"I think so. She was overcome with grief."

The detective nodded, flipping a page in his notebook.

"I asked Corrie if there were any strangers at the party and she didn't seem to know."

"There were a lot of people," Sarah said.

"But anyone out of place? I can't stress enough how important these next few hours are, Sarah."

"You think I don't know that?" she snapped, bracing her hands on the edge of the counter.

The detective sat back.

"I understand you're in shock and you're in grief, but try to allow your mind to wander back. Return to the party. Did you get a bad feeling about anyone? Did you see Sammy arguing with anyone?"

Sarah sat heavily in a chair and took a deep breath. She tried to push the pain surrounding Sammy off to the side as she returned to the party. Had anything unusual happened? Anything that foretold the horror that lay ahead?

She shook her head as the memories rolled past. She remembered Sammy in his Total Recall costume, weird dead alien baby hanging from his stomach, standing at a long, cobwebbed-draped table and talking animatedly with a group of men as he popped appetizers in his mouth. She glimpsed him on the porch with Corrie, laughing and holding his arms out as if shocked at how many people had come to the party. She recalled him dancing in the great room to Michael Jackson's, *Thriller*, but he looked rather drunk and fell twice.

"There's nothing, Detective. Nothing that sticks out. It was typical Sammy. He was laughing and happy, and everyone he came into contact with shared his expression. There were no fights, no evil men lurking in the shadows. I mean, unless you consider a hundred people dressed as monsters and zombies sinister."

The detective smiled.

"I can imagine picking out the bad guys in such a group is challenging. Let's take a different approach," he said. "I need a list of everyone at the party. Just start listing names. I hope to contact everyone who attended within forty-eight hours. Between you and Corrie, perhaps we can get the majority identified."

Sarah glanced at Corrie and doubted she'd be much help.

"Hold on," Sarah said. She jumped from her chair and hurried into the kitchen, where men in uniform moved meticulously through the room dusting for fingerprints. Sammy's black leather planner was sealed in a plastic bag.

She returned to the great room.

"There's a black planner in the kitchen. It looks like it's already been put in an evidence bag. Sammy will have a list in there with phone numbers and emails. That won't cover everyone, but it will come close. The other guests will be friends of guests or people who tagged along. I won't have all those names, and neither will Corrie. You'll have to get them from the guests themselves."

"Okay," he nodded, writing in his notebook. "Let me also ask you this. Why were Sammy and Corrie living in this house? I admit it surprised me when the call came in."

"A man named Dane Lucas renovated it. He does restorations, and stumbled upon this house during a summer vacation. Two years ago, he started restoring it. He knows Sammy through some Gothic house group online. The man offered to let Sammy rent it for the winter. He was traveling out of the country and needed someone he trusted to move in and make sure everything functioned. Sammy jumped at the chance."

Detective Collins frowned, an expression that added ten years to his boyish face.

"And Sammy was aware a family had died in this house a century ago?"

"Yes, unfortunately, Sammy loved creepy stuff. He wrote horror comics for a living." Sarah paused, putting a hand on her chest. Each time she spoke of Sammy, it was in the past tense. How could that be?

"Are you okay, Miss Flynn?"

Sarah nodded, and then shook her head.

"I have to call my mom," she started. "No, I have to go to her house. She's watching Isis. I need to take Corrie with me."

"Who's Isis?"

"Corrie and Sammy's two-year-old."

The detective looked sad for a moment, and then nodded.

"Write down your cell phone number and expect to hear from me."

CORRIE

I KNEW he wasn't gone. I knew it even as I watched the sheen slide from his eyes and vanish into the shadows beneath the great oak tree. I knew it before he first whispered into my ear, only hours after his death as I sat trembling in the claw-footed bathtub at his mother's house staring at the pink and black water swirling around me, and the gleam from the iridescent bath bubbles scented with vanilla caramel.

"Gorey."

I jerked my head so hard, I strained a muscle in my neck. It was a sick pet name. At least, Sarah called it sick, but I liked the nickname. Sammy was a horror buff. It made sense that he called me Gorey and Morticia and even Carrie White, but he saved that last one for my especially difficult PMS weeks. He made sure to remind me to "plug it up" during those emotional meltdowns, which always got a laugh and a much-needed decompression for me. Sammy had a gift. No matter how angry I became, he knew how to bring me back to sanity. He joked a lot, but never out of cruelty. He seemed to tap into a cosmic timeline that pinged him at the exact moment a little humor might deflate the monster within me.

So, when I heard Sammy whisper "Gorey" into my ear in his sweet, lilting way, I didn't cry out in fear. I closed my eyes, leaned my head back against the hard lip of the bathtub, and smiled.

"I knew you wouldn't leave," I told him.

How could I remember the final look in his eyes, you might ask? His last breath? And to that, I am silent. Because I don't know. How can I have no memory of the night after I fell asleep and simultaneously have that memory, that single image captured as if by a photo and printed on my brain, so I must look at it again and again and worse, I must question what it means. How could I have been there if someone else killed him?

29

$\mathcal{N}$ow
Corrie

I STOOD near the back of the room. The temperature, cool when I walked in, had grown stifling. My black dress clung to my skin, growing sticky with sweat, the neckline too tight. A line of people in dark suits and dark dresses blocked the shining coffin, but I sensed it hunched in the front of the funeral parlor. A void seemed to exist there, a black hole of indescribable emptiness. Sammy, larger than life, could never occupy such a space.

Three days that encapsulated a lifetime had transpired since Halloween night. Moments drifted in and out of my thoughts. The anguished cry of Sammy's mother when Sarah broke the news. The sound of Isis's laughter, foreign and heartbreaking in the silent house of my dead husband's mom. Sarah trying to force-feed me oatmeal as I lay in bed with my teeth clamped shut. I had become like a child, worse than a child. My own daughter would open her damn mouth and eat. I refused even basic life-giving necessities and forced my sister-in-law to set aside her own grief and care for me.

The guilt lay heavy, and yet I could not shrug off my anguish.

A dreamlike quality descended over the scene. I watched people lose shape and merge into a single stream of black, pricked through with sallow skin and dark eyes.

"Corrie?" The whisper stole through the cottony barrier that filled my ears. I turned and saw my sister, Amy, her hand outstretched, a series of rings glittering from her slender fingers.

People stared. Their eyes devoured me.

Sarah appeared on my other side. Amy's and Sarah's hands held me. I waited for them to grip hard, pull me toward the coffin, force me to gaze at the empty shell he used to live in. I couldn't, I wouldn't.

I twisted away and pushed through the door, smacked into a hard man wearing a brown coat and black slacks. I slammed onto my butt.

"Mrs. Flynn?" Detective Collins bent low, offered me his hand, and I took it if only to get up faster and escape.

I didn't look into his eyes, just brushed him aside and clicked toward the door, my stupid heels sounding vain and dramatic in the marble foyer. I burst through the doors and gulped the cold air, grasping the iron rail as my legs wobbled beneath me.

People moved through the parking lot. Their eyes followed me. Someone broke from the group, but I turned quickly away, slipping behind the funeral home. I kicked off my shoes and crept into the garden, empty of flowers in November. A white swing hung in a gazebo and I sat down, and then curled onto my side, pulling my knees to my chest and weeping into my hands.

"Shh… it's okay." I heard his voice and felt his hand on my back rubbing.

Sammy gave the best back rubs.

I didn't dare look at him, nor lean into the sensation, because the moment I did, he would vanish.

∾

Sarah

. . .

SARAH SAT on the couch next to her mother, watching her tea grow cold. The guests had left, Corrie slept in a room upstairs, likely sedated, and Isis had gone to the hotel with Corrie's sister.

Archie, Sarah's West Highland white terrier, lay in a little dog bed sleeping with one eye open as Corrie and Sammy's cat, Dracula, stalked him from the hallway.

A clock ticked from the kitchen, the cuckoo clock that Sarah and Sammy had loved as children. They would race to the kitchen every hour to watch the little Danish man and woman slide out in their wooden shoes for a kiss. If the clock chimed now, Sarah might scream or cry or cease exiting. She hoped it was one-fifteen or some middle hour that wouldn't result in an overreaction to the damn clock.

Her mother leaned her head back and closed her eyes. Her face looked ruddy, mascara streaked beneath her eyes, the pink lipstick long ago rubbed from her lips by kissing friends and family, hands and cheeks and lips.

"I've got to take a walk, Mom," she murmured and stood. She'd abandoned her signature white t-shirt and jeans for proper funeral clothes. Her black slacks were wrinkled, her matching black sweater too warm in the once-cozy, now claustrophobic house.

She passed houses, trees, a little girl diving from her porch into a pile of multi-colored leaves, but she saw only one thing: Sammy, his face powdered and strange, staring up from a bed of dark satin.

Had Sammy wanted a funeral? A burial? A polished mahogany casket and a trail of people looking into his dead face?

Sarah wondered why she'd never thought to ask him. They'd had a thousand conversations, why not one of the most important of all?

Corrie hadn't known either, but then again, Corrie could barely take a sip of water without dropping the cup since Sammy's death. For three days, she'd wandered in a fog of grief so heavy her mere presence in a room made it hard to breathe.

It didn't seem real, or possible, that Sammy had died.

"Sammy," she whispered and saw again his face, eyes pressed closed, his lashes long and dark as if they'd put mascara on them. Drained his body and pumped it full of chemicals, plastered on powder to hide what they were seeing - not Sammy, but a dead body that no longer contained Sammy at all.

Beneath his suit, Corrie had provided a Werewolf in Paris t-shirt. Beneath that, his flesh was likely a mass of stab wounds. Did they bandage those?

"Hi, Sarah."

Sarah jerked up at the sound of her name.

Lisa Priss or Prim or something-or-other jogged by in neon purple leggings and a black all-weather jacket, her blonde curls piled on her head and her face heavily made up.

Sarah gave a little wave and cut down a path that led into the trees. She didn't want to chat with a woman from high school she barely remembered. Most of all, she didn't want to explain all the cars in her mother's driveway, all the long faces.

Their freshman year of high school, Lisa had developed a crush on Sammy. She walked her yipping Chihuahua by their house at every opportunity. She wore ridiculous outfits like miniskirts and teeny-tiny jean shorts. Sarah and Sammy would dive to the floor when they saw her coming.

"Blonde vampire passing in three-two-one," Sammy would whisper, and then they'd crawl to the window and peek out as she glanced back at the house forty or fifty times, hoping for a glimpse of a boy who would never reciprocate her feelings.

Lisa had bought her childhood home and now had a husband who did some kind of boring finance thing, and two kids or two dogs.

"Tragically typical," Sammy would have called her.

"Will I ever stop hearing your voice in my head?" Sarah whispered, picking up speed as the forest trail sloped down toward a weedy pond.

5

*T*hen
   Corrie

"Coffee?" Sammy smiled and held out the chipped *Everything Tastes Better with Cat Hair* mug he offered me every morning. I took it, grateful, and slumped into the armchair facing the hard surface of the lake beyond. We had claimed the great room in Kerry Manor for the panoramic window the designer had installed. It wasn't in line with the home's original architecture, but he told Sammy he had to take a handful of allowances. How could you blot out the sweeping views of Lake Michigan?

Other than the window, the room lived up to its Gothic beginnings. The vaulted ceiling comprised an intricacy of deep grooved wood rising to a ribbed pattern, ending at a dangling, tiered chandelier. Upholstered furniture in dark colors clustered around the room. Thick, burgundy curtains butted arched windows, which faced the courtyard.

I had grown to love the hand-carved fireplace and the pagan figurehead in its center, which we referred to as Loki. Sammy had lined up several horror movie action figures across its ledge, including the Michigan Wolf Man, Freddy Krueger and something that resembled a half-man-half spider.

I looked out the window and sipped my coffee, marveling at the changing landscape.

October signaled the shift. In some divine orchestration, the whole earthly realm seemed to agree it was time to remodel the house. Green leaves melted into reds and gold. Orange wood lilies and opal trillium receded into the forest floor and took with them the vibrant green ferns and grass. Pumpkins appeared, stacked at the end of dirt driveways, and Indian corn lay in bushels on people's doorsteps.

Sammy loved October, and before the first leaves fell, he fantasized about Halloween costumes and rum-laced apple cider. He watched horror movies and insisted we add pumpkin pie spice to everything from chili to pancakes.

Sarah once told me that Sammy was an October baby, though he was born in July. Since birth, Sammy had loved the full harvest moon, and the gold-flecked painter's brush that turned down the world of color.

As a boy, he painted the walls of his bedroom Halloween orange and began a collection of monster-face masks that would put a Halloween store to shame.

At the age of ten, he nearly sent his mother to an early grave when he jumped from the attic one October morning wearing a devil's mask. Poor Helen fell flat on her back, and Sammy's dad whipped him with a belt for the first and only time in his young life. Sammy's mother had told me the story half a dozen times, and claimed still to this day she didn't like to open the attic door.

In our house, Halloween trumped Christmas. We didn't merely carve pumpkins, we carved a dozen, at least. Sammy took hours scouring pumpkin patches for the perfect ones - the bigger, the better. Halloween night involved a massive celebration. Last year, we road-tripped with Sarah to Salem, Massachusetts, and spent the evening attending a witch's ball at a huge old church transformed into a dance club.

This year, we would host a Halloween party at Kerry Manor.

"Okay, we're out of here, sweet cheeks," Sammy told me, kissing my temple.

I leaned down to hug Isis. She licked the side of my face and grinned.

"Icky, Isis," I said, wiping her slobber from my cheek.

"See you in a few hours," I told them.

Sammy wrote comic books for a living, which left him ample time to lean over my shoulder and attempt to read my lines before I finished writing them. Fortunately, most days he packed up Isis and went into town to give me a reprieve. He rented a small office comprised of two rooms attached to the back of a boutique clothing store. In one room, Sammy covered the floor with craft paper. Isis could sit in a rainbow explosion of crayons and draw to her heart's content. At two-years-old, she didn't draw so much as scribble and occasionally eat a crayon. Toys and a small mounted television occupied her time when the coloring grew boring.

I had abandoned my own office, a therapy practice I shared with a colleague, for what I termed a writing sabbatical. My clients had been recommended to other therapists, and I was fulfilling a lifelong dream of writing a novel.

"Now, if only I could actually write it," I muttered, deleting my last line and starting again.

"One for sorrow, two for mirth..."

The child's rhyme, sung in a high, girlish voice, drifted through the house.

I paused, blinking at the handful of words I'd just typed.

I glanced toward the hall. Had Sammy and Isis returned? Certainly not. It took more than a half-hour to drive into Traverse City.

I strained, listening, but the sound didn't come again. Sammy's mother loved to buy Isis toys that sang and talked. The previous Christmas, she gave her a cow that cackled madly when you pressed its foot. Apparently, she'd also given her one that sang creepy nursery rhymes - great.

I returned my focus to the screen. My protagonist had just discovered her mother was dead. Writing the scene felt impossible.

I thought of my own mother, her gaunt face against the white of the hospital pillow, her hair thinly arranged in a dark halo around her head.

She needed a liver transplant, but alcoholics didn't get liver transplants. They died instead.

"Three for a funeral, four for a birth." This time, a burst of laughter followed the song.

I sat up so quickly, my laptop plummeted to the floor.

"Damn."

I got down on my knees. A small plastic chip had splintered from the side, but otherwise the computer remained intact.

"Is someone there?" I called, stepping into the foyer.

Sun slanted through the stained-glass window at the top of the stairs, but hardly enough to illuminate the darkness in every corner. I roamed from room to room, listening, waiting.

I wandered into the kitchen, the bathroom, and lastly back to the stairs. I did not hear the child again.

"Because there is no child," I said out loud. The instant the words left my mouth, I paused, as if I'd offered a challenge and now the child would have to reveal herself.

Silence greeted me.

I searched every room, peeked beneath beds, which gave me a shiver or two, and decided Isis must have a horrible new toy I would dispose of when I came across it.

I had only just settled back into my space on the couch when Sammy and Isis returned in a tornado of sound and movement.

Isis tugged at the blanket wrapped around my feet and demanded cookies.

"Lunch first," Sammy announced, giving me a smack on the lips.

I followed them into the kitchen.

Sammy continued singing whatever rock song he'd been listening to in the car. He pulled the high chair from its cupboard and slopped sandwich fixings onto the counter.

I stretched, grateful my little stream of chaos had returned to distract me from the blank screen.

"Get some writing done?" Sammy asked, lifting a squealing Isis into her high chair. He gave her jarred peaches and half a turkey sandwich, and settled an array of toy figures on her tray.

"Yeah," I shrugged and gestured to the now-closed laptop I had set on the kitchen counter.

"Good because there's a zombie movie marathon happening in," he looked at his watch, "twenty-five minutes."

"Oh my, I didn't realize it was a movie day."

He grinned.

"This is the winter of our discontent. How better to while away the hours than watching zombie movies?"

I cocked an eyebrow.

"We could rake some of those leaves in the yard. In a week they'll be waist-high."

"Leaves, schmeaves," he grumbled. "Anyway, I bought some monster bags for the Halloween Party and we need leaves to fill them out. Best to put that off until the week before the party."

"How are your peaches, Honey Bear?" I asked Isis, kissing the top of her head.

"Mmm-good," she mumbled, chewing a mouthful of fruit and stomping a pink princess toward a group of unsuspecting penguins who were about to be knocked to the floor.

I caught them as they fell and returned them to her tray.

"Why hasn't anyone invented a sling shot that catches falling toddler toys and returns them to their original spots? They'd make a fortune," Sammy exclaimed.

"Maybe I should do that instead of writing a book."

"No way," he grinned, taking a bite of Isis's sandwich. "You'll see, Corrie. Next year at this time, we're going to be sitting back and reading about Corrie Flynn, the New York Times Bestselling Author."

"I'd be happy if next year at this time, I had a rough draft," I admitted, putting the bread and turkey back in the refrigerator.

"You will," he assured me.

"I found a little room upstairs I might turn into a writer's room. It has an old desk and a window that looks out on the courtyard," I told him.

"Ooh, tucked away clacking at the keys like Hemingway, huh?"

"I'm pretty sure Hemingway managed more words in a day than I produce in a week."

"You'll find your groove, babe."

Isis finished eating, and Sammy helped her down. She raced into the great room with her toys clutched in her hand. Sammy and I followed her.

"Oh," I said, remembering the child's song. "Does Isis have a new toy that sings nursery rhymes?"

Sammy plopped on the couch, wrinkling his brow.

"My mom got her that little cat piano that sings."

I frowned.

"I don't think so," I murmured.

"Come snuggle with me," Sammy said, patting the place beside him. "Zombies aren't the same if you're not clutching me in terror whenever they feed on a new victim."

I SAT at the little wooden desk tucked into the alcove, the gray sky washed in gloomy darkness. The room lacked an overhead light, making up for it with antique lamps and sterling candlesticks. I lit candles, imagining the person, likely a man, who sat at a desk like this one-hundred years ago. I knew nothing of the Kerry family except a tragic fire stole most of their lives. Did he sit in this room and pen letters to his family? Tell them of the trials of life in northern Michigan and close his envelopes with a wax seal?

"No," I murmured, surveying the space. The man of the house would have done those things in the study. This room likely belonged to the mother. Perhaps a sewing table sat near the window, so she could watch her children play outside.

The tiny black cursor blinked at me from the solid white screen of my laptop. *Write*, it seemed to say. *Write... write... write.*

I stood and stretched, missing our cats for the first time since coming to Kerry Manor. Helen had taken them in. They would be fat when we retrieved them after months of eating tuna from the can. Each time we visited, I found them lazing in her sunroom, their bellies turned up and their eyes rolled back.

When I first started my novel, both cats flocked to me as if they understood the absolute necessity of a cat to a writer. They would curl on my lap, on a stack of books perched near my desk, or on the windowsill in my writing room, which doubled as a guest bedroom. That, however, existed in our actual home - a little bungalow in Traverse City. Kerry Manor was off-limits to pets.

"Maybe that's why I'm blocked," I mumbled. "I don't have my furry muses."

I walked around the room, sliding my hand over furniture, looking closer at the neat grooves in the old wood. This room was far from where the fire had occurred and likely contained all of its original wood. A small closet, only waist-high and pointed at the top, adorned one wall. I pulled on the little iron handle, but it didn't budge. Perhaps a veneer had been put on the wood, causing the door to stick. I tried a second time. The door began to open and then was wrenched back - as if someone who sat on the other side had pulled it closed.

I took my hand away and stared at the door.

Only a child could sit comfortably in such a closet, and Isis was not in the house. I was alone.

"Don't be silly," I whispered, echoing a sentiment my older sister told me when I crept into her bed late at night during our younger years. I had often woken from nightmares, and I would have liked to crawl into bed with my mother. Unfortunately, most nights she drank until she passed out on the couch. If I did go to her, her skin would be slick and pungent. She'd swat me away as if I were a giant mosquito attacking in her sleep.

My sister was a much safer option.

I gripped the handle and pulled, but it didn't budge. I folded my hand into a fist and knocked.

Silence.

Shaking my head at my misgivings, I stood and returned to the desk.

As I started to sit in my chair, a knock sounded behind me, small and hollow. Just one.

The silence that followed had substance. It crowded the space, pressing in until even air seemed hard to come by.

I had not moved. My hand stood poised over the back of my chair, my head slightly rotated toward that little door, my ears straining to hear.

I lifted one leaden leg and then another, until I crouched again before the little door, my heart hammering against my ribs. I swallowed the saliva coating the back of my throat and lifted a hand to the tiny metal handle.

The metal felt icy, sticky even, and I jerked my fingers away.

Don't be silly. I heard my sister's voice a second time, but it had lost its power to deflate the terror ballooning at the backs of my eyes.

I returned to the handle, cold, and pulled. The door swung open easily, and I fell back with a thud, landing hard on my butt.

I scrambled away, pushing my palms and heels into the polished wood floor, sure something or someone would come crawling out on hands and knees, teeth snapping at my face.

Instead, I stared into thick darkness. A musty smell wafted out, as if it had been closed for a very long time. No yellow eyes peered from the dark. No monster bounded from the deep. The little closet sat empty, the dust on the floor undisturbed.

ow
Corrie

I CAN'T REMEMBER how long it felt like Sammy and I were just pretending to be grown-ups. Playing house, mimicking our parents (his more than mine), but we were not really like those adult people. Even after the wedding and the baby and the mortgage, I still found myself elated by this enormous secret we shared: it was all just an illusion, time had stopped at twenty-one. After all, he was still Sammy. Sammy, whose gangly arms and legs were always stuffed into funky '70s band t-shirts and torn, faded jeans. He was cool in that way smart guys obsessed with Star Wars are cool. His always-laughing face was long and thin and made longer by his shoulder-length auburn hair that his mother called amber waves of grain. He hated and loved that.

We rolled through life together like a single, solid wave, as steady as the tide. We were that connected. Soul mates, love of my life, the One... I got it. I understood every single cliché, every ridiculous label, every Disney-concocted fantasy of happily ever after. Not in an arrogant way, either. I didn't stand on some

pedestal of love and pity the rest of the world for their discon-
nected and dysfunctional relationships. I knew how lucky I was.
That's the truly awesome power of an overwhelming love - it builds
this perfect bubble around you, and you sort of forget everything
else.

When Isis came along, we welcomed her into the fold as if she
had always been. Our creation, our love child. During her first year,
she slept between us at night. Sometimes I would wake to see
Sammy's enormous brown eyes gazing at her with this mystified
expression, as if she was an alien who teleported into our bed at
three a.m. I knew the look. I experienced the same awe, and when
he looked up into my eyes, that knowing passed between us word-
lessly. That was our bond. We didn't need vocabulary. We could
have been mute and still reveled in the knowledge that we understood the other completely.

Those days have begun to feel like a dream. I remember them,
but I can't recreate them. It's such a horrible curse - the way my
mind shifts to the present and slowly releases all that came before.
I'm sure it's still stored in there, but I can't reach in and grab it. I
can't smell his skin after a long day at the beach or hear the funny
pitch of his laughter after he's just smoked a joint. All the nuance
has blurred and faded.

"Momma?"

I opened my eyes, pushing myself up to sitting in bed.

Isis stood at the foot of the bed in her kitty pajamas, clutching
her stuffed Gizmo.

Sammy had relinquished control of much of his monster
memorabilia to Isis after her second birthday, when suddenly her
eyes lit up every time she entered his study. Gizmo had been the
first to go, and when he handed her the bulge-eyed Mogwai, she
had jumped up and down and raced through the house to show me
her new friend. The items still off-limits to Isis had been moved
into Kerry Manor's study, but even those were likely smothered in
her sticky fingerprints.

The study had been Sammy's favorite room in Kerry Manor. I
had often found him there, comfortable in a throne chair with its

ornate high back, his feet tucked into a pair of Bigfoot slippers, giggling as he read a *Tales from the Crypt* comic book and listened to Bill Evans light across the keys with haunting clarity.

I have not been in the study since the morning after I found his body. I walked in once, in the hours after it happened, and clutched the scattering of papers on his desk. I crumpled them into a tiny ball and shoved them in my mouth and tried to stifle the sobs erupting from the mysterious cellar in the darkest parts of my being. Eventually when I choked, I spit them out and raced from the room.

"Dada..." Isis continued, as if Sammy was hiding under the covers like he always did and would spring out to scare her at any moment.

I pulled back the comforter to reveal the empty white sheet and patted the silhouette of his body I couldn't see, but felt sure was there.

We had returned to Kerry Manor the day before, four days after Sammy's death. My sister and her husband accompanied us, so I wouldn't be alone in the house, though all of them - Amy, Todd, Sarah, and Helen argued with my choice to return. Isis and I could stay with any of them, but I refused their offers. If I wanted to be close to Sammy, I needed to be at Kerry Manor.

Isis crawled onto the bed and laid her head in my lap. She stuck her index and middle fingers in her mouth and sucked. I stroked her wispy blonde hair that shot like sprouts from her soft, pink head.

Sometimes Sammy had called her his hairless princess because her blonde strands grew in so slowly.

"There's my sweet girl," Sarah said, appearing in my doorway. She held a canister of cheese puffs. "Did she wake you?"

I shook my head and turned to look out the window at the lake. Sarah bore such a striking resemblance to my dead husband that something ripped open every time I looked at her.

She knew as much and kept her distance. I hated to put her in that position. Surely, as Sammy's twin, her own loss struck a deeper chord than mine, but my grief trumped my compassion.

"Icy? Cheese puffs?" Sarah shook the canister, but my daughter burrowed under the covers next to me.

"It's okay, Sarah," I told her. "Thank you."

She left, and I tugged Isis from beneath the blankets and pulled her back onto my lap. My pajama bottoms were damp from the sweaty, nightmarish sleep I'd had. I shivered as her warmth seeped into my clammy skin.

She tilted her face to mine and repeated her earlier plea.

"Dada?"

I rested my palm on her forehead and tried to look into the dry emptiness that rose up to meet me at her question. How could I tell my two-year-old child her father was gone forever? That his body lay in the cold, hard ground, but his soul had escaped the confines of this desperate life for something sweeter?

"Dada's not here, Honey Bear."

"Dada's in heaven?"

I looked at her sparkling eyes nestled in her perfect round face.

I nodded and pulled her closer.

ow
Corrie

"TODD IS happy to ask the people renting your house to leave, Corrie," my sister Amy told me, folding tiny pairs of mismatched pants and shirts Isis had destroyed with a variety of chocolate fudge-pops and grape juice.

I sat at the kitchen table in Kerry Manor, staring dazedly into my coffee cup, watching the oils swirl and create strange patterns. I saw Todd walking hand in hand with Isis on the frozen beach. Her winter jacket enveloped her tiny body like bubble wrap.

We had been back in the house for two days. Someone had removed the Halloween decorations, mopped up the fake blood - and the real - and unraveled the spider webs.

"I don't want to do that," I responded, loathing the prospect of returning to the house we had created as a family.

What would the first seconds be like? Swinging open the blue door, marred by the claws of our two cats, and smelling, for the first time, our little home without Sammy? How could I step into that foyer, painted with our favorite poetry in elegant black calligraphy I had spent hours perfecting while Sammy read the poems aloud?

"Your lease here is up on May, you have to go back sometime..."

Was that true? Did we have to go back? What if we never went back? I could pack a suitcase for Isis and myself, and we could fly to Costa Rica or Australia. I had always wanted to hike the rain forest and listen to monkeys chatter from the trees overhead. Isis could chase birds on the beach, and I could learn to be a tour guide or a snorkel instructor.

Or if I was really desperate, I could continue my therapy practice. Costa Rica was likely filled with expats dying to pour out their woes on some other first-world prat.

"May is six months away, Amy."

"Sure, but in the meantime, you're stuck in this creepy house all by yourself. I'm worried about you, Corrie."

Amy awkwardly rubbed my back, and I continued to stare out the window and refuse the lurid images from Halloween that the oak tree conjured. Sammy's face, streaked with sweat and then later, streaked with blood.

"Todd and I would love to take Isis, maybe for a week. She can play with Tyler and Adelaine. Plus, we have tickets to Elmo on Ice." Amy sat down across from me at the kitchen table.

I looked up at my sister. Her freshly dyed blonde hair was neatly arranged in a French braid, not a single strand out of place.

"All-Together-Amy," I murmured, echoing a nickname Sammy secretly called my sister.

Amy had responded to our mother's chaos and alcoholism by constructing the perfect life. She and Todd bought a sunny yellow house in a subdivision of Stepford two-story family homes, each adorned with two rose bushes, a single lilac tree, and a little concrete pathway that led to white doors hung with decorative wreaths, no matter the season. The rooms were color coordinated with paint and artwork and even figurines to match.

When Sammy and I visited, we slept in the ocean room with

deep aquamarine paint, sand dollars decorating our bureau, and a giant photograph of a sailboat drifting on a calm sea.

When we'd gone down for coffee one morning, Sammy had opened the cupboard and laughed.

'Which mug do you want?' he'd asked me.

I had looked up to a shelf of tidily arranged, identical white mugs in three perfect rows. Our own coffee cupboard was comprised of two dozen mismatched mugs in different colors, some chipped, all connected to a memory. Sammy loved to buy mugs at truck stop gas stations during road trips. *Arkansas* or *Wyoming*, they'd announce in huge black letters against a painted backdrop of rushing streams or snowcapped mountains. We picked up mugs at thrift stores, traded mugs with friends, and Sammy had at least five advertising his favorite horror flicks.

"What did you say?" Amy asked.

I felt guilty for the comment, and guiltier for all the times Sammy and I laughed at how hard she tried to put everything in its right place. It was only funny from the bubble of Corrie and Sammy – but here in this untethered place, floating in a vast terror, I understood her desire to keep it all together perfectly.

"Nothing," I sighed, rubbing at my face, where dark circles spread beneath my eyes like spilled ink. "Isis would love that."

"She would," Amy agreed. "And you need a break. I know Sammy's mom loves to take her, but she needs time to grieve. This will give all of you a little time to put the pieces back together."

I snorted but said nothing. The pieces had been stabbed to death. They sat in the cold, dark earth. There was no putting them back together.

Amy stood and moved around the table, wrapping her arms around me and pressing her face into my disheveled hair.

I smelled her perfume, something strong and heady, the perfume that assails you when you walk through a department store.

"You will get through this, Corrie. You don't believe it right now, but I know you. You're strong."

She pulled away and moved to the kitchen counter, pulling

dishes from the sink and loading them efficiently in the dishwasher.

~

I LAUGHED and clamped my hand over my mouth as if I'd committed a sin. The graveyard yawned darkly beautiful in the moon's light. Splashes of white and gray headstones rose like teeth.

"And I in the beast's mouth," I murmured, sitting on the damp leaves that blanketed the cemetery floor.

I clutched a canvas sack, which held a Ouija board, four reiki candles, a book about using the board, and a pair of Sammy's worn socks. I wanted something that held remnants of him, and it didn't get much more potent than those. This was just the kind of thing Sammy would do, as a joke, and my laughter bubbled when I imagined him waving the socks wildly in the air and demanding their owner reach out from the spirit world.

A mass of withering flowers lay near my elbow, their scent grossly intoxicating. I closed my eyes and searched for a breath free from the scent.

The gates to the cemetery had been closed hours earlier, at dusk. I had walked around them but felt like a trespasser just the same. Despite my layers of clothes, goosebumps rose along the back of my neck.

As I sat in the pervading darkness, terror edged in, but I shooed it away with thoughts of hearing Sammy's voice drifting up from the mound of fresh dirt beside me. I didn't look too closely at that pile of earth. I couldn't truly consider what lay within it.

I pulled out the Ouija board, unwrapped the plastic sheath and stuffed it into my bag. I lit two candles and set them on either side. The cheap board felt flimsy beneath my desperate fingers, a child's toy. I set it on the dirt and took up the little plastic dial.

I had never used a Ouija board but couldn't shake the idea when it struck me that morning. I knew he was close, Sammy. He'd been close since it happened. I saw him slipping around corners, sensed him watching me. I needed to bring him into the light.

"Sammy?" I asked, placing the dial in the board's center and moving it slowly in a circle.

My hands shook, and I stared hard at the black letters.

"Sammy, if you're here, move the pointer."

The candles flickered in the night breeze and I shifted my gaze to them. If one blew out, would I believe he stood nearby? Was that rustling in the leaves my dead husband reaching from beyond the grave?

I closed my eyes and waited. Seconds ticked by, and then minutes.

Nothing happened.

I opened my eyes and stared at the board until the black calligraphy blurred and my tears wet the dirt beneath me. I took a handful of the dirt in my hand and clutched it to my chest.

The silence turned into pain, unbearable pain. How could I go on living with it? One of these nights it would tear me in two and I would bleed to death on the cold, dark floor in Kerry Manor.

"Please," I whispered, pushing the dial toward the letter S. "Please."

A movement caught my eye deeper in the graveyard, and I stared into the darkness, searching the shadows. I saw the whisper of a hand behind a tall tombstone.

I jumped to my feet. It was Sammy.

He slipped away, his shape dissolving into the darkness as my eyes trained hard, tried to ferret him out.

I ran toward the headstone. In a little grove of trees, something moved. I sprinted into the trees, glimpsed his face from the shadows, his brown eyes sparkling in the moonlight.

"Sammy, please," I gasped, a stitch clutching my side.

A creek ran along the back of the cemetery. Thick trees arched over the running water, blotting the light. I perceived movement. He'd gone there. He was hiding near the stream bank.

I stumbled through sharp branches, sliding in the slick leaves along the bank. My shoes stuck in mud and I almost lost one, wrenching it out before the damp earth swallowed it.

"Gorey..." I heard my pet name whispered from his lips.

My heart spasmed at the sound, and I cried out, searching. I crashed down the bank into the river, the water icy as it swirled up to my thighs. I pushed through the stream - slow, cold. For an instant I saw his reflection in the moonlit water. I whipped my head around, but he was not behind me. I stood, panting, listening, but the presence had gone.

I was alone in the night once again.

hen
Corrie

"I HAD a bizarre death dream last night," Sammy announced, grabbing the box of donuts Sarah had arrived with. "Yes! Apple fritters."

"A death dream?" Sarah asked, frowning. "Corrie, I got you blueberry, and a chocolate with sprinkles for Isis."

I smiled and shook my head.

"No donut for me yet. I need at least two cups of coffee before I can disrupt my perfect caffeine buzz with sugar."

"Corrie doesn't play with the white wizards until after ten a.m.," Sammy said, taking a huge bite and rolling his eyes with pleasure. "Ugh, yes, come on dopamine, have your way with me."

"The white wizards?" Sarah laughed. "Death dreams and white wizards. You guys think Kerry Manor is getting to you?"

"The white wizards," Sammy continued, winking at me, "are sugar and salt. We call them that because, well," he gestured at the donut. "Need I say more? The death dream was..." He paused, scratching the back of his neck. "Freaky. I was covered in blood and my life was fading. It didn't hurt, but I was staring up into a starry sky and watching the world recede into a pinhole, and I knew when it went black, I would be gone, over, poof!" He wiggled his fingers.

"But you didn't die, right?" Sarah demanded.

"Nope, woke up just before."

"Why do you say it like that?" I asked her.

"Because if you die in a dream, you die in real life," she said, pulling a glazed donut from the box. "At least that's what we always believed growing up."

Sammy grinned.

"Thanks to Grandma Fiona, who liked to tell us stories about the Wolf Man and Sasquatch and fifty different tales from her childhood. She was a master of horror and didn't even know it"

"I'm sure we have Grandma Fiona to thank for Sammy's obsession with monsters," Sarah said, grimacing as she traced a finger over the crown molding surrounding the doorway. "The house is overkill."

"Grandma Fiona bought me my first ever horror comic," Sammy beamed.

"What happened to her?" I asked.

I had heard references to Fiona over the years, but she died before I met Sammy.

"Lung cancer," Sarah explained. "She smoked a pack of day from the time she was twelve years old. At least, that's our mother's story."

"A nasty way to go," Sammy said, grimacing. "I wouldn't wish it on my worst enemy."

Sarah nodded.

"Where's Isis?" she asked.

"Playing in the great room. Sammy found an old dollhouse in the crawl space beneath the house. Isis has claimed it."

"Sounds gross. Was it cloaked in spiderwebs?"

"Yep, but otherwise in perfect condition. It's weird. Most of the stuff down there is molded, but this dollhouse is flawless. Come check it out." Sammy stood, stuffing the rest of the fritter in his mouth.

"Can I take one to Isis?" Sarah asked, plucking the chocolate donut from the box.

I would normally say no. I preferred Isis not play with the white wizards in the morning either, but I nodded instead. She would squeal with glee when she saw Sarah approaching with a donut.

Isis sat on a shag rug in front of the fire, gazing into the doll-house. We had brought the rug from our house, and though it didn't fit the decor, Isis often napped on it, so it was a must-have item.

"It's huge," Sarah marveled.

The house stood a good two feet above Isis sitting on the floor.

"Sawah," Isis yelled, standing and running to her aunt.

Sarah lifted the chocolate donut, and Isis slid to a stop on the wood floor. "Choc-it!"

She grabbed the donut and took a bite before looking back at me for permission. I nodded at her.

"Play," she mumbled through the donut, dragging Sarah to the dollhouse.

"Gothic Revival with some personal touches," Sarah said, touching the gabled roof on the dollhouse. "Even a little widow's walk. I bet this thing is worth a fortune."

"We'd have to sell our daughter along with it, I'm afraid," Sammy told her, leaning over and taking a bite from Isis's donut.

"Daddy!" she shrieked, swatting him away.

He settled on the couch next to me, and we watched Sarah plop next to Isis on the rug, peering at the old-fashioned furnishings arranged in the tiny rooms.

"WHAT'S YOUR BOOK ABOUT?" Sarah asked, picking a red crayon from the box next to Isis and coloring in a flower.

"Mine," Isis announced, snatching the crayon from Sarah's hand. "Please," she added in the same abrupt tone.

"Isis, remember what we talked about?" I asked her, gently removing the crayon from her hand. "If you want people to color with you, you have to share. You can't just snatch the crayon away."

She stared at the crayon, reaching out, but I held it away.

"Please?" she asked a second time, looking at Sarah.

"Sure, go ahead, Icy, but I'm coloring the grass with this green one. Okay?"

Isis bit her lip, staring enviously at the green crayon. Finally she huffed and accepted the red crayon, scrawling red streaks across Sarah's newly colored grass.

I grinned and shook my head.

"Toddlers. Why is everything more wonderful if someone else has it?"

Sarah looked up and laughed.

"I'm afraid that problem extends way beyond the toddler years."

"True enough," I sighed and pushed my hands through my hair, knowing I still hadn't answered the question. "In my mind it's about a woman who..." I paused, searching for the words.

Sarah set the crayon aside.

"Joins the circus? Is looking for her long-lost love? Has a sex change?"

"Ugh." I pressed my hands into my face. "Is it terrible if I'm still not sure what it's about?"

"No, you'll get there. Just keep at it, Corrie."

"Maybe I'm having a midlife crisis," I complained, stretching and wincing on the hard little sofa. "I'd like to know who designed this furniture. It's clearly not someone who considered comfort a high priority."

"I'd extend that question to this whole house," Sarah remarked. "Don't get me wrong, I appreciate the craftsmanship, but why on earth did anyone want to revive Gothic to begin with? I saw black wallpaper in the dining room. Black! As far as living here – no, thanks. You must really love my brother," she laughed.

"I do." I smiled and slipped off the couch onto the floor, pulling my knees into my chest and rocking back and forth. "Ooh, that's better. It grows on you," I added

"Me too," Isis announced, coming to lay next to me and rolling back and forth. She giggled and climbed on top of me. "Fly me, mama."

I grinned and propped her on my feet, lifting her high.

"Now you," she bellowed hopping over to Sarah and pushing her on her back.

"Yes, ma'am," Sarah laughed, floating Isis on her feet.

From upstairs there came a faint creaking, as if someone had taken a step.

"Did you hear that?" I asked Sarah.

Sammy had gone into Traverse City for a meeting with his editor.

She turned and shook her head.

We both sat still. I shushed Isis when she cried out to be lifted again.

The sound came again, like rafters sighing - or was it a footstep?

"This is an old house," Sarah answered, tilting her feet so Isis could lay across them.

"I'm just going to listen in the hall."

I stepped into the foyer.

Shadowy stillness hovered at the top of the stairs, and yet I felt distinctly that something lurked up there, just out of sight. I clutched the ornate banister and studied the gloom beyond the bit of colored light through the stained-glass window. The darkness seemed to draw the light in and devour it.

"Show yourself," I whispered, challenging the black emptiness.

The foyer seemed too warm and airless. I held my breath, unable to look away because the moment I did, something would race down the stairs behind me.

Suddenly I wanted to gather Sarah and Isis and run into the daylight.

"Hey."

A high, horrible scream punctuated the stillness as Sarah's fingers closed on my elbow.

Sarah gasped and stumbled back, and I realized it was I who had screamed.

I stuffed my fist into my mouth, shaking my head, my eyes surely as wide as hers.

"Oh my God, I'm sorry," I said, the sound of my words breaking the spell, the terror dissipating.

Isis ran into the foyer, brown eyes huge in her baby face.

"Mommy?" Isis asked, bottom lip quivering.

I gathered her in my arms and looked apologetically at Sarah.

"I was standing here listening and maybe imagining. I'm so sorry. I can't believe I screamed like that."

Sarah grinned and shook her arms out.

"Whew. Damn, Corrie, I thought someone was up there. I was ready to run to the kitchen for a butcher knife."

The rigid muscles of my face softened. Isis planted a kiss on my cheek.

"Mommy scared?"

"No, honey-bear. Not now anyway." I turned to Sarah. "Maybe I do find this house a tad spooky. There's a bookstore in Northport. Fancy a trip into town?"

Sarah shifted her wide brown eyes to the top of the staircase for just a moment.

"Yeah," she agreed. "Let's get out of here."

 ow
Corrie

"I KNOW you don't want to hear this, honey, but everyone is worried about you," Sarah told me, setting a bowl of steaming tomato soup on the table in front of me. She had made a tiny sour cream heart in the center of the bowl.

I stared at it and thought of Sammy. He and his twin were so similar it was scary, which made me laugh out loud. Scary had risen to a whole new level in my life during the previous days, and to consider a glob of sour cream scary was downright hilarious.

"This is what I'm talking about," she said, sitting across from me at the table and taking hold of my clammy hands. "Are you weeks away from the loony bin?"

I shook my head and suppressed my laughter.

"I'm sorry, I realize it's not funny. None of this is funny." The smile fell from my face. "Sammy's constantly in my thoughts, and I see this little heart and it reminds me of something he would do or say, and then I'm laughing because I can't help it. And I don't know why it's funny, and I don't understand why I can't help it..."

"It's okay," she told me, giving my hands a squeeze. "I've laughed in church and at funerals, and even one time when I was getting fired. I'm no stranger to the awkward laughter stuff. He's in my head too. He's constantly commenting on things in typical Sammy fashion."

"Thank you," I told her, wishing I could share with her the other stuff too - glimpsing him, feeling him near me.

"That being said, I think you need to talk to a therapist." She spoke the words slowly, gauging my reaction.

"The therapist who needs therapy," I murmured.

Sarah nodded and tucked one of my curls behind my ear.

"Where'd you go last night, honey? Amy mentioned you went out for a few hours?"

I flinched away and shrugged.

"I drove around. I needed to clear my head."

Guilt swirled in my stomach. I flashed on the cemetery and Sammy's brown eyes gazing at me in the stream. Sarah would love to see Sammy, hear his voice. Was I wrong to hide him from his twin?

"How's Brook?" I asked, hoping to shift the conversation.

Sarah frowned.

"I haven't seen her since..."

She paused, and I knew she'd started to say Halloween, but Halloween had become synonymous with Sammy's murder.

"You should call her," I said. "She seemed nice."

Sarah studied me, and I took a sip of the hot soup. I wasn't hungry, but if I wanted Sarah to relax, I had to take a few bites.

"She is nice but... with everything that's happened, dating seems trivial."

I nodded.

"But it's not. That's how it starts."

For a moment, I drifted back nine years to the balmy summer evening when I first met Sammy.

We were both walking out of a ridiculously bad horror movie. My girlfriend had dragged me along because she liked the lead actor. I'd dropped my notebook. The cover depicted a cow quoting the famous Rumi poem: "out beyond ideas of rightdoing and wrongdoing, there is a field..."

Sammy, alone at the theater and wearing ripped jeans and a Creepshow t-shirt, picked it up, glanced at the image, and laughed before handing it back to me.

When he looked at me, really looked at me, I experienced the strange pull I'd heard people talk about – love at first sight, instant attraction – and I tried to say something witty and indifferent, even though my heart had stopped beating, and I recognized in his gleeful brown eyes that he felt something too. Maybe not the same thing, how could I know? But something...

"May I?" he had asked, taking my notebook back. He flipped to the last page, pulled the pen from the spiral binding, and wrote his name and his phone number in surprisingly readable print.

"Will you call me?" he asked, handing my notebook back.

I was silent and oddly breathless, but I managed a nod, and then my friend Rita dragged me away with a long glance at my future husband that seemed to say 'she's not usually this crazy.'

Fourteen months later, we were married.

"You're staring into your soup like there's an eyeball floating in it," Sarah said, forcing me back to reality.

I stirred the sour cream into a swirl and took another bite.

"No eyeball, just memories. They're like landmines. No matter which direction I choose, I step on one."

∾

Sarah

SARAH SAT IN DETECTIVE COLLINS' office and drummed her fingers on the arm of her chair. Exhausted and wired, she flipped between drooping eyelids and a desire to pace the cramped office. Sammy's death had stolen her sleep. She laid awake most nights thinking about Halloween night, scanning the faces from her memory, desperately searching for the shred of evidence that would reveal Sammy's killer.

"Forensics reported no evidence on Corrie's dress," the detective announced, not bothering with introductions.

He swept into the room with two cups of coffee, slopped one in front of Sarah, and dropped into his chair. He fixed her with a cold stare.

"Okay..." She struggled to sit up careful not to spill coffee on her white t-shirt.

"There should have been bacteria from the lake, blood from touching Sammy, sweat, fibers. That dress should have told a story, and it did. It told us that someone had laundered it before we got there."

Sarah frowned, sipped her coffee, and then shook her head.

"Wait, what dress? I burned the Frankenstein's Bride dress."

"I'm sorry, you what?" the detective asked, his eyebrows meeting the sheaf of blond hair that rested on his forehead.

"I burned the dress," Sarah repeated, feeling a flush rise into her neck.

"It was evidence, valuable evidence, and you burned it?"

"I wasn't thinking about your valuable evidence, Detective. My sister was half-drowned and someone had murdered my brother."

"I understand that, Sarah. And I'm not trying to be insensitive, but for Christ's sakes, Corrie's clothes could have contained important information. What she wore that night mattered as much as Sammy's clothes."

"Well, it's gone. The dress is gone."

He sucked in his cheeks and looked away from Sarah.

"Why did you burn it?" he asked, his eyes narrowing on her face.

Sarah opened her mouth and then closed it.

"I didn't think. After I pulled Corrie from the lake, I stuck it in the bathtub. When I went back to clean the house, it was hanging there. I grabbed it and threw it in the fire. I didn't want it to remind Corrie. I wanted to protect her. If it was so important, why didn't you guys take it when you were there?"

"You failed to mention it to us, that's why. Corrie said her dress was in the laundry room. There was a black dress hanging there, and we took that one."

Sarah shrugged.

"She probably assumed that's where I put it."

The detective sighed and shook his head.

"I'm guessing this means you haven't made any progress on finding Sammy's murderer?" Sarah asked, irritated with the detective's tone.

He set his hands on the table and studied her. Sarah wished she hadn't asked the question.

"I'm very curious about the block of time your sister-in-law doesn't remember. I'm also curious about her suicide attempt. In our line of work, that indicates a guilty conscience."

Sarah glared at him.

"You're wrong, Detective. And you don't know Corrie. She loved Sammy, they loved each other. Their relationships was like something out of a fucking fairy tale. Corrie wasn't trying to kill herself, she was trying to numb the pain. She couldn't handle finding Sammy dead. She still can't. I'm terrified for her. Have you considered that Corrie was drugged? What if someone slipped a roofie into her drink?"

"A roofie?"

Oh, come on, don't make me feel stupid. Isn't that what the date-rape drug is called?"

"It is sometimes called that, yes."

"Why didn't you guys test her blood?"

"Because we had no reason to suspect she'd been drugged. And if I might remind you, you gave her a sedative yourself, and then took her to your mother's house. If you were concerned, you might have taken her to the hospital."

"My brother was fucking dead! I was out of my mind. We all were!"

Sarah stood, bit back more angry words, and stormed out of the office.

She sat in her car and blasted the heat. Her hands shook as she gripped the wheel.

"Corrie would never hurt Sammy," she grumbled, pulling out of the parking lot.

ow
Sarah

AFTER SHE SPOKE with the detective, Sarah went home and tried to work. She sketched roof-lines until her eyes blurred, but they were all wrong, and ended up crumpled in her recycling bin. Finally, she got in her car and drove to Kerry Manor.

The house was quiet when she arrived. Corrie might be napping, and Sarah had no interest in waking her. She doubted Corrie was getting much sleep, other than little sips stolen when the exhaustion became too much to bear.

Sarah stood in the foyer of Kerry Manor and considered her mother's ominous feeing upon first entering the house. Did she sense it? Or had the dark premonition already come to pass? The opportunity for an intuitive warning fading as quickly as a dream once the sleeper has awoken.

She stepped into the great room, glanced at the ugly doll house tucked in the corner. Sammy had found it in the crawl space, a dark hole in the butler's pantry that Sarah had looked in on Halloween night. Sammy had wanted to put huge rubber rats with glowing eyes in the space, and then stack the extra wine behind them so people would be forced to crawl into the black hole to refill their drinks. Corrie had given him a firm 'no,' and Sarah reminded him of his lack of liability insurance.

The square of wood contained a tiny metal handle. Sarah pulled up it up and recoiled at the blast of cold, acrid air that gusted out.

She listened for Corrie, and hearing nothing, switched on her phone flashlight and dropped into the hole, crouching and waving the beam across the dirt floor. A few old crates stood further back, thick with cobwebs.

In another corner, her light bounced over a heap of rags. She shuffled closer, recoiling at the dark, red-brown stains marring the light fabric.

❧

Corrie

I STOOD DRINKING my coffee on the porch. I wore only a thin nightshirt, and the crisp November air had teeth. Shivering, I sipped the scalding coffee, allowing the extremes of hot and cold to burn out the thoughts always gathering like storm clouds in my head.

"Corrie?"

I head Sarah's voice but didn't turn. I couldn't face her today. My dreams had been troubled, flashes of Sammy's face filled with fear. I doubted there would ever come a day when he didn't haunt me.

The glass door slid shut and Sarah paused beside me, putting her hands on the rail.

"Corrie, I found something," she said.

I nodded but trained my eyes on the horizon. The sun had already risen, and the lake was perfectly still, not a ripple in sight.

"I found a towel, Corrie, in the crawl space. It was covered in something that looked like dried blood."

Sarah's words hung in the air - not an accusation, but perhaps the start of one.

Sammy had been her twin, her other half. It made sense she would hunt for the truth at whatever cost.

I closed my eyes and felt him there behind me. He'd widen his eyes and say something funny. *Uh-oh, Gorey, you're in for it now.*

"Corrie," Sarah's tone sharpened.

I wondered how long she'd been saying my name.

"Look at me, damn it!"

She grabbed my arm and jerked me around. Hot coffee spilled from my cup, splattering us both.

"Oh damn, ouch," she hissed, pulling her white t-shirt away from her body.

The liquid scalded my bare thighs and knees, and a few drops splashed onto my feet. I barely noticed it as I sank slowly to the porch. I wrapped my arms around my legs and buried my head in my knees.

"I'm sorry," Sarah whispered. "Are you okay?"

I nodded.

"Before Halloween, Sammy said something," Sarah continued.

I wanted to put my hands over my ears and scream, but now and then her voice merged into Sammy's. If I didn't look at her, I could almost believe he stood above me.

"He said you'd been acting strangely, disappearing in the house for hours at a time. He searched everywhere and couldn't find you."

"That never happened," I said, snapping up to look at her. "Why would he say that?"

Sarah's brow was furrowed, her mouth turned down. She looked on the verge of tears. I had only seen Sarah cry twice in my life - when her and Sammy's father, died and more recently the night of Sammy's murder.

"I don't know why he said it, Corrie." Sarah crouched before me. "But things aren't adding up. Do you see that?"

I nodded, and like a song I couldn't get out of my head, the vision of that night - blood in the water, on my hands, on the rocks - drifted through. A river of memory drowning me.

"Oh God," I moaned, feeling the familiar pain in my chest like something sharp had lodged there. I wanted to tear open my ribs and wrench it free. "How will I live without him?"

I howled, and Sarah fell back, landing with a thud.

I didn't care. I moved onto my hands and knees and screamed into the deck, pushed my face down until my nose touched the smooth boards, snot and tears pooling beneath my face. When my throat grew hoarse, I cried, resting my forehead down.

Sarah's hands found me. She didn't force me up, just rubbed my back in small circles, whispering over and over, "It's going to be okay."

But I knew better.

~

Sarah

SARAH RELUCTANTLY LEFT Corrie on the porch. Her sister-in-law had refused to come back in, citing a need for more fresh air, though Sarah had seen her lips growing purple and the goose-bumps covering her arms and legs.

The towel in the crawl space had unnerved her, but what did it reveal? It might have been there before Sammy's death. It belonged at the police station. They could forensically test it for blood, blood spatter, all those little nuanced things criminologists did.

Instead, Sarah fished the towel out and stuffed it into a trash bag before throwing it in the garbage can.

She wandered into the study, empty and cold. Sammy's stuff lay strewn across the desk. A child-sized Chucky doll stood in one corner, a plastic machete clutched in his chubby baby hand.

Sarah heard the sliding glass doors open and sighed, relieved that Corrie had at least come in from the cold.

A notebook filled with Sammy's drawings lay open on the desk. He'd been working on a new comic book series featuring a man who peered into a dollhouse and became trapped inside. He was being stalked by a wicked little girl with long blonde hair.

"Creepy," Sarah muttered, returning the notebook and picking up a plastic bobble-head of Pennywise the Clown from Stephen King's, *It*. The clown grinned from the red gash in his white face.

Sammy had loved the darker side of life, but what would become of his lifelong collection of horror? Would Corrie save it for Isis? Sarah imagined Isis arriving at school show-and-tell with a Barbie-sized Freddie Krueger.

"Swamp Man," Sarah murmured, smiling as she touched a finger to the webbed feet of one of Sammy's original figures. He had gotten it on their tenth birthday, a gift from Grandma Fiona. Sarah, despite her lack of interest in horror characters, had grown jealous of the gift. She had received an art set, beautiful and useful - but the way Sammy gazed at the figure, how he propped it on his dresser and only touched it gingerly, made the toy seem otherworldly, special.

The sound of a child singing drifted into the room.

Sarah paused, listening.

Isis was staying with Amy.

Sarah stepped from the study, gazing down the dark hallway that led to the front of the house.

"One for sorrow, two for mirth, three for a funeral…"

She followed the voice, pausing at the great room. The voice sounded like Corrie, and yet…

Sarah took a breath and stepped into the doorway.

Corrie sat on her knees in front of the dollhouse. She held a tiny bureau in her hand and leaned forward, placing it in a room.

"Is there a child in here?" Sarah asked, scanning the room but already knowing the answer to her question.

"What?" Corrie looked up, her expression distant. She stared at Sarah for a moment before her eyes cleared. "What did you say, Sarah?"

Sarah faltered. "I thought I heard singing."

Corrie shrugged and looked back at the house before climbing to her feet.

"Not from me. Maybe one of Isis's toys? She has a little green dog that breaks into song at the oddest times. Sammy's going to take the batteries out one of these days."

Sarah bit her lip, watching her sister-in-law lumber across the room. Corrie stood in front of the fireplace and gazed into the flames.

"He *was* going to, you mean?" Sarah said.

Corrie turned back, her expression puzzled.

"Oh yes, of course. Was."

hen
Corrie

I OPENED the door and gave Helen a kiss on the cheek.

"Welcome to Kerry Manor," I said, moving back so she could walk through.

"What do you think, Mom?" Sammy asked, spooking his mom from behind.

She jumped, startled, and I shot Sammy a 'don't give your mother a heart attack' look.

"Sammy, don't make me paddle your bottom in front of Corrie," his mother told him through gritted teeth.

He stuck his butt out and grinned. She smacked it before pushing him away.

"I think it's…" she paused.

I could see her searching for kind words when she wanted to say what a handful of others had said - it's creepy, spooky, strange.

"I guess it's perfect for your Halloween party. Beyond that, I don't think I'd want to spend the night."

Sammy clutched his heart.

"You wound me, Mother."

She grinned and touched the embellished molding that surrounded the doorway into the great room.

"My poor little Isis probably gets lost in here."

"Not yet," I told her, taking her coat and hanging it on the wrought iron coat tree near the front door.

"Are you kidding me, Mom? This is Disneyland for Isis. She loves it."

"She loves it, or you love it?"

"Well, you know I love it," he admitted, grabbing me and twirling me around the room. "The question is, does my bride love it?"

I looked into his laughing brown eyes and nodded.

"I love you," I told him. "If you love it, I love it."

"Oh, Corrie," his mom said. "How did he ever find you?"

Sammy flopped on the couch and propped his legs on a velvet footstool.

"Well, it all started on a sunny afternoon in August," he began.

I grinned and patted her arm.

"Have a seat. I'll bring coffee while Sammy regales you with tall tales."

"Thanks, dear. No sugar, just cream," she said.

"No sugar?" I asked, surprised. His mother usually added a heaping tablespoon of sugar to her coffee, tea, oatmeal - you name it.

She rested her hands on her voluptuous hips and belly.

"I'm cutting out sugar. At least in my coffee, to start. We'll see how it goes." She winked at me.

"House-frau, bring me the canapés as well," Sammy called, blowing me kisses.

"I don't even know what canapés are," I told him. "But I'll bring you a coffee."

I selected Sammy's favorite mug, which depicted a werewolf howling at the moon, and a purple flowery one for Helen. I leaned in and inhaled the coffee before pouring the three of us steaming mugs.

Through the window, I watched the waves lap rhythmically at the shore. A crest of white washing in, massaging the stones, then pushing back out. Frothy white clouds marred the blue sky, and I hoped they would part in the afternoon so we could take Isis to play outside. Methodically I prepared our coffees, pulling cream from the refrigerator and sugar from the cupboard, stirring and setting the silver spoon in the sink.

I arranged the coffees on a tray.

As I walked from the kitchen, I glanced at the counter and paused. Next to the carton of cream, a small plastic bottle of blue antifreeze sat open, the red cap resting beside it.

"Where's the sugar?" I asked, scanning the counter.

I distinctly remembered taking it out and scooping sugar into Sammy's coffee but I hadn't put it back, had I?

"Need help, babe?" Sammy called from the living room.

I heard him get up, knew he'd walk in any moment.

I dropped the tray of coffees on the floor. The glass shattered, startling me from my momentary reverie. Before Sammy could burst into the kitchen, I grabbed the antifreeze and stuck it under the sink.

Sammy rushed in, jumping back before he stepped in the broken glass and spilled coffee.

"Whoa, what happened?"

Helen followed, her face pinched with worry.

"I stupidly tried to balance them in one hand," I lied, grabbing rags and dropping to the floor. "I've got this." I shooed them away. "I'll bring fresh cups in just a minute."

"No, babe," Sammy said grabbing the broom. "I don't want my Gorey cutting her pretty fingers."

I nodded but didn't trust myself to look at him.

"And I'll get the coffee," Helen added.

"I broke the werewolf mug," I said miserably, holding up a piece of glass.

"Guess I'll have to switch to my Zombies in Love mug, then," he told me.

When I didn't respond, he leaned close and tilted my face toward his. "Honey, it's okay. It was just a mug."

I nodded, fighting tears at the backs of my eyes and glancing toward the cupboard beneath the sink.

I OPENED my eyes and stared into the dark canopy that hung suspended above our four-poster bed. My heart thudded in my chest, and I balled my fists at my sides. My entire body buzzed with adrenaline, as if I had not just woken from a deep sleep, but had been running a sprint.

Sammy snored beside me.

I turned and stared at his profile in the dark.

Whatever had awoken me had not awoken him.

I lay still for another minute. It must have been a dream. I rolled to my side and closed my eyes.

Close by, something thumped against the ground.

My eyes shot open, and I stared in the direction of the sound. It had come from the opposite side of the room. A tall bureau stood there. Next to that, a pile of Sammy's clothes sat on a large chest.

I stared into the darkness, tracing the outline of familiar shapes, halting at something that didn't fit. The top of the object was rounded like a head, though it stood only a few feet tall.

I squinted, trying to make sense of it. One of Sammy's life-sized comic book figures? I hadn't seen one when I went to bed. In fact, he'd only brought two into the house, and he kept them in the study.

I closed my eyes and blinked them open, expecting the shape to disappear, a late-night trick of the mind - but no, it hovered there at the edge of the chest.

It was watching me.

My stomach clenched at the thought, and I reached a clammy hand beneath the covers until I found Sammy's arm.

"Sammy," I whispered, watching the silhouette in the darkness. Had it moved?

"Sammy, wake up!" I said louder.

He mumbled and pulled his arm away.

The silhouette stepped away from the wall. It moved toward a small shaft of moonlight on the wood floor. I saw the feet of the thing, a child's feet, streaked with black.

"Sammy!" I screamed, sitting up and fumbling for the lamp beside my bed.

He shot up next to me, eyes and hair wild as the light cast away the shadows.

"I'm up, I'm up," he bellowed, pushing the covers off and stepping from the bed.

I turned, pointing at the child, but no one stood next to the chest. No child or anything resembling one. The wall was empty, the floor bare except for a blanket discarded by Isis.

"What is it, Corrie? Isis? Is Isis awake?" He rubbed his eyes and blinked at me.

I opened my mouth, ready to blurt what I had seen, and then I closed it. The way he looked at me gave me pause, as if I were delicate, unbalanced.

"No, I... I thought I saw a rat running along the floor."

He frowned, sitting heavily on the bed.

"A rat?"

It was hardly a believable story. I'd never been afraid of rats, and on more than one occasion I'd rescued the little rodents from our cats.

"Yes. I'm sorry, Sammy. I was half asleep, and it spooked me."

Sammy yawned and lay back on his pillow, reaching a hand to rub my back.

"It's okay, babe. Juts go back to sleep. Lucas had an exterminator out here a week before we moved in. There are no rats."

I nodded.

"Kill the light," he murmured, closing his eyes.

I reached toward the light switch, watching the empty space where something, someone, had stood moments before. I was irrationally sure when I flicked off the light, the person would reappear

- only visible in darkness. I turned the switch and held my breath, but the room remained empty.

As I shuffled back beneath the comforter, I wanted to pretend I had imagined it, but I knew better. A child had been standing in our room.

*ow
Sarah*

RELUCTANTLY, SARAH WALKED INTO DETECTIVE COLLINS' office. He'd called that morning and asked her to come in. For reasons she didn't understand, the thought produced a withering sense of dread.

"Do you recognize this person?" he asked when she stopped in front of his desk.

Sarah studied the picture of a young man with striking green eyes and long black hair past his ears. His mouth was set in a grim line.

"No, should I? Did he kill Sammy?" She studied the detective's face, but he gave nothing away.

"I'm not sure. But I do know he was at your brother's party and he wasn't invited."

"And?" Sarah waited for the detective to elaborate.

"He has a history with Kerry Manor. He's tried to burn it down twice. Last year he was arrested for vandalizing it during the renovations, and he attacked Dane Lucas, the man who bought the house."

Sarah's eyebrows rose and she leaned closer to the picture, trying to draw him out from that night. The problem was that everyone wore costumes. She might have had a half-hour conversation with him and not known it because he was tucked behind a goblin mask.

"Why? What's his issue with Kerry Manor?"

"He claims it's haunted," the detective said, lifting the photo up. "More than haunted, he called it evil the last time he got arrested."

"What makes him say that?" Sarah asked, chilled by his comment.

"Something that stems from his childhood, according to another detective here. The kid's name is Will. Six years ago, he witnessed his father murder his mother."

Sarah grimaced, shaking her head.

"That's terrible, but..."

"But what does it have to do with the house? Yeah, that's what I asked. Will says they stumbled on Kerry Manor a week before the murder during a day at the beach. His father went in the house and had a strange experience. Will insists that something evil entered him in the house, and they took it home. Eight days later, his father strangled his mother in the bathtub."

"And what happened to his father?"

"He killed himself in jail."

"Good grief," Sarah murmured. "No wonder the kid's messed up."

"The father said the same thing. He insisted when the police arrived that he hadn't done it. He had no memory of the incident, but an evil little girl had followed him from Kerry Manor. She had killed his wife and was framing him."

"So mental illness runs in the family?" Sarah asked, but her words sounded hollow. She thought of the gaps in Corrie's memory.

"It hadn't, before the murder," Detective Collins continued. "The father's record was pristine. Not a single incident of domestic violence, not even a drunk driving. But the son fixated on his father's claims. He's been trying to destroy Kerry Manor ever since."

"Where is Will now?"

"That's what we're trying to figure out. I have a guest at your brother's party who saw him. He knew Will from school and recognized him. Will wore a black ninja costume that concealed the lower part of his face. He's only seventeen and still a minor. Unfortunately, he doesn't have a home, per se. He stays with friends, changes locations pretty regularly."

"Can't you find him in school?"

"He took online classes and graduated early. He's not in school anymore."

"Why would he kill my brother, though? I mean, Sammy wasn't the one restoring the house."

The detective shrugged.

"Why do crazy people do crazy things? We'll probably never have an answer to that question."

∾

CORRIE

I UNLOADED THE DISHES. We had bought this coffee mug in New Orleans when I was pregnant with Isis. It was bright pink and black with a colorful skull grinning out from the bone face. I put it in the cupboard, exhausted, though I'd spent most of the morning in a heap of blankets on my bed.

I was a therapist. I knew the signs of grief, depression, hopelessness. But what did any of those labels matter when you waded through it, the muck as high as your neck, the future only more of the same?

At some point I had to pull it together. I understood that on a theoretical level, but how did people actually do it? I usually counseled them to find a hobby, make friends, go for walks in nature.

I laughed and clutched the edge of the counter. For the first time in my life, I understood why people cut themselves. They sought relief from the despair trapped inside, mistakenly believing they could cut it out.

"Corrie?" I looked up to find Sarah in the kitchen doorway, an envelope in her hand.

"Hi," I said, and then returned my gaze to the dishes, still troubled each time I looked at Sarah and saw Sammy tucked in her features.

"I spoke with Detective Collins this morning." She came to stand near me, opening the envelope. "He asked about this person. Apparently, he was at the party. Do you recognize him? He was wearing a ninja costume."

I glanced at the photograph of a young man. Startling green eyes looked out from his pale face, as if the picture had taken him by surprise.

"No." I shook my head.

"His name is Will. He has a pretty bizarre history with Kerry Manor."

"Yeah?" I unloaded several plates, knowing I should listen to Sarah, but I felt as though I were receding down a long dark hallway, getting further and further away from myself.

"Corrie? Corrie!"

"Huh?" I snapped my head up and realized she'd asked me something, maybe had been talking for a while.

"I asked if Sammy ever mentioned him. Maybe he and Sammy had an encounter before that night?"

I glanced at the picture again.

"He's just a boy," I murmured, rubbing my temple with one hand and bracing myself against the counter with the other.

"Are you okay?" Sarah asked.

If I looked at her, her forehead would be marred with little lines of worry.

"No, I'm fine. I'm going to finish the dishes and take a nap. I'm not feeling well."

~

Sarah

SARAH HUGGED Corrie goodbye and walked to the front door. She opened and closed it with a bang, and then slipped into the hall closet, tucking behind a rack of coats.

Not sure what compelled her to hide in the house, she waited, listening to Corrie putting dishes in the sink. Sarah could see the great room through a slit in the hall door.

After several minutes, Corrie walked by clutching one of Sammy's shirts, breathing in the fabric. Though Sarah could not see her face, she suspected Corrie's eyes held the same glazed expression that had come over her in the kitchen.

Corrie sat heavily on the couch. For several minutes she didn't move, and then something fell to the floor. Sammy's shirt.

"One for sorrow, two for mirth."

Sarah froze when she heard the song and squinted forward. Corrie sang in the voice Sarah had heard before, a child's voice.

Corrie stood, and her body looked different. Her head was high, her eyes bright and fierce. A little smile played on her lips, and she skipped across the room to a playpen in the corner. She reached down and pulled out one of Isis's dolls.

Sarah recognized it as the Raggedy Ann doll her mother had given Isis at her last birthday.

"Dolly's been bad," Corrie said, holding the doll out in front of her. "Dolly has to go to the room. Bad Dolly made Mommy drop her ironing."

Corrie tucked the doll beneath her arm and bounded from the room, running up the stairs.

Sarah slipped out, pressing against the wall and listening to Corrie's footsteps in the upstairs hallway. Stepping lightly, Sarah hurried up the stairs.

She saw Corrie disappear into the master bedroom. Sarah

waited, counting off sixty seconds, and then followed, pushing the door open quietly.

The room appeared empty. Sarah crept to the bed and peeked beneath it, and then moved to the closet to peer behind Corrie and Sammy's clothes, her eyes lingering for a moment on Sammy's Bigfoot slippers.

Where had Corrie gone?

Sarah moved along the perimeter of the room, touching the paintings, oil portraits of another time. The huge wardrobe stood near a vanity arranged with Corrie's makeup and a scattering of Isis's toys. Sarah looked behind the wardrobe, but found no other door Corrie could have gone through.

Above her, she heard movement. Had Corrie somehow climbed into the rafters?

Sarah looked at the ceiling, following the line of footsteps across the room, and then the distinct clap of bare feet on stairs.

She tiptoed across the room and tucked herself behind the long drapery that shielded the gloomy day.

A tiny metallic pop met her ears, and then the wall to the right of the wardrobe swung out, revealing a dark staircase.

Corrie stepped from the shadows, her eyes glassy, one of Isis's teddy bears clutched to her chest. She looked into the bear's face, running her hand over the shaggy brown fur. Sarah saw Corrie's lips moving but could not hear her words.

A little stone of fear rested in the pit of Sarah's stomach as she watched Corrie.

Corrie started to sing, "One for sorrow, two for mirth." She swayed from side to side, her voice high and unnatural.

She wandered from the room, petting the bear and leaving the wall open behind her.

"Three for a funeral, four for a birth," she sang as moved away down the hall.

Sarah waited until she heard Corrie's footsteps on the main staircase, and then quickly shuffled to the dark stairway.

She crept up the stairs, inhaling dust and a smell of smoke, as if a candle had just been extinguished. At the landing she stared into darkness, fumbling her hands along the wall for a light switch but finding none. She fished out her phone and pressed the flashlight icon.

She shone the light across the room.

An old brass bed, child-sized, was tucked in one corner. Several of Isis's toys lay strewn along the floor.

On a little table beside the bed lay a doll, odd and misshapen.

Sarah walked closer and stared at the antique and ugly thing. Its cracked, leathery body looked like real skin, with little patches of matted black fur poking forth.

"Cat's fur," she whispered, imagining who would fashion a doll from the corpse of a cat.

Someone had sewn hair to the doll's head and this hair, she was sure, was human. Long and blonde mixed with other colors, what might have been golden red, and darker black shot through with gray. The mother's hair, she thought.

Crude mismatched buttons were the doll's eyes, and a jagged line of red yarn created a mouth twisted in a lopsided smile.

Beneath her, something banged, and Sarah dropped the doll, startled. She took a moment to understand what the sound had been.

Corrie had closed the door to the secret room.

ow
Sarah

SARAH CLICKED the light on her phone and pressed against the wall, expecting to hear Corrie's footfalls on the steps. Instead she heard Corrie skipping back down the hallway, the muffled nursery rhyme drifting through the floorboards.

After several minutes, she turned the light back on, wanting to search the room but overwhelmed with fear that Corrie had just trapped her inside.

Sarah crept down the steps.

"I'm fine," she whispered, nudging her panic aside to focus on the dark wall before her. When Corrie had emerged earlier, she'd heard a click. There had to be a handle of some sort.

Sarah glided her phone's light up and down the wall, searching.

"There's nothing," she moaned, feeling a growing heat in the stairwell. She pulled her t-shirt away and waved it, wiping sweat from her brow with her forearm.

Holding the phone in one hand, she allowed her free hand to

roam across the wall, searching for an abnormality, a little crevice, something. Minutes ticked by, but the wall was flat and unblemished.

She glanced at her phone, knowing there was no reception.

What would happen if she banged on the door? Would Corrie let her out?

She leaned forward, resting her forehead against the wall and it swung out, sending her sprawling to the floor in the master bedroom. She rolled sideways and sat up, listening. Had Corrie heard?

No footsteps started up the stairs, but Sarah waited, oddly afraid that Corrie would step into the doorway at any moment and fix her with that blank stare.

When her sister-in-law didn't appear, Sarah hurried from the room and down the stairs. She paused at the great room and then peeked around the corner. No sign of her. From deep in the house, the study perhaps, a high, childlike giggle rang out. Sarah slipped out the door and ran to her car.

～

"I'M HAPPY YOU CALLED." Brook leaned over Sarah from behind. Her wavy dark hair, streaked with purple, brushed Sarah's cheek.

Sarah leaned back against her chair and shut her eyes.

When she'd returned home from Kerry Manor, she'd dialed Brook without a second thought. Each time she drifted away from the memory of the awful little attic, Corrie's childlike voice would pop into her mind and conjure the experience again.

She needed a friend, she needed her twin. He was her sounding board, her voice of reason, but he was dead. She missed him, and the missing had a life of its own - like a ghoul hunkering in the corner, slobbering at her with its needy, desperate eyes. She wanted to shut it in a closet, return to business as usual, get on with the falling-in-love with Brook thing. But she couldn't.

She imagined Corrie in that huge, empty house, singing like a little girl. In a day or two, Amy would return Isis, and then what? Was she safe with her mother?

Brook spun Sarah's chair around. She straddled her, sitting on Sarah's lap, and looked into her eyes.

"I read if you stare someone in the eyes for four minutes, you'll fall in love with them," she said, her eyes searching Sarah's face.

Brook's skin was smooth and pale, unblemished. She wore dark eye makeup that caused her green eyes to pop like jewels in her pale face.

When Sarah had introduced Brook to Sammy at the Halloween party, he called her Elvira and winked at Sarah, hinting that he approved.

Unlike many of Sarah's friends, Brook teetered on the edge of something playful and dark. She was not a jock. She wore long necklaces with silver spiders and cat's eyes. When she'd arrived, Sarah spotted a guitar propped in her passenger seat.

Despite barely knowing her, Sarah suspected if she confided everything to Brook, she would believe her.

"Did you know about Kerry Manor before Halloween?" Sarah asked, planting her hands firmly on Brook's thick thighs. Through her jeans, she felt her warmth.

"Yeah." Brook nodded. "I was obsessed with the house for about a year when I was thirteen."

"Really?" Sarah asked. "Why?"

"I grew up in Suttons Bay, pretty close to Northport. Old-timers still talked about Kerry Manor, and kids went up there to peek around. It had the same kind of allure as the old asylum. Abandoned, spooky, the perfect place for a séance."

"A séance? You're kidding, right?"

Brook turned her eyes into tiny slits and let out a diabolical cackle, leaning her head back and exposing her soft, pale throat.

"My girlfriend and I conned our neighbor into driving us up there with a Ouija board we bought at Walmart. Scariest half-hour of my life. To be honest, that's why I went to your brother's party. Gloria invited me, and I like Gloria, but she's not the usual type I chum around with, if you know what I mean?"

Sarah grinned, imagining Gloria pumping her arms as she sped around the skating rink, insisting that all things in life were a competition even if you were traveling in a circle.

"I can see how that would be the case."

"But when she mentioned Kerry Manor, I was all over it. I'd never gotten the house out of my head, and I'd never gone back. Figured if there was a whole house full of people, I'd be safe."

Sarah lifted her eyebrows.

"You were afraid to go back?"

Brook crawled her hand, thick with silver rings, up Sarah's arm and traced her collarbone.

"Yes, I was."

Sarah wanted to kiss her, to wrap her arms around Brook and inhale her scent - an alluring mixture of coconut oil and rosemary.

Brook turned her head to the side.

"What's going on behind those chocolate eyes?"

Sarah sighed.

"Too much. I want you to tell me what happened at Kerry Manor. Will you do that?"

Brook frowned and then nodded.

"Yeah, but let's crack open that six-pack first. My memory improves after a beer."

Brook started to climb off, but Sarah held her in place for another moment. Brook leaned in and kissed her, her lips deliciously soft. Sarah pulled away, knowing if she kissed her much longer, they'd find their way to the bedroom.

Archie plodded from his dog bed and settled beneath her chair.

"It was around midnight when we got to the house," Brook started. "Our neighbor sat in his car and listened to the radio while we snuck in. The house was boarded up, but Kim hoisted me up on her shoulders, and I crawled through a broken window. The house smelled wet and smoky, which seemed strange since the fire happened like a hundred years ago. I had to reach out and pull Kim in through the window too. The second we got inside, we were both scared shitless, but neither of us wanted to bitch out. We set the Ouija down in the big room, probably had a fancy name back in the day. There was some old furniture, spray paint on the walls, a mattress in the corner, which grossed us out pretty good. Your typical abandoned house. We lit a few candles and sat down by the Ouija board, but before we could try it out, we heard someone moving upstairs. It sounded like a little kid skipping. We practically tripped over our own feet running to the window. Kim dove out headfirst and fractured her wrist. I went a little slower, but I swear I heard a little girl coming down the stairs, singing."

Brook held up her arm, awash in gooseflesh.

"Your friend fractured her arm? Because of a noise?"

Brook rolled her eyes.

"Fear is a powerful emotion, maybe more powerful than love. Whatever we heard, it wasn't human, Sarah, and it was real. As real as anything else in this fucked-up world."

"What was she singing?" Sarah asked.

"I couldn't make it out. A kids' rhyme, I think."

"Did the neighbor take you to the hospital?"

Brook shook her head.

"We snuck out. We would have been in deep shit. He took us back to Kim's house, and we were practically bouncing into the roof of his car with the adrenaline rush. When we got home, we saw Kim's arm, and by morning it was the size of a baseball. She told her mom she tripped over a pile of laundry."

"Did you ever go back?"

"Hell no. I had to sleep with the light on for a year. I still get the creeps when I hear nursery rhymes. It sounds dramatic, I know, but it left an impression. So, tell me why you're curious about Kerry Manor. Is it because of your brother, or…?"

"Obviously it's because of my brother," Sarah snapped, immediately regretting her tone. "Sorry. I feel like I'm in an endless loop of acting like an ass and apologizing for it lately."

Brook smiled and clinked her can against Sarah's.

"I've been doing that my whole life. Though I prefer the term bitch."

"Thanks," Sarah said. "I mean it. Thanks for coming here and for not making me feel crazy."

"Crazy is subjective," Brook said. "Now answer me this, Sarah Flynn. Do you think something supernatural killed your brother?"

hen
Corrie

"I HAD THE STRANGEST DREAM," I told Sammy, stopping behind him at the stove and wrapping my arms around his waist.

"Not another merman dream, I hope? I can't compete with a Fabio-esque man of the sea."

I laughed and leaned my head between his shoulder blades. Several years before, I had dreamed of falling in love with a merman who lived in the great lakes. He took me beneath the water to live in his pearl-walled cave. I told Sammy of the dream, and ever since he claimed to live in terror I would one day abandon him for my dreamland merman.

"No merman," I said, sniffing the air. Sammy was making his famous peanut butter pancakes. "I was a little girl living here in Kerry Manor."

I moved to the refrigerator and pulled out butter and syrup, setting them on the kitchen counter.

"It's grainy, but I was angry in the dream because my older sister had a doll I wanted."

Sammy turned from the stove and cocked an eyebrow. "Maybe a deeply buried subconscious resentment of Amy? Should we call the psychoanalyst?"

I wadded up a paper towel and flicked at him.

"Do we have one of those on speed dial now?"

He batted it away and nodded.

"Yes, we do. Gotta make sure my family is well adjusted. For Christmas this year, we're starting family therapy."

"Ha." I grabbed plates and knives. "I'll give you some family therapy," I laughed, holding a butter knife in the air.

"You wouldn't," he groaned, grabbing his chest. "You know if I die first, you'll be stuck with my ghost."

"Well, that's reason enough to keep you alive. Anyway," I continued. "In this dream, I wanted my sister's doll and couldn't have it, so I killed her cat and made a doll from its skin."

Sammy turned, grimacing.

"Okay, now we're definitely signing up for family therapy."

"Stop it," I scolded him jokingly. Though a tiny part of me truly wanted him to stop. The dream had unnerved me.

"Isis still asleep?" I asked him.

"In the great room. She woke up crying this morning, and you know what's weird? She wasn't in her room, but in the bathroom. In the tub!"

"What?" I asked, frowning. "I've never seen her climb out of the crib. How?"

Sammy shrugged.

"Apparently you're both adventurous at night."

"I wasn't last night, was I?" I asked. Several times Sammy had found me sleepwalking through the house at night. It concerned me, but not nearly as much as the thought of Isis making her way to the bathroom in the dead of night. "I don't remember getting up."

"I don't think so," Sammy said. "But I slept hard last night. I didn't even pee."

I smiled.

"That is miraculous."

Isis was curled on a blanket in the great room. Sammy had not yet built a fire, and a chill lingered.

"Hi, Honey Bear." I lifted her from the floor and carried her to the couch. She turned her sleepy face at me and then dozed back off. I cuddled her, pulling a throw from the floor to smooth over us.

A dull aching lingered just behind my eyes, and my mouth tasted of pennies.

"Babe, can you grab me a glass of water?" I called to Sammy, brushing a lock of hair from Isis's forehead and kissing the perfect patch of skin beneath.

The dream from the night before was already slipping away. Still, the satiny texture of the cat's soft skin after the fur had been shaved off lingered at the tips of my fingers.

"What a terrible dream," I whispered, kissing Isis a second time.

ow
Sarah

"TED MORGAN?" Sarah asked the man who stepped from the white pickup truck with a decal plastered to the side that read Morgan's Building and Construction.

"The one and only." Ted closed his door. "And you are?"

"Sarah Flynn." She thrust her hand toward him and he took it, giving it a shake.

She watched his mind work, and when he placed her name, he looked puzzled.

"You're related to-"

"Yes. Sammy was my twin."

"My condolences, Miss Flynn, or Mrs....?"

"Ms. Flynn. And I appreciate it. I came across something strange at Kerry Manor, and wondered if you could help me."

He leaned back against his truck.

"Sure, go ahead."

"I found an attic above the master bedroom. It was hidden behind a paneled wall. When I looked at the house plans, it didn't show up. Why wasn't it renovated?" Sarah asked. She had pulled up the house's master plans on Dane Lucas's website, but the attic was nowhere on them.

"I don't know anything about an attic in Kerry Manor," Ted said.

Sarah opened her bag and drew out the set of folded house plans.

He squinted at the house plan, shrugging. "It's been a busy year. I must have missed it. I didn't exactly go around tapping on every wall and searching for the hollow one. How did you find it?"

Sarah thought of Corrie and shuddered.

"I was exploring the master bedroom."

"Hmph. Well, best if you tell Corrie and her little one to steer clear of it. I can't say if the floor is sound. Probably lead paint all over the place. The usual culprits. I'll get to it in the spring. To be honest, I figured Corrie'd move out after..." He didn't say 'Sammy died,' but Sarah nodded.

"Me too. Hoped, actually. Maybe you could give her a little nudge, say there's more work to do."

He lifted an eyebrow.

"Is there a reason you'd like me to do that?"

Sarah had a dozen reasons. Unfortunately, they all stemmed from the paranormal, and Sarah didn't much feel like seeing his expression if she told him her concerns.

"I think it's traumatic for her to be there. Someone murdered Sammy in the back yard. If not for Corrie, at least for Isis. It's not a healthy place for either of them to be."

"Have you told Corrie that?"

"Of course," Sarah snapped. "But she's not exactly in her right mind."

"To be honest, Ms. Flynn, it's not my place to ask Corrie to vacate. Your brother's agreement was with Dane Lucas. He's the owner of Kerry Manor. Overseeing the renovations is where my business with the house ends."

Sarah stared at him, weighing her next words.

"Did anything strange happen during your renovations?" she asked.

The builder gazed at her appraisingly.

"Explain strange."

Sarah faced him.

"I can't explain it, because I don't know what it might have been. Sounds, things moving, stuff like that."

"I had thirty guys working out there on any given day. It was nothin' but sounds and movement."

"Did any of them describe anything bizarre?"

He sighed and rested his large hand on the hood of his truck, as if that small connection might keep the haunted things away.

"I know what you're getting at - the Kerry Manor urban myths. I've heard a few stories, but I didn't experience nothing like that."

"Okay, but did anyone else?"

"I don't want to read about this in this newspaper."

"You won't."

"Maybe a handful of comments. I had a guy email me, he thought one of the other workers was bringing their kid to the site."

"Their kid?"

"Yeah, a little girl. He kept hearing her singing. I talked to the other guys, and they swore up and down they weren't bringing no kids. Then later, two more of 'em admitted they heard a little girl singing too."

Sarah nodded for him to go on.

"One guy, Ralph, real quiet type, walked off the job and said he wasn't comin' back."

"Why?"

"He said he felt weird givin' me a reason because he didn't have one he could put his finger on, just a feelin' what we were doin' was wrong, renovating the old Kerry mansion. But Ralph's been livin' in these parts a long time, his dad's an old codger, and I've no doubt those superstitions passed on to his son."

"Will you give me Ralph's phone number?"

"Sure, but he moved on down to Florida 'bout three months ago. His dad lives in town. The big old rambler across from the library."

"I know it," Sarah said, picturing the old farmhouse with its peeling paint and shingles half-falling off the roof.

"Anything else?" she asked.

The man sighed, and Sarah knew he'd had an experience, something he didn't want to divulge. But sharing the other men's complaints had warmed him up.

"I stopped out at the property one night, eleven or so. I forgot my power drill out back. I smelled smoke. I was sure that little shit who's tried to torch the place a couple times must'a come back to finish the job. I went runnin' into the house, mad as a wet hen, wavin' a crowbar with a mind to scare him off. There was fire in the back of the house, I saw it. It burned my eyes. I ran down the hall, and then" He wrinkled his forehead and held out his empty palms. "Poof, gone. I'd been workin' with some varnish that day, staining the stairs, and I figured the fumes..." He waved his hand in the air, but Sarah knew neither of them believed fumes caused him to hallucinate the fire.

"I pretty well wrote it off until my wife told me the history of Kerry Manor, the little girl burnin' up her family. I'll tell you, I was happy to be rid of the job. Paid mighty fine, but money ain't everything."

"Do you regret assisting with the renovations?"

The man shrugged.

"Somebody was gonna do it. Might as well have been me."

"Thanks for your time," Sarah said, turning away.

"One more thing," the man said.

Sarah turned back.

"Your brother, he called me a few days before it all went down and asked me some of the same questions you're askin' me now."

"Sammy called you wondering about strange experiences in the house?"

The man nodded, pulling a pouch from his back pocket and tucking a wad of tobacco beneath his lower lip.

"Yep."

Sarah drove home mulling over the man's words. Somehow, the most disturbing piece of all was that her brother had called the man only days before his death.

ow
Corrie

"Juicy, juicy," Isis bellowed, leaning from the cart and grabbing at a stacked display of juice boxes. I handed her a box and steered the cart down another aisle. I tried to think about what we needed, knowing I should have made a list. I had not gone to the grocery store since Sammy's death. The freezer full of frozen casseroles ensured I didn't have to, but that morning I realized I had no coffee creamer and Isis was out of baby vitamins. I hated to go, and almost called Helen, but couldn't bring myself to ask for the favor.

"Cookies," Isis squealed, waving at a shelf. I plucked a box of chocolate chip and dropped them in the cart.

"Cream and vitamins, cream and vitamins," I whispered. I could do this. I had to do this.

"What was that, ma'am?" a voice startled me, and I glanced up a moment before I crashed my cart into the young store clerk stocking cans of soup.

"Oh, nothing. I'm sorry." I turned the cart and went to the

checkout lane, the cream and vitamins forgotten in my haste to leave the store.

I could feel the tendrils of panic rising into my belly. Soon they'd wrap around my lungs and squeeze. After that, I'd see the black spots begin to dance behind my eyes. I needed to get to the car before that happened.

I fumbled money to the cashier and hurried toward the door, glancing at the bulletin board heavy with fliers advertising everything from free kittens to reiki massage. One image caught my attention and I paused, my panic momentarily forgotten.

A spectral figure, almost transparent, stood beneath three bolded words: "They're Not Gone." I read the paragraph beneath quickly with Isis pulling on my arm. The flier described a gathering for those who had lost loved ones and wanted to reach out, make contact.

At the bottom of the paper, small tabs held a web address. I ripped one off and stuffed it into my pocket.

Isis dug through the paper bag of groceries, searching for the cookies.

I took a deep breath and lifted the box from her hands, oddly calm. The panic attack had not taken me. I no longer felt the vice surrounding my lungs.

"Here, honey." I handed her a cookie and pushed the cart into the cool November day.

Sarah

"Mr. Pulver?" Sarah stood on the sidewalk in front of the old house.

A thin man, with an orange hunting cap tucked over his ears, likely nearing ninety, sat in a rocking chair reading a book. He looked up and squinted toward Sarah.

"Who's there? Melissa with the Girl Scout Cookies?"

Sarah walked closer and waved.

"Sorry, no cookies here. My name's Sarah Flynn. I was hoping to ask you a few questions."

She glanced at the cover of Mr. Pulver's book, which read "Fancy Cat Breeds" in tall black letters. In a photo beneath the title, a woman held a huge, fluffy gray cat with yellow eyes.

He sat up in his chair and set the book aside, tapping the cover.

"Ever seen a Norwegian Forest Cat, Sarah? Big as a bobcat, and fierce too. Thinkin' bout gittin' one fer security."

"A cat?" Sarah asked skeptically. "I hate to tell you, sir, but my impression of cats is when trouble arrives, they run and hide under the bed."

He stared up at her, his little blue eyes watery, and chuckled.

"True enough, but it's not burglars I'm worried about. They say cats can sense evil. Did you know that?"

Sarah sat on a wooden porch swing.

"Yeah, I have heard that. Funny you should mention evil, Mr. Pulver. I was hoping to ask you some questions about Kerry Manor."

The man frowned and picked the book back up, holding it against his chest like a talisman.

"Sure, sure. I've got stories and memories. What would like to know, Miss Sarah?"

"Everything," she admitted.

He grinned and reached into his mouth, popping out his bottom dentures.

"These lowers give me trouble when I'm talkin' too long," he admitted, plopping them into a water glass. "James and Winifred Kerry built Kerry Manor in 1883. Winni, as they called her, was pregnant with their first child, a girl they named Stella."

Pulver leaned back in his chair, eyes half closed as he talked.

"In 1872, Traverse City saw its first railroad, and life was booming in these parts. James Kerry was a businessman and realized there were opportunities to be had. He moved his growing family from somewhere out east. Rumor says an Ottawa trapper told Kerry of the rugged beauty at the tip of the Leelanau Peninsula, and the man became obsessed with building his mansion at the place where civilization ends. Back then you were hard-pressed to find a doctor, or even a grocery to buy a loaf of bread, up there. I can't say how his wife felt about the move, but he constructed his mansion and they moved right in. According to my pa, there was never no trouble at Kerry Manor until after the girl-child, Ethel, went into the asylum."

"Why was she institutionalized?"

Pulver shrugged, spotting something over Sarah's shoulder and twittering his fingers.

"Here kitty, kitty, kitty. Come here, Mickey."

Sarah turned to see a fat tabby cat lazily wandering from the neighbor's yard. He trotted up the steps and planted himself just out of reach of Pulver's outstretched fingers.

Pulver sighed and waved his hand dismissively.

"He likes to play hard to get. Five minutes and he'll be in my lap, purring like a lawn mower."

Sarah smiled, watching the cat crane his neck and vigorously lick his belly.

"My pa knew Ethel, went to the same school, though he was a few years younger. Said before she went to the asylum she was a pretty typical kid, got into a few scraps now and then. But after they released her, she was odd, real sneaky-like. He saw her push another little girl out of a tree. The girl broke her arm, and it could'a been worse according to my pa. Could'a killed her if she'd landed on the rake lyin' down below."

"What did everyone think at the time?"

Pulver shrugged.

"It was a different time. People didn't sit around mullin' over why a kid was bad or good. Kids was just kids. But after she burned her family up, well, that changed things, didn't it? They decided James Kerry must have been beatin' her or somethin'. Not that it was out of the ordinary to take a belt to your young ones in those days."

"I'm curious how they knew Ethel Kerry started the fire?" Sarah asked.

"She nailed the door closed on her family and hid in the dumb waiter upstairs. Hammer and nails was on the floor in her parents' bedroom where they found her dead, so they put two and two together. I ain't no detective, but the writing was on the wall."

"What happened to Kerry Manor after the fire?"

"It sat. There was a lot of superstitious folks in those days. Nobody wanted to live in that house. Later on, other kinds of stories came out of the house. People who went there and came back funny-actin'. Almost like there was a bad luck charm on Kerry Manor, and if you got too close, it'd grab hold and follow you home."

"By the time I was growin' up, my pa was right spooked by the old place. Me and my brothers wasn't allowed anywhere near it. Course, that made it all the more enticing. I went once in high school with a few buddies. We threw some rocks at the windows - that kind of thing."

"Did anything happen?"

Mickey hopped into Pulver's lap, turning twice before settling into a little ball of fur, head tucked near his back legs.

"Not to me, per se, but my friend Jerry went up real close to the house to peek in. He came away screaming, blood runnin' down his face. Somethin' stabbed a piece of glass into his face. He thought he saw someone movin' inside, and then a hunk of glass came flyin' out the window and lodged in his cheek. We ribbed him about it good, said he prob'ly stuck his face too close and a piece stickin' from the frame got him."

"Do you think that's what happened?"

"No." Pulver smoothed his liver-spotted hands over the cat's back. They seemed to stiffen, and he massaged his knuckles, opening and closing his fingers. "Jerry was the toughest kid I knew, and he didn't tell no lies. I don't think a one of us doubted his story. It was just our way to rag each other."

"Did you know they restored Kerry Manor?" Sarah asked.

"Heard somethin' bout that." He nodded, his hand drifting to the side to rest on his book of fancy cats. "Damn fool thing. That house is as haunted as a plague graveyard. Best if they'd burned the whole place to the ground, trees and all."

ow
Corrie

I SAT in the circle and wrinkled my nose at the incense wafting out from the ceramic turtle to my right. The worn, red and purple rug beneath me scratched at my bare calves, and I welcomed the sensation because I was uncomfortable.

There were no eyes on me. Everyone kept their polite distance, glancing at the wall hangings or closing their eyes and humming along to the ambient music drifting out from the laptop perched on a small glass side table.

Dede, the spirit guide, sashayed into the room with bells clanging on her wide hips. They were silver and copper and hung above her camel-colored tulle skirt on a belt of leather and beads. She sat in the single opening of our circle on a turquoise meditation cushion that barely supported her voluptuous bottom.

I struggled to hold my lips in a straight, grim line. This was one of those moments. When Sammy and I would have shared silent laughter, and later in bed, we would have bellowed like children. Everything about the scene had the surreal quality of a bad movie. I was visiting a spirit guide who'd converted her garage into a New Age hovel, complete with mandala wall hangings and wooden statues of pregnant deities.

"Let us begin," Dede told the group, turning down the lights.

The candle flames flickered on our ghoulish faces.

"We will connect now. Turn your left palm up and your right palm down. Take the hands of your brothers and sisters."

I pressed my clammy left hand into that of a man wearing a baby blue polo shirt. Sweat stains spread beneath his armpits, and he gave me a tiny, tight smile. I felt his anxiety streaming into my palm, and I gave it a little squeeze because I knew he sensed mine as well. My right hand went into the palm of Miss Cleo. Or that's what Sammy would have called her. She was a heavyset black woman in a burnt orange tunic rimmed with purple lace. Her thick braids were piled on her head in a sort of crown, run through with strings of colored pearls. She rubbed her thumb along my wrist and murmured something that sounded like "it's all gonna be okay," though I may have imagined it.

In the center of our circle stood a small shrine erected on a wooden block. On the altar, Dede had placed an Egyptian Book of the Dead, a string of maroon prayer beads, and photos or trinkets from our loved ones. I could see Sammy's glasses sticking from beneath the photo of a slender, blonde woman leaning down to smell a bushel of pink roses. I knew the woman belonged to the man in the blue polo. He had not told me this, and I had not seen him put the picture on the altar, but still I knew.

Half-melted candles surrounded the shrine, and their tiny flames flickered and danced. I stared at the candle in front of me and watched it dip and rise, undulating from side to side like the sinewy body of a snake charmer. As I stared, the flame grew taller and more pointed. It rose until it stood higher than all the other flames, and when I realized that the woman in bells had shifted her attention toward me, I broke my gaze and the candle shrank back down.

"Sing through this body, speak through this body, I summon thee, I summon thee..." she chanted, and her eyelids flickered and she swayed from side to side. The bells on her skirt jingled, and my hands grew moist. The candle flames brightened, and the shadows in the surrounding faces deepened.

Nausea crept over me. It began in my throat with a trickle of saliva that seeped back and down, lingering. The nausea dropped into my chest, and then my belly. Only after it washed through my gut did it race back up into my brain, where the entire world tilted on its axis like a rolling ball.

I clenched my eyes tight, and the vision of blood-soaked towels stuffed into a black plastic bag raced behind my eyelids and sent lightning bolts of dizziness through my whole body. I slumped forward and my curly hair caught a flickering candle flame. It burst like a firework, as if I'd hosed myself with a can of hairspray, which I had not.

Startled cries rang out. The man in the blue polo patted at my burning hair, and seconds later, the woman in bells threw a glass of tepid water onto my head. I gasped and rolled away from the flames. I folded myself into a tiny ball and sobbed into my sweater, which I'd bunched up to my mouth, ignoring my exposed stomach and back.

Everyone was murmuring and moving, and someone turned the lights back on.

Time passed, and then I heard tinkling bells as Dede sashayed back across the room and knelt on the floor behind me. She rolled me over, and suddenly I saw her differently. Her face was warm and kind, filled with compassion.

"Let me help you up."

I struggled up to sitting, my hair dripping little rivulets onto my collar. I touched the piece of hair that had been singed, and the end was crispy.

"Here," she said, and clipped the hair with scissors. "Now it's a reminder, a scar, and you'll cherish it."

She put the piece of hair she had cut into a pocket in her skirt.

"Do you mind?" she asked, and I shook my head.

I didn't speak as she guided me to my feet and through the beaded curtain that led down a dark hallway, and then into a small house. She led me to her kitchen table, where I sat on a high stool and rested my elbows on the smooth red surface of her kitchen table. Everything in the kitchen was red. The toaster and coffee pot and dishtowels and throw rugs. The kitchen table was red, and little red cushions rested on the stools surrounding it. Red roses sat in a white vase on top of the refrigerator.

She returned with a t-shirt that boldly stated, *Take Back the Night*. I took off my shirt and slid hers on, too overwhelmed to feel awkward at my nudity.

"So, tell me about Sam," she said gently, setting his eyeglasses on her table.

I stared at the silver frames against the red surface. I reached out and touched one lens, knowing if I put them on, I'd develop an almost immediate headache.

Blind as a vampire bat, he had told me the first time I tried them out.

"Lots of red in here," I said.

"Muladhara," she told me. "It's the first chakra, or the root. Red is the color that symbolizes it. It's about our connection to earth and groundedness. It's also about safety and survival. This is my root chakra room."

"Hmm..."

"And red makes me think of love, not to mention I like the color." She winked at me and looked back at the glasses.

"Safety and survival." I repeated her words, and then more images of red besieged me. Red on my white dress, on my pale hands, on the stones, at the edge of Sammy's mouth.

The woman watched me but said nothing.

"Sammy was my husband, but he was murdered."

She nodded, as if affirming something she already suspected.

"And these were his." She touched the glasses, and I thought I saw her shrink from them, but couldn't be sure.

"Yes."

"Why did you come here?"

I stared at her watching me, and then I said the first words that popped into my mind.

"To see if he knows..."

The woman crinkled her forehead.

"To see if he knows what? That he's dead?"

"Yes," I replied quickly. "I can still feel him, and I wonder if he realizes he died."

The woman turned to the stove where her teakettle whistled.

She took the kettle – red – and grabbed two mugs from the cupboard. She prepared our teas, adding ginger and elderberry syrup.

"Skull cap tea," she told me, handing me a mug.

I took a sip and, despite the syrup, grimaced at the bitter flavor.

"It will soothe your grief. It's pouring off you in waves."

"Can you sense him? Sammy?"

I knew she could. How else had she known his name?

"Yes, I sense him. But I cannot separate what's coming from you and what's coming from him."

"I don't understand."

"Well, it's like there's no distinction between the images and thoughts he sends me, and the ones I pick up from you. You must have been very close."

"We still are."

The woman smiled and nodded.

"I've often dreamed of a love like that. A love that withstands even death."

I took another drink and stared at the woman hard.

"I need to contact him. I need someone that can help me reach him."

"I'm not a medium, not in the usual sense, anyway. My gifts are more like enhancement. If an energy is there, I can draw it out. But I have the sense you're looking for something..."

"More real," I blurted, not knowing what it meant. "I want someone who knows about death, not just light and angels and energy. I need Hermes, the God who can travel into the Underworld and bring Sammy back."

The woman dropped her gaze, frowning. She stayed quiet for a moment more and then seemed to come to a decision. She left the room, and I waited, glancing toward the window and the dark night.

Returning, she handed me a small sheet of parchment paper.

"There's a book I've heard of. It contains a story, and rumor has it, it's a true story. My advice is that you start there. It may not be easy to find. It's been out of print for a few years."

I looked at the sheet of paper and read *The Summoning by Fletcher Wolfe*.

hen
Corrie

"I AM the eternally gorgeous Bride of Frankenstein," I told Sarah, holding up the moth-eaten wedding gown I had bought at the Salvation Army. Sammy's mother had improved upon the dress, adding green lace and black stitching. I would dye my creamy brown hair black for the occasion and pile it high on my head, run through with cobwebs and bones.

I heard Sammy downstairs, directing his mother.

"Yes, exactly. Little fangs come out of the baby's mouth. Head blown partially off."

Sarah cocked her head.

"He's wearing a Total Recall costume? Veering from the traditional horror cast?" she asked.

"Yep, he says he's overdone Dracula and the Werewolf, so he's onto space aliens."

"Humph, well, I'm sticking to my usual slutty chick in a position of power role. I think this year, I'm getting a Sexy Construction Worker outfit."

"Positions of power, huh?"

"Hell yeah. What's more powerful than holding a jack hammer between your legs?"

"I don't think that's where you hold one," I laughed, and laid the dress back on the bed, careful to keep it on the plastic sheet Sammy's mother had laid out.

"We could shorten this up, maybe bring down the bust a foot or so, and you'd be right there with me," Sarah said, touching the beaded neckline.

I grinned and imagined Sammy's face when I showed up as Sexy *Bride of Frankenstein*.

"No way. Two shots, and Sammy would try to reproduce in the laundry room."

Sarah guffawed and yelled to Sammy.

"Corrie wants fishnet stockings with her costume, Mom."

"Fat chance," Sammy called back. "Plus, that dress is going to have a train. No one will even see your stockings, love."

I shook my head and listened to Sarah and Sammy argue back and forth about the importance of nylons, no matter how long the skirt.

"Icy's with your sister?" Sarah asked, holding her white t-shirt away from her stomach and inspecting a tiny stain. "Damn, I must have spilled iced tea."

"Yeah, she's staying the night. I told Amy we needed your mom's undivided attention for the costume prep."

"And a night alone?" Sarah asked, winking at me.

I grinned.

"We're always grateful for a night alone. After we're done with the costumes, we're headed downtown to get fat on pastries, drink too much coffee, and catch a movie at the State Theatre - the perfect Saturday night."

"What's playing?" Sarah squatted down as our two cats lumbered in. They rarely went anywhere without the other.

"Honey, come here, sweet girl," Sarah cooed, beckoning to our older female cat whose gray fur was silky soft. Dracula pushed Honey out of the way and reached Sarah's outstretched fingers first, planting his plump orange body in Honey's path.

"We're seeing *Gone with the Wind*. I had to promise Sammy we'd watch *The Exorcist* tomorrow to make up for it."

Sarah laughed, gently pushing Dracula onto his side and rubbing his belly. He affectionately bit her hand. "I hate to say it, Corrie, but I find both of your tastes in movies rather appalling. Isn't there a new X-Men or something a little more action-packed showing?"

I sighed and gave her a dreamy look.

"Wolverine can't hold a flame to Rhett Butler."

I leaned down as Honey sauntered my way. As my fingers reached for her, she stopped, her hair standing on end.

"Hey, pretty girl. What's that look for?"

Her green eyes grew wide and she bared her teeth, hissing before she raced from the room.

"Jeez, way to make a girl feel loved," I called after her, laughing.

Sammy rushed into the room and ripped open his green button-down shirt to reveal a grotesque baby torso dangling from his stomach. Kuato, the mutant seer from *Total Recall*, had been Sammy's costume choice, and I recoiled at its vacant, staring eyes.

"God, Mom is good at this shit," Sarah said, touching the waxy face and grimacing.

"Last chance to go as the mutant hooker with three boobs," Sammy exclaimed, lunging toward me.

I swatted him away.

"Ooh yeah," Sarah agreed, her face lighting up. "Corrie, that would be hot and gross! It's perfect."

I shook my head and rolled my eyes toward Sammy.

"Can you imagine him if I had three breasts? Like a dog in heat."

Sammy dropped to his knees. He whimpered and wrapped himself around my feet, legs and arms in the air.

"Do you ruv me?"

"Too much," I groaned, nudging the dead baby with my foot. "But that thing gives me the creeps. I don't think you've outdone Dracula. You could go as Nosferatu this year?"

"1998, love. Remember? I was Nosferatu, and you were my

busty victim covered in little bite marks. Ugh, in that sexy gray dress with the lace..." He rolled around and howled.

"Get a room, or a dog house," Sarah laughed.

"Speaking of getting a room, who are you bringing to the Halloween party this year, sis?" Sammy asked, propping himself up on one elbow.

Sarah scrunched her face and shrugged.

"Nobody currently in my sights, but Gloria is planning a ladies-only skate trip, so maybe I can rustle one up."

"Ladies only or lesbos only?" Sammy asked, grabbing my ankle and trying to lick it.

"Stop that," I said, "down, Fido."

"All dikes. I hope, anyway," she said, pushing a finger into one of the rubber baby's bloodshot eyeballs. "Last year she brought her very straight sister on our ski trip, and I spent half a night coming on to her before someone broke the news. Usually I have a pretty good sense for these things, but damn, the woman is almost six feet tall and has her hair buzzed clear off."

"But tell us about the skate part," I said, sitting on the edge of the bed.

"Roller skates. Yes, it's as ridiculous as it sounds. This is what happens when you become friends with a woman who has spent her entire adult life as an event coordinator on a cruise ship."

"Ah, the Glorious Gloria. She is quite a trip," Sammy said. He crawled to the bed and climbed on next to me. "Why don't you go out with her? She's got those dreamy blue eyes you love so much."

"I prefer brown eyes," she said, leaning over to flick his ear.

He rolled off the bed with a thump.

"Don't go there, Sarah-Bo-Berra, or you'll start an ear-flicking feud they'll write about in history books," Sammy called from the side of the bed. He dove out of sight and shot a rubber band at Sarah, who batted it away.

"Corrie, how exactly do you manage a two-toddler home?" She threw a pillow at Sammy, and he caught it mid-air, flinging it back where it struck her square in the face.

I laughed and shook my head.

"It's quite nice, actually. Every day is a play-date for Isis."

~

"CORRIE." I popped open my eyes to find Sammy inches from my face, his eyes wild and his hair standing on end as if he'd been running his fingers through it.

"What? Isis?" I sat up, and pain leapt through my right shoulder blade and snaked up my neck. I had an instant headache.

I looked around and realized why. I had fallen asleep on the floor of the study. I pressed my hands into the hardwood and tilted my neck to my left shoulder.

"Ouch, oh shit, ugh."

"Here," Sammy massaged my neck, searching my face as if I'd fallen.

Had I fallen?

"How did I get in here?" I asked him, rewinding back to the night before when we'd climbed into bed together. We had made love, and I'd fallen asleep tucked in the crook of Sammy's arm.

"I was wondering the same thing. I practically went mad trying to find you. I've been calling your name for ten minutes."

"Really?"

He helped me up, and I lumbered from the room feeling like I'd aged a decade in one night.

I sat heavily at the kitchen counter, sensing Sammy's gaze.

"What?" I asked him.

"What? I just found you asleep on the floor in the study, and you have no memory of how you got there."

"Coffee would probably help." I winked at him, but he didn't smile. "I sleepwalked. What's the big deal?"

He pressed his mouth in a line and turned, filling the kettle and setting it on the stove with a huff.

"I'm sorry, why are you mad at me right now?" I asked, unable to keep the irritation from my voice. I would need a visit to the chiropractor to get this kink out of my neck. "I'm the one who slept on the floor."

He turned and braced his hands on the counter.

"I'm not mad at you, and I'm sorry it's coming off that way. I'm worried about you."

"Sammy, people sleepwalk all the time. I knew a girl in college who wrote her entire thesis on the subject. It's not exactly a phenomenon."

The cold light of morning barely illuminated the kitchen, but I could see the weariness plain in Sammy's face.

Was he overreacting? Or was I under-reacting?

He ground the coffee, and when he turned back his features had softened.

"Corrie, don't take this the wrong way, but are you okay?"

"What's that supposed to mean? We had a great day yesterday. Why are you ruining it over something so stupid?"

He took my hands across the counter and squeezed.

"Yesterday was great. I loved it, it felt like old times."

I frowned.

"Old times? What are new times, then?"

He stayed put, gazing into my face.

"You've seemed different since we moved here. You sleep a lot and forget stuff."

I bit my cheek, my hands tightening around the glass of water Sammy had set in front of me.

"I sleep a lot?"

"You never took naps before. Now you take them every day, and after you wake up you seem wonky, like you're in a trance."

"I don't want to talk about this anymore," I said, standing abruptly and nearly knocking my chair over backwards. It wobbled and landed back on its feet.

"I'm going to take a shower."

I stormed from the kitchen, refusing to look back. As I walked up the stairs, I rubbed my neck and tried desperately to remember when I had woken in the night and made my way to the study.

ow
Sarah

"WILL?"

The young man spun around. His eyes had the wild look of someone getting ready to run.

"Please," Sarah held up her hands. "I just want to talk to you."

He remained still for another moment, his hand held midair.

"What do you want?" he asked finally.

"I want to talk to you about Kerry Manor."

He took a step away.

"I didn't have anything to do with that murder," he spat.

"I believe you," Sarah reassured him. "But I think you can help me. Please?"

Will shoved one hand in his pocket and looked beyond Sarah, studying the parking lot and the park beyond.

"Not here," he said finally. "This isn't my place. There's an arcade on Front Street. I'll meet you there."

"An arcade?" Sarah asked, dubious. It didn't seem like the ideal location to talk about murder.

"My friend owns it. There's a private room, and it's easy for me to get out if I need to."

SARAH'S SHOES stuck to the sticky floor as she wound through the arcade. Lights flashed from the tops of games, and little electronic voices shouted, 'you lose' or 'add one dollar now.' A group of young men stood around a pool table, lining up quarters on the edge and haggling one particular kid who was wrestling his own pool cue from a long black case.

Sarah had not been in an arcade in years. They seemed a thing of the past, and yet here in downtown Traverse City, tucked away, one still existed. Sarah stopped at a little Plexiglas window.

The girl behind the glass looked all of fourteen -years-old; she stared at Sarah, but said nothing.

"I'm looking for Will," Sarah told her.

The girl stood, face expressionless, and opened the door beside her.

"He's back there."

Sarah walked past, glancing at the girl's desk, where a battered copy of Rolling Stone lay revealing the non-smiling faces of the band U2. The hallway contained only two doors, one marked restroom and the other a mystery. She opted for the mystery door.

The room matched the arcade, with dim lights and sticky floors. A Pac Man game towered in the corner, and several well-loved couches butted around a large, scarred coffee table. Will sat on one couch, his hands fiddling with a small pocketknife he opened and closed.

Sarah stared at the knife and gave Will a look she hoped would deter him from using it.

He looked surprised, and then glanced at the knife.

"It's not like that," he told her, tucking the knife in his pocket. "My dad was an Eagle Scout. He taught me to take my knife every-where. It's not for violence."

Sarah nodded, thinking the same dad he spoke of had murdered his mother.

She grabbed a plastic folding chair and perched on the edge, preferring not to get too comfortable next to the troubled young man.

"So what do you want?" he asked.

"My brother was the person murdered at Kerry Manor. A detective told me you were there that night."

Will's face grew red, and he sprang from the couch.

"I told you, and them, I didn't have nothin' to do with it!" he shouted.

Sarah leaned back on the stool, glancing at the door. Over the sounds of the games and the well-insulated walls, no one would hear her if she screamed.

"I'm not here to accuse you," she said calmly. "I want to know what you think."

"What I think?" he sneered.

"Yes, what you think. I know you suffered a tragedy you believe was connected to Kerry Manor. I'd like to hear more."

Will glared at her. He seemed to size her up, questioning whether she might actually believe him.

He took his knife back out and flicked it open, closed, open. He paced away from her.

"Whoever killed your brother," he said in a rush, "was forced to do it."

"Forced how?"

"By the evil spirit that lives in the house." He spoke the words with his back to her.

She wanted to laugh. In a movie, this was the part where she'd laugh, the kid would get mad, and later the evil spirit would kill her for her disbelief. The kid would get the last laugh. Instead she squeezed the chair beneath her and braced for the possibility his words were true.

"You don't believe me, right?" he asked, spinning around.

"Well, I don't want to," she sighed. "I prefer murderers who can be incarcerated. But I'm learning things, strange things about Kerry Manor. You're not the first to…"

"I know," he said. "I've spent the last five years of my life researching Kerry Manor. There are at least three deaths I'm aware of, four now that your brother is dead, and half a dozen other… things."

"Three deaths?" Sarah asked, incredulous. "At Kerry Manor?"

He shook his head and slumped back onto the couch.

"Before your brother died, there'd been only one at the house itself – well, more if you include the original family that died. The first after the fire happened in 1965. It was a doctor who worked at the Northern Michigan Asylum. His wife killed him in Kerry Manor."

Sarah frowned.

"How do you know?"

He rolled his eyes.

"This is the twenty-first century. Have you heard of the internet?"

"Don't trust everything you read online."

He snorted.

"I'm not stupid. The stories online are a place to start. I found the wife."

"The wife? The murderer?"

He nodded, head high.

"She's not a murderer. That's what I'm trying to tell you. A spirit made her kill him. She woke up in a pool of blood in Kerry Manor. She found her husband in the kitchen, dead, stabbed to death with a piece of broken glass."

A tremor of fear coursed through her as she recalled the story of Mr. Pulver's friend with glass sticking from his cheek.

"How did you find her?"

"Her name was public record. They institutionalized her after the murder at the Northern Michigan Asylum. When the hospital closed, they released her."

"Released her? No prison time?"

"They considered her insane when she committed the murder. Of course, they released her. She lives in Petoskey now with her sister. She takes care of old people."

"And she spoke to you about these things? After all these years?"

He cocked an eyebrow.

"She did when I told her about my dad. But it's also because I believed her. Do you know how rare that is? To find someone who truly believes? I mean, look at you. You're sitting there just searching for a way to poke holes in my story. You don't want to believe it, so you'll find a way not to. I know the truth. I watched it happen with my own eyes. My dad was the best person I've ever known. He was honest and kind and loved my mom like... like people in romantic comedies, or some shit. After we went to that house, he was scared. He confided in me. I was only twelve, but I knew something was wrong. He said a girl followed him from the house. She was torturing him, and he was terrified she wanted to hurt Mom."

"And then your father killed your mother?"

"Except it wasn't him. It was just like the doctor's wife. He blacked out, and when he woke up, Mom was dead in the bathtub. They arrested him. The prosecutor made up some fool story that he wanted to have an affair with his secretary. Bullshit! He and my mom used to laugh about what a ditz his secretary was. Our criminal justice system is a joke."

Sarah tried to imagine the young man before her as a twelve-year-old boy - the only believer in his father's innocence.

"Why did he commit suicide? I mean, doesn't that imply guilt?" She realized she'd just echoed the words of Detective Collins, and immediately regretted them.

Will glared at her and shook his head.

"He killed himself to get rid of the spirit. He couldn't take it anymore. He wrote me a letter and told me everything. I tried to stop him. I called his lawyer, but it was too late. By the time I got the letter, he had already done it."

"I'm sorry," Sarah breathed. She too had lost her father, but not under such horrendous circumstances, and not while she was still a young girl. "What other things happened at Kerry Manor?"

"I'm sure there's more than what I know," he said. "But I have a file on my laptop of every incident I've uncovered. Give me your email, and I'll send it you."

Sarah nodded.

"Okay, yeah, that would be helpful." She noticed he had glanced toward the corner when he mentioned his laptop, and she saw a green duffel bag next to a stack of neatly folded blankets.

"Do you live here?" she asked.

His jaw tightened, and he shook his head.

"I crash here once in a while."

"You're seventeen?"

"Eighteen in four months."

"And then what? College?"

He shrugged and took the knife back out, opening it and closing it.

"Maybe. Why do you care?"

Sarah stood.

"I don't, just asking." She handed him a card from her wallet.

"Sarah Flynn, Architect," he read out loud.

"Yep, that's me."

"You build houses?"

"Design them. I leave the building to the professionals."

He nodded and stuck the card in his back pocket.

"I'll email you tonight."

SARAH CLICKED the email from truthteller333@mail.com. Will had compiled a Google document that spanned five pages, including links to online articles, forums, his personal notes, and a detailed timeline.

"Damn, this kid is organized," she murmured, wondering at his persistence. His parents were both dead, after all; there was no one to exonerate.

"He did it for himself," she said. "Because he had to know for sure."

The document started with the original tragedy at Kerry Manor. It listed the names of the five members of the Kerry family offering a handful of details about each. There was a paragraph about Ethel, who had potential behavior problems at school and allegedly spent six months in the Northern Michigan Asylum for the Insane.

The next incident occurred in 1928 and involved a little boy who nearly drowned while swimming in front of the partially burned mansion. He insisted he saw a little girl watching him from the window, and then suddenly she was in the lake, pulling him beneath the water. His father resuscitated him, and the incident was reported to a local journalist, who wrote a piece reflecting on the tragedy that occurred in the house nearly three decades before.

Sarah read on. A girl claimed she was shoved from her roof by a ghost who followed her from Kerry Manor. A young woman was institutionalized, insisting she was being haunted by a child's spirit after visiting Kerry Manor. The doctor's wife, who murdered him at Kerry Manor and claimed she had no memory of the event. There were several reports by people who visited Kerry Manor and heard a child singing. Five articles linked to the murder of Will's mother, Beverly, and an entire page was devoted to his father's strange behavior after their visit to Kerry Manor. Finally, lastly, Sarah read about her own brother's murder, and followed links to two news articles.

Sarah leaned back in her chair and blew out a long, heavy breath.

She had followed Will's links and read articles posted by journalists who clearly had an open mind when it came to paranormal possibilities. She had also read two forums where several people spoke of second- and third-hand stories about strange, and often tragic, events that occurred shortly after family or friends visited Kerry Manor.

Sarah closed her laptop and walked to one of several windows in her study. She braced her hands on the window ledge and looked at the steadily darkening sky. The sun had set and left a purple horizon, soon to be black.

Something was clearly wrong at Kerry Manor. Sarah felt as if she was staring at a huge table scattered with puzzle pieces, unsure of the image she was meant to create.

ow
Corrie

I WAS twenty-one and Sammy was twenty-three years old when he proposed marriage on a gondola in Las Vegas. It was cheesy and romantic. We drank champagne, and Sammy sang *Moon River* in his Sinatra voice. As the gondola veered back to the Strip, beneath the dazzling lights of the Venetian, Sammy fumbled onto one knee and pulled out a ring - a woven band of gold with an emerald in its center.

"Will you be mine, forever?" Sammy asked, and I stared into his earnest eyes and tried not to burst into tears.

"Who else would have me?" I grinned, wanting to joke through the spasm of happy grief that overwhelmed me.

"Nope, it has to be proper," he said. "Will you marry me?"

"Yes, in a heartbeat."

We ate caramel crepes at the Paris to celebrate, and then returned to our own, less fancy, hotel in downtown Las Vegas. We sat in our room at the Golden Nugget, on a comforter that smelled of cigarettes, and plotted our future adventures.

"Sammy, what if we become like all those other boring married couples who resent each other, but stay together because it's easy or comfortable or they have kids?"

Sammy lay half-naked on the bed, wearing a pair of sagging gray briefs. We had barely made it into the hotel room before we tore off our clothes and made love on the bristly carpet.

"That will never happen to us, Corrie," he said in a rare serious moment. "This love we have is cosmic, lifetimes in the making. This world," he waved his hand dismissively, "can't touch what we've got."

"Cookie!" Isis announced from the back seat, pulling me from my memories.

I glanced in the rearview mirror at Isis holding a partially eaten cookie she'd found in her cup holder. Someday I would take her to Las Vegas for a gondola ride. I would repeat that day with our daughter.

"And maybe with Sammy too," I whispered, turning into the empty parking lot of the last bookstore on my list.

The Antiquarian was a squat brick building with a wooden sign and a wrought iron eagle perched near the door. I glanced at the other five bookstores on my list - a slash through each of their names. No one had the book.

I unloaded Isis from her car seat.

"Last one, honey, I promise. Then we'll go get a snack."

"A cupcake?" Isis asked, her brown eyes growing wide.

"Sure, baby."

I pulled up her hood and tucked her tiny hand into my own. She hopped up and down as we hurried across the parking lot. The bookstore was in Ludington, two hours from Kerry Manor, and further than I had intended to travel. I should have called ahead, but the experience of driving, having a purpose outside of Kerry Manor, was oddly seductive. I dreaded returning to the shadowy house.

I pushed the door open into a dimly lit store stuffed with old books. Bookcases stretched from floor to ceiling, crammed so close it was more like a maze than a store. As we meandered through the space, Isis trying to touch stacks of books I feared would topple on her head, a middle-aged man stepped from the shelves.

Startled, he dropped the books in his hand.

"Oh, I'm sorry," I said. "You must not have heard us come in."

He bent and scooped the books up.

"Nope, these books are as good as earmuffs." He adjusted his glasses and smiled. "What can I help you with?"

"I'm looking for a book: *The Summoning* by Fletcher Wolfe."

The man stared at me, his eyes searching, and I knew he had the book.

"You have it?" I asked, breathless.

He nodded and frowned, patting the books in his hand.

"It's rather strange that you'd ask. I received this donation of books this morning. I had just set out to put them away." He lifted a book from the top of the stack. I saw the black title on a dull gray background, an ethereal white figure set deep into the background.

"May I?" I asked, reaching my hand out.

He handed me the book, his expression curious.

"How much?" I asked, though I didn't care. I would pay a thousand dollars if he asked. Ten thousand.

"It's yours," he said.

"Excuse me?"

"It's meant to be yours. I couldn't possibly take any money for it. But how about you, little lady? Every child gets a free children's book just for walking in the store."

Isis tucked herself behind me, peeking between my legs.

"She'd love it," I said. "Isis, would you like a new story book?"

She grinned and bobbed her head, yes.

Isis picked out a worn copy of *The Giving Tree*, and we left. As we drove home, I fought the urge to pull over and open the book. I wanted to devour the pages, and yet felt strongly I had to read *The Summoning* at Kerry Manor.

~

Sarah

. . .

"THAT WAS A VERY LONG TIME AGO," the woman said, tilting her head to look at Sarah through narrow spectacles with stylish black rims. Her lips were painted a dark red, and silver streaked through her waist-length black hair. She wore a long black dress, and Sarah thought if she'd ever met a witch in real life, this woman was it.

In Will's *Kerry Manor document*, Sarah had found Delila's story especially intriguing. After looking up her number online, she called the woman and asked for a meeting, surprised when she readily agreed.

"But it happened? You're the Delila from the story?"

The woman laughed and shook her head.

"Oh no, not at all. That Delila died many years ago, in Kerry Manor perhaps. But I share her name, yes, and her memories."

Sarah sat in the woman's kitchen. A wall window revealed the forest, branches tangled, a little glass greenhouse nestled at the edge, bursting in green and color despite the November chill.

Sarah drank warm cranberry juice sweetened with agave nectar - Delila's secret recipe, she claimed.

Delila held up her gray coffee mug cup painted with dark swirls.

"I made these," Delila said, nodding at the glass. "After that summer, I did so many things. For a moment, I feared I'd lost everything. Some days I expected to die, and other days I imagined I'd lost my mind and I would live forever in that huge asylum, listening to the mad cries of the other patients."

"You were committed then?" Sarah asked, returning to her seat.

"Who told you this story, dear? Could they have skipped over that most important part?

"A young man. His name is Will."

"Will Slater?"

Sarah nodded, hoping she was not breaching a confidence that Will and Delila shared.

"An absolute tragedy what happened to his family. Although tragedy implies something accidental, and it surely was not."

"Why were you committed, Delila? What happened in Kerry Manor?"

At the mention of the name, Delila clutched the lace tablecloth beneath her fingers and closed her eyes.

"I used to believe that old adage *sticks and stones will break my bones but words will never hurt me*, and then I met Ethel."

"The Ethel who burned her family?"

"Yes. She was long gone when I encountered her, but her presence, her spirit perhaps, remained."

"She haunted the house?"

"After the day I got rid of her, I blocked everything out. For two years I pretended it never happened, and then one night, Christie's little girl started singing Ethel's nursery rhyme. I near died in my chair. After that, I knew I had to unearth... something. I'm still not sure what, but I couldn't live with this horrible, terrifying mystery. What if I woke one morning, and she again stood behind me in the mirror?"

Sarah saw a drop of Delila's cranberry juice slip down the outside of her mug, staining the white lace. The red fanned out in a tiny flower.

"I became very interested in the occult. Christie hated it. She believed in not speaking about the things that scared or hurt us. Today, they'd call it denial. Christie was on the outside looking in. She glimpsed the supernatural for an instant. It's different when it moves in and takes up shop in your little life. There's not enough room. I don't understand what Ethel wanted, but I learned things about her. I learned that she too was in the Northern Michigan Asylum for the Insane. Her parents sent her there, just one year before she killed them. I learned of a brotherhood of doctors who experimented on patients who were touched by the supernatural."

"Can you tell me the story, Delila? Of Kerry Manor?"

"I will, yes, I will. But first, I need to know what's at stake here. Why have you come, young lady?"

Sarah pictured Sammy and tears pricked her eyes. She pulled in a heavy breath and let it out slow.

"My brother was murdered at Kerry Manor on Halloween."

Delila's eyes opened wide, and her mouth fell open. She touched a gold cross suspended around her neck.

"They have not found his murderer?"

Sarah shook her head. "But it's so much more complicated than that. His wife has been acting strangely since it happened. Sometimes she sings... an old song, and she sounds like a little girl. She has lapses in memory. She has no memory of the night my brother died."

Delila looked grave.

"My heart goes out to you, Sarah. Another life stolen by Kerry Manor." She shook her head, disgusted. "In August 1961, I visited Kerry Manor with my future husband. It was an abandoned house, a place kids explored, but for me..." She paused, searching for words. "It had an energy, an attraction I guess. I returned to the house late that night with my niece, Christie. She was my niece, but I was only two years her senior - we were more like sisters. Christie walked around outside, but I insisted on going in the house. I always had an adventurous spirit, often to my detriment, I fear. I walked into the house, and the moment I stepped across the threshold, I sensed a presence. I should have turned and left instantly. I heard the voice of a little girl. She was singing a nursery rhyme."

"What was it?" Sarah whispered.

"One for sorrow, two for mirth-"

"Three for a funeral, and four for a birth," Sarah finished, grinding her teeth and wondering when she would wake up from this horrible nightmare.

"The girl attacked me, the spirit. She wasn't physical, but she had power. I started to scream and she clawed my face, though later I tried to convince myself that I clawed my own face, got spooked, panicked. Except the next morning she was there. Everywhere I went, she hovered in the shadows. Her laughter and songs invaded my dreams, my every thought. But she was not merely a nuisance. She hurt me. Somehow, she gathered energy and hurt me. I was terrified she would hurt Christie. After a few days, Christie's husband had me committed."

"Her husband?"

Delila smiled and shook her head sadly.

"I didn't blame him. Well, maybe I did at the time, but to them I appeared insane. I had lost my marbles. They didn't know what to do, and just down the road was this magnificent place filled with doctors who could save me."

"The asylum."

"Yes. And later I realized they had saved me, for if I had not gone into the asylum and met the people who could rid me of this spirit, she would have driven me to my death."

Delila took a sip of juice, but her hand shook, and she returned the cup with a clank to the table.

"Don't let my age fool you," she told Sarah. "I'm as steady as a boulder. This," she held her shaking hands in front of her face "is fear."

"How did you get rid of her?" Sarah asked, sliding to the edge of her seat.

"There's an odd little place on the grounds of the old asylum. Kids these days call it the hippie tree. Are you aware of it?"

Sarah nodded.

She had heard of it. Kids liked to go there to graffiti and smoke pot. One of her clients claimed people called it a portal to hell.

"All urban legends begin with a kernel of truth," Delila said. "I believe that. And in the case of the hippie tree, I know it to be true. We trapped her there - Ethel, or whatever dark thing Ethel had become."

"How did you know what to do?"

"There was a woman at the asylum, Sophia. She could see spirits. Today they'd call her a medium. She was the first person who saw Ethel, who finally proved to me I was not insane. She told me about another patient at the asylum. He was an alcoholic who'd gone in and out of the hospital several times. He too had been directed to the asylum because a spirit haunted him. This man told me where to go and how to rid myself of Ethel."

"And it worked?" Sarah asked

Delila nodded, but her eyes clouded and her mouth turned down.

"And yet... terrible things still surrounded Kerry Manor. I returned to that basin of trees at the asylum, years later, and I searched for the child's dress Christie and I had nailed into the tree. It was gone."

"A dress?"

Delila nodded.

"Christie went to Kerry Manor and retrieved an item of Ethel's, a green dress. We did a ritual in that basin of trees. I fear the act only detached Ethel from me, and it was only a matter of time before someone would come along and release her. I must tell you, Sarah, I learned many things after that summer. I spent years visiting a therapist who did exorcisms."

"Exorcisms?"

Delila nodded.

"Until you're touched by the unseen world, all these words are just hocus-pocus, scary bedtime stories. But he told me tales of unimaginable things. He reckoned Ethel wanted to possess me. She was waiting for me to break down enough to become available to her. Your brother's wife sounds as if Ethel has possessed her."

Sarah bit her lip and studied the woman before her. Delila's eyes bored into her own. The woman believed every word she spoke.

"What do I do if she is possessed?"

"My friend is dead now some twenty years," Delila admitted, "but I'm still in contact with his daughter. Let me reach out to her. The people who work in this field must do so in obscurity. Our society is far too scientific to allow their stories into the light, but they exist, my dear. I will say this: I wonder if the key is not the asylum."

"The asylum?"

Delila nodded.

"Ethel went there herself, you see. It all started there, and life is a circle. Fear not, Sarah. Fate has brought us together. You might suppose you did this on your own, but if you pay attention, you will notice tiny nudges from the unseen world."

hen
Corrie

"MAYBE YOU SHOULD CANCEL THE PARTY."

I paused in the hallway at the sound of Sarah's voice. I must have been asleep for more than a few minutes if Sarah had arrived and I wasn't even aware of it.

"That seems a little drastic," Sammy told her.

I heard him pacing around the room.

"What's drastic is insisting on throwing a giant party with a hundred people in this house when Corrie's..." Sarah trailed off, and I strained forward wondering what she was about to say.

"She's just off," Sammy continued. "I think it's this novel. She's blocked, and I'm sure it's bringing up stuff from her past about her mom and dad. Things she's never dealt with as an adult."

"I know her mom died of alcoholism, but what happened to her dad?"

"He left when the girls were little. Just took off one day and never came back."

"That's terrible, did she ever try to find him?"

"She looked him up on the Internet but didn't get a hit. I'm not sure she really wanted to find him."

"I wouldn't discount all this, Sam," Sarah said. "I know your Halloween party is your precious little pet, but the stuff you're telling me about Corrie is not good. You're finding her wandering around the house at night and she has no memory of it the next day. She was holding one of Isis's dolls in the lake like she was trying to drown it? That's the stuff of horror movies, brother."

I frowned, shaking my head, and almost stepped into the room to refute the insane comments.

"Don't you dare mention that to her," Sammy said.

I heard him moving closer to the hallway and considered revealing myself, but suddenly I felt ashamed. Had I done those things?

"I won't mention it to her, but you sure as hell should. My advice? Say you want to get into some therapy and move back home. This place is disturbing. It's obviously bringing up weird stuff for Corrie, and it's your job as her husband to do the right thing. She'd never suggest it because she knows you love this house, but come on, Sammy. Since you guys came here, Corrie's not been well."

I listened to Sammy's sigh and could imagine him resting his head against the fireplace mantel, biting his lower lip as he battled his desire to stay in Kerry Manor with his larger desire to save me, his wife, from an apparent mental breakdown. But I wasn't having a breakdown, so why...

"Corrie?"

I looked up, startled, to see Sarah standing in the hallway.

"Oh, hi," I said trying to appear sleepy. I rubbed my eyes. "I thought I heard you guys talking down here. Did I sleep for long?"

I walked into the living room, where Sammy looked rattled. He replaced the expression with his usual grin and snaked an arm around my waist.

"How did you sleep, my love?"

I nodded and yawned. "Good. Was I out for a while?"

"Two hours, about," Sammy said.

"Isis is napping?"

"Yep, both of my princesses were catching their beauty sleep. Sarah wondered if we wanted to go get lunch after Isis wakes up?"

I nodded, willing Sammy to open up and tell me the truth. Instead, he looked away, offering a thumbs-up to Sarah.

"I'm dying for some chicken wings," he announced.

∾

I LAID on the rug watching Isis line up a row of little plastic people near the dollhouse.

"Hey, baby." Sammy came into the room and squatted beside me, leaning over to kiss my temple.

"Mmm, hi," I told him, growing drowsy as the fire seeped out, wrapped me in a coil of heat.

"Listen," he said. He sat on the floor next to me and rolled me to face him. "The party is not important, Corrie. I know I make a big deal out of it, but I'm not against canceling the whole thing. I'm not against moving home, either."

I sat up, agitated by his question.

"Sammy, we've sublet our house out until May. We can't move home."

"Then we could move in with my mom, or even Sarah, until the lease runs out. Or rent a different place, whatever."

"Where is this coming from?" I asked, thinking back to the conversation I'd overhead between Sammy and Sarah several days earlier.

He tilted my chin up and studied my eyes. I saw the familiar love always present in Sammy's face, and something else - worry.

"I've noticed a change in you, honey. It's not bad," he added. "But I get the feeling this place doesn't agree with you. Maybe it's taking a break from your practice, or writing your book, but I'm afraid all this change has been too much. I wonder if we shouldn't backpedal a bit. We're so far up the Peninsula. I go into town every day, but sometimes you're here with Isis for days at a time. This is a lonely place, it's big, and to use everyone else's words, 'creepy.'"

I blinked around the room and considered his statement. Had I changed? It was a huge leap taking the break from my practice, and the book - frankly, the book was resting in purgatory with only a few hundred words added weekly. But surely, we couldn't blame the house.

"No," I shook my head. "We have to stay. This is where we're meant to be right now. I'm sure of it."

He took my face in his hands and kissed me. For a moment I melted into him. He nuzzled my cheek.

"Maybe we should take Isis to my mom's tonight? We could make dinner, spend a few hours warming up the bed." He kissed my chin and eyelids.

"Daddy, look," Isis announced, pointing to her house.

All her figures were laid on their backs in the study. Only one figure remained upright. A little girl with blonde hair, which she'd placed in an upstairs bedroom.

"Where's all the furniture, honey?" Sammy asked, leaning toward Isis and peering into the house.

"It's gone, Daddy. The fire burned it up."

Sammy frowned and touched one of the little figures.

"Are they taking a nap?" he asked.

But Isis didn't answer him. She walked the little girl figure back and forth in the bedroom and finally tucked her into a tiny wooden cabinet and left her.

"Snack?" Isis shifted her eyes from the house and gazed at me.

"Sure, boo-bear. Apple? Or smoothie bites?"

"Moothie bites," she announced, jumping up and running to the kitchen.

"Your mom and Sarah are going to dinner tonight," I reminded Sammy. "And then to watch that new movie with Scarlet Johansen."

"Oh dang, that's right," Sammy said, still staring into the doll-house. He touched one of the prone figures a second time. "Sarah and Scarlett, how tragic unrequited love is."

I stood and laughed, fluffing his hair. His sister had a serious crush on Scarlett Johansen. She never missed one of her new releases. The previous Christmas, Sammy had a t-shirt made for

Sarah with a picture of Scarlett superimposed holding Sarah's hand as they stood in front of Niagara Falls.

I found Isis in the kitchen tugging on the refrigerator door from her footstool.

"Isis, when you block the door, it won't open," I told her, moving her and her footstool out of the way.

I pulled open the door, and the lights flickered.

"Mommy, lights," Isis announced, pointing at the ceiling.

"I saw, boo-bear," I told her, filing through the freezer for the plastic bag of smoothie bites. I grabbed them just as the lights flickered and then went black.

"Damn. Oops, naughty word. Isis?" I reached down expecting to feel her soft blonde head, but my hand waved through the air.

"Isis?" I said louder, walking my hands down the refrigerator and then reaching into the darkness. She didn't respond, and my pulse began to race.

"Sammy?" I called, moving cautiously along the counter toward the doorway. The great room had a fire. We could sit there and wait for the power to come back on. I glanced toward the dark window expecting to see lightning, but only more blackness greeted me.

I paused, listening. If Isis were hiding, she'd eventually give in and giggle. Unlike most two-year-olds, Isis was not afraid of the dark. Sometimes she and Sammy would climb into the furthest reaches of the closets to crouch in total blackness when we played hide-n-seek. I heard a shuffle near the kitchen island and blindly moved toward it.

"Got you," I said as my hands found her. I touched the top of her head, but as my hand drifted down, I realized her hair was too long - very long, and tangled. She was too tall. This child stood above my waist, and Isis barely reached my thighs. My hands shook as they roamed from hair to face. Cold, waxy skin drifted beneath my fingers.

In the darkness, I stared down shaking, my mouth opening and closing like a fish plucked from the water and laid on the beach.

A terrible scream exploded from my chest, and almost instantly the lights flashed, on illuminating the kitchen. My hands were poised in front of me, but no child stood beneath them.

Sammy raced into the room, Isis propped on his hip.

"What? What's happened?"

Sammy's eyes darted around the kitchen.

Isis watched me with round, frightened eyes.

"I... the power went out. You have Isis?"

I tried to take her from Sammy, but she wrapped her arms around his neck and held on, burying her face in his shoulder.

"The power went out?" Sammy asked, puzzled.

"Yes, didn't it go out in the whole house?" I searched the kitchen with my eyes. Where had she gone?

"And that's why you screamed? Good God, I thought you'd seen a knife-wielding lunatic peeking in the window."

I shook my head, started to mention the child, and then I registered Sammy's face, the lines of worry etched there, the fading shock.

"I couldn't find Isis. I panicked."

"She wandered in a few minutes ago. I figure you were bringing her snack to the great room."

"Snack?" I asked, staring at the floor where I was sure the small outlines of two feet had stood, their remnants already vanishing. I squatted down and touch the place. It did not feel warm, but I did feel something.

"Let's go out to dinner," Sammy announced, swinging Isis high. "We'll drive down to Glen Arbor to Art's bar. You want tater tots, Isis?"

"Taters," Isis shrieked, kicking her legs and smiling.

"Sure," I mumbled miserably.

Sammy pulled me into a hug, crushing Isis between us. She laughed and wrapped an arm around my head.

I smiled and tried not to see the question in Sammy's eyes.

"IT'S AVAILABLE RIGHT NOW?" I heard Sammy's voice and paused.

I had woken again from a long nap that left me groggy and disoriented. It had taken several minutes of staring into the canopy of our bed before I remembered where I was.

"Dada, look, gween," Isis announced.

"Yes, it is green. Good observation, Isis."

"Gween gass," she announced.

"We'd be looking to move in early November. No, we left our furniture at our own house in Traverse City. We're sub-leasing it for the winter. Okay. Sounds good. I'll come in next week to fill out the application."

My head pulsed, and I experienced a strange sense of rage. For an instant I wanted to run into the room, snatch Sammy's phone from his hand and throw it in the fire. I touched my temple and felt the steady thrum of my pulse, almost hot to the touch. I hoped I wasn't coming down with something.

We were only two weeks from the Halloween party, and I didn't want to be recovering from a cold or the flu.

I stepped into the doorway. Sammy held his cell phone clutched in his hand. Isis sat on the floor, coloring a flattened paper bag.

"Who were you talking to?" I asked.

He held up his phone, where Sarah's face appeared on the screen.

"Hi Corrie," she waved.

"Hi." I waved back as Sammy ducked from the room, pecking me quick on the cheek. I watched him slip down the hallway and wondered who he'd been talking to before Sarah.

ow
Sarah

SARAH KISSED her mom on the cheek and handed her a wriggling Isis.

"How's my sweet girl?" Helen asked, bouncing her granddaughter up and down.

"Gizmo," Isis announced, proudly holding up her stuffed toy.

"Oh my, that Gizmo is a special critter, isn't he?"

"Cookies!" Isis shouted, pointing at Helen's counter stacked with plates of cookies.

Sarah grabbed her one and settled Isis in front of an episode of Sesame Street before returning to the kitchen. She plopped on a barstool.

"How's Corrie?" Helen asked, returning to the counter.

"Okay," Sarah lied. "She said she got a new book and planned to spend the day reading."

Helen stood at the kitchen island, kneading and pounding dough as if she wanted to bake her grief into a cookie and feed it to someone else.

"What do you think happened, Sarah?" her mother asked,
Sarah leaned against the counter and shook her head.

"I don't know, Mom. I keep replaying the night in my head. Was
there a psychopath there and none of us knew it? Did Sammy get in
a fight with someone? He had a lot to drink." She bit back any
mention of Corrie, still not able to consider any real possibility that
her brother's wife was also his murderer.

"Not Sammy," Helen said, taking the dough she'd flattened and
pushing it back into a ball to start over. She sprinkled flour on the
top and shoved her hands deep into the creamy softness. "He never
fought. He wasn't a confrontational man."

"Well, he didn't fight back, that's for sure. But someone might
have attacked him. Maybe he made a snide comment, or…"

"It wasn't his fault," Helen snapped, and her voice wavered. She
closed her eyes.

"Oh, Mom. I know that." Sarah stood and wrapped her arms
around her mother's soft body. She leaned on her mother's shoulder, wishing she could ease her pain. Unfortunately, she couldn't
even ease her own pain.

"I'm so worried for Corrie. What if he comes back? What if he
murders Corrie and Isis? What if we lose them all?" Her voice rose,
a hysterical edge slipping in.

"Shh," Sarah whispered, glancing toward the living room where
Elmo sang about brushing his teeth. "Mom, here." She pulled out a
chair. "Sit for a minute." Sarah sat across from her and took her
hands. "That will not happen. I've been going out to the house
almost every day. I think it was just a horrible, crazy thing that
happened. Some lunatic showed up at the party, drank too much,
and who knows - maybe he confused Sammy for someone else. I
don't think anyone had it in for Sammy, and I don't think anyone
will hurt Corrie and Isis. Okay? I believe that."

Helen's gray eyes searched Sarah's. Sarah wondered if she did
believe it. She wanted to.

"I keep baking," Helen murmured. "It's like after your daddy
died. I couldn't seem to sit still. I woke up at two a.m. this morning
and started baking. Yesterday, I went downtown and dropped off

platters of cookies at shops, the hospital, even a gas station on one-thirty-one."

She laughed a dry, humorless croak and rubbed her face.

"I'm so tired, Sarah. I'm tired and I'm scared half to death. I'm scared for you, for my other half of Sammy and Sarah."

"I'm okay, Mom. I am. My heart is broken, and none of us will ever be the same. But we will make it through this."

"I didn't like that house," Helen muttered. "The first time I stepped through the door, I had a terrible feeling."

"You did?" Sarah asked.

Sarah recalled her first morning visiting Kerry Manor. She pictured Sammy in the kitchen, his hair rumpled. 'I had a death dream last night,' he had announced.

Had Sammy dreamed of his own murder?

"I didn't tell Sammy," Helen continued. "I should have. I will live with that regret for the rest of my life."

"Sammy wouldn't have listened, Mom. He was so excited to rent the house for the winter. He would have said you were being paranoid."

Helen stood back up and shuffled to the kitchen island, grabbing a handful of chocolate chips and dropping them in her mixing bowl.

"You're probably right." She stirred in the chocolate chips as the timer on the oven sounded behind her.

"Here, let me," Sarah said, jumping up, but Helen shook her head.

"No, please. The busier the better for me right now."

Helen put on a pink oven mitt decorated with dancing pigs and pulled out two cookie sheets covered in peanut butter cookies.

"Something came in the mail yesterday for Sammy," she said, sliding the pans onto hot pads.

"Really?" Sarah walked to the table in the front hall where Helen stacked the mail.

A brown paper package addressed to Sammy sat on the bureau. The return address included the name *Mystic Moon* and a location in California.

Sarah carried the package back to the kitchen.

"What are you doing?" Helen asked as Sarah ripped open the package.

"I'm opening it."

"Shouldn't we give it to Corrie?"

Sarah didn't stop.

"Corrie has enough to deal with. We can handle errant mail that comes to your house."

"Yes, I wondered why he had it sent here."

Sarah folded back the paper and stared at a book.

True Cases of Possession by C.M. Riley.

She glanced at her mother, still hammering the dough, and tried to keep her face impassive.

"What is it?" Helen asked not looking up.

"Just a book. I'll take it to Corrie this afternoon."

"Tell her I'll keep Isis tonight. I'd like some company."

~

CORRIE

"How long have you been out here?" Sarah asked when she found me sitting along the hardened shoreline.

I had put on one of Sammy's huge and hideous Christmas sweaters over a pair of flannel pajama pants. My hair was knotted, and I knew my face was haggard from crying and the cold.

Once upon a time, I would have cared. I remembered considering how well I handled grief. After my mother's death, I missed only three days of work, and I never once broke down at the office. I showed up every day with my slacks ironed and my stupid happy face because God forbid I made anyone uncomfortable.

"Isis stayed with my mom," Sarah told me, although I hadn't asked.

Later, I would lie in bed and cry for Sammy and hate myself for how I was failing our daughter, but right now, with the frigid wind blowing in from the lake, and the words from *The Summoning* rolling through my mind like a hurricane, nothing mattered,

I'd been sitting on the beach for two hours. My backside was numb, and the horizon had taken on a dreamy quality I quite liked. Out here life seemed less sharp, less real.

Sarah sat next to me and picked up a flat stone. She threw it at an angle toward the water. It didn't skip, but plopped with a little splash.

"Sammy was the stone skipper," she said. "We counted six skips one time."

"He wanted to teach Isis. He tried a few times when we first moved in here, but every time he threw a rock, she cried and demanded he retrieve it. I remember him wading in, water to his crotch, trying to get one of those stupid rocks."

Sarah laughed and threw a second stone. It dropped with a loud plunk.

"He was a great dad."

"Yeah," I murmured, unable to accept the word 'was,' as if he'd never be a great dad again.

"I want to help, Corrie. I feel like Sammy's up there watching us right now, saying 'Come on Sarah, take care of my wife, help her through this,' and I'm down here twiddling my thumbs and rocking back and forth on my heels. I don't know what to do."

I looked at her sideways and shook my head.

"No one can help me, Sarah. Not even me."

"That's not true. I refuse to believe that. You've got everything to live for, Corrie. Isis is just a baby, you have her whole life ahead of you. The only way she can know Sammy, truly know him the way you did, is through you."

I listened and nodded and understood that Sarah, and likely everyone else, feared I would kill myself.

"I'm not planning to commit suicide," I told her.

"That's not what I'm saying."

"But it's what you're thinking, right? I'm a mess and that means I'm a danger to myself. Who knows what I'll do?"

"Is that how you feel?"

I laughed, but it sounded dry and humorless.

"Sure, sometimes. But I would never do that to Isis. My mom didn't kill herself in the traditional sense, but she did it just the same. I would never leave Isis without either of her parents."

Sarah scooted close and wrapped an arm around my back. I felt her heartbeat against my side. I had forgotten the sensation of being held. Sammy always held me. He was a man who loved to hug, spoon, cuddle. Until Sarah pressed close, I didn't realize how empty my world had become since Sammy left it.

I rested my cheek against her hair and gazed at the stones.

ow
Corrie

"MOMMY, PHONE," Isis announced, shaking my knee.

I had been gazing into the fire, lost in another reverie. "I hear it, baby." I scooped her up and hurried into the kitchen, grabbing the phone.

She pulled it out of my hand before I could talk.

"Dada?" she asked.

I let out a little strangled gasp and jerked the phone away. I watched her face crumple, her brown eyes filling with tears. "Oh no, sweetie, I'm sorry. Don't cry." I kissed her tears.

"Gorey?" I heard his voice, Sammy's voice, from the dangling receiver. I stared, transfixed, moving the phone slowly to my ear.

"Corey, are you there?" Sammy's voice did not come through the phone. Instead it was a man's voice I didn't recognize.

I closed my eyes, leaned my head against Isis's warm, wet cheek. "Yes, this is Corrie."

"Corrie, hi. Gosh, I'm sorry about that. I heard Isis. I hope I didn't upset her."

Isis wiggled in my arms and I set her on the floor.

"No, it's okay. She's... she's fine. I'm sorry. Who am I speaking with?"

Laughter on the phone.

"Guess I should have started with that. It's Gunner from the Halloween party. You met my wife, Micah. We have a boy the same age as Isis."

"Yes, Gunner. I remember you. How are you?"

"I'm okay. I'm calling, actually, to ask about you. I wanted to right after, but figured you'd need time."

"Sure, thanks. I'm fine. That's a lie, of course, but we're getting there - one day at a time."

"Yeah, good, I'm happy to hear that, Corrie. Sammy was an inspiration and a friend, and our whole community, the comic artists up here, have been devastated by the news. We're creating a comic book in his honor. All of us donating a strip. I won't bore you with the details, but I'll send you a copy as soon as it's finished."

"Thank you, Gunner. Sammy would have loved that." He would have; in fact, it was just the sort of thing Sammy would have organized for someone else.

"I have another reason for calling," Gunner continued. "Micah's taking Jared to the Children's Museum today. She'd love to take Isis."

Isis had run back into the kitchen. She waved her pink sippy cup in my face.

"Juicy?"

I took the cup and unscrewed the lid.

"Isis, would you like to go to the Children's Museum today? With a little boy your age named Jared?"

Isis hopped up and down.

"For play?"

"Yes, to play. Does that sound fun?"

She nodded her head.

"Sure, Gunner. I think Isis would really enjoy that. I'd take her myself, but..." I imagined a string of excuses but let them all die on my lips.

"Jared will be over the moon," Gunner said. "I'll let Micah know. She'll probably be to Kerry Manor around two. Is that good for you?"

"Perfect."

"Great. And Corrie, if we can do anything, please let us know."

He hung up the phone, and I stayed on the line listening to the staticky silence, willing Sammy's voice to drift across the veil and whisper my name.

～

Sarah

SARAH PUSHED through the door into the arcade's back room.

Will sat at the cheap folding table, his black hair shaggy across his face, a pencil propped on his lip.

"I need your help," Sarah told him, holding out a bag of chips and a bottle of Mountain Dew.

He wrinkled his nose. "And this is what? A bribe?"

"Isn't this what your kind eats?"

He rolled his eyes, snatching the chips from her hand. "Not that stuff," he nodded at the soda, "tastes like battery acid."

He tore open the chips and paused, studying Sarah.

"I don't play well with others. You'd be better off teaming up with a cop. Isn't that how it works in the crime shows?"

"I'm pretty sure if I took my concerns to the cops, they'd lock me up and throw away the key. Plus, the police are too…"

"Stupid?"

"No." She imagined Detective Collins' suspicious gaze. "They're too closed-minded - not open to consider other possibilities. Not that I blame them."

"Explain," he said.

"Before my brother died, he said his wife Corrie was acting strangely. He found her sleepwalking several times. Once she was holding a doll in the lake. I've noticed things too. She…" Sarah paused, but Will did not look skeptical. "She changes, gets this dazed look on her face and sings like a little girl."

Will stuffed a handful of chips in his mouth and crunched loudly, wiping the orange dust on his dark jeans. He stood and wandered away from her, pausing at a large picture of Pac Man dressed as a super hero.

"Too risky? Or time for a new adventure?" she heard him mumble.

"Are you talking to yourself?" she asked.

He turned and grinned. "Of course, I'm talking to myself. Sometimes I need expert advice.

Will reminded Sarah of her twin. A more brooding version of Sammy, but similar nevertheless. She wondered if she desired to draw him closer for that reason alone.

She glanced at the table where he'd been sitting and saw a newspaper lying open. A picture of Kerry Manor perched above a caption that read: *How Much Tragedy Is Too Much Tragedy?*

He saw her looking.

"They're starting to take notice." Will tapped the paper. "There's an op-ed in there from a guy demanding Kerry Manor be demolished."

"Do you believe the destruction of Kerry Manor will... end it, kill it?" She struggled to find a phrase that didn't sound insane.

He stared off, and then shook his head.

"No, but it's a start."

"Maybe, helping me is a start, too?"

"I'm intrigued," he admitted. "But Sarah, this isn't a joke. That house harbors something evil, and I'm not sure if it can be stopped."

"I spoke with Delila," Sarah said.

Will perched on the edge of the table.

"And now that you've had adult confirmation, you believe me?"

"No. I already believed you, as much as my rational brain allowed, anyway. I was curious about her story. It reminds me of what's happening with Corrie. And Delila got rid of Ethel."

"She trapped her."

"At the asylum."

Will nodded.

"Do you know the place? The Hippie Tree?" Sarah asked.

"I've been there a time or two. I don't like it. Lots of kids hang out there, get stoned, spray-paint the trees. Dancing with the devil, if you ask me."

"How can we find out more?"

"I have some connections. Give me twenty-four hours, and I'll take you to meet someone."

Sarah bounced on the balls of her feet, feeling lighter than she had in days.

"Is it absurd that I finally feel closer to the truth? Could you be the key to figuring all this out?"

"I am a paradox wrapped in an enigma sealed in a Monopoly game."

"Huh?"

"Exactly."

~

CORRIE

"CORRIE! WHAT ARE YOU DOING?" Sarah's voice sliced through my thoughts.

I looked up, surprised, but continued cutting. As I brought the knife back down, I felt the sharp blade cut into my index finger, but it was as if my brain was too slow to catch up.

Sarah whipped the knife from my hand and flung it away. Blood splattered us both. I blinked at her face speckled in red, wondering at the shock in her eyes.

"What? My God," I said. "I lapsed for a second, it's only a little..." But then I looked down and saw it was not only a little cut. I had several long gashes on the backs of my hands, another on my right forearm - and almost worse, a bird lay on the chopping black, its head severed and its legs sliced clean away from the black, oily body.

I swallowed rising bile and spun away, trying to breathe, but I couldn't force the air. My ribs had locked tight around my lungs, blocking passage for the next breath.

Sarah took my elbow and guided me to a kitchen chair. I sat stiffly, refusing to look in her eyes.

What could I say? I tried to think back. When had I come into the kitchen? Picked up the knife?

"Where's Isis, Corrie?"

I looked at Sarah, bewildered, and then terror tore me in half before I remembered - Micah, the woman from the party, had picked her up.

"She's okay," I whispered. "She's on a play date with Micah and Jared."

Sarah nodded, a stunned expression frozen on her face. She moved methodically through the kitchen, leaving and returning with peroxide and a roll of gauze. Kneeling in front of me, she poured peroxide into my cuts. They fizzed and oozed, but I did not look at the wounds. Instead, I looked at Sarah with her blood-flecked white t-shirt. I saw drops of red in her blonde hair and realized I did not know what blood belonged to me, and what belonged to the bird.

After she wrapped my wounds, she cleaned the kitchen, meticulously wiping up blood and scrubbing the counters until they gleamed. She disposed of the bird and the blood-soaked paper towels in a trash bag, and walked them to the garbage can outside.

I wanted to run up the stairs and cower in my bed, but no, I couldn't. I had to face Sarah.

"Corrie," she breathed when she returned.

I knew what she would say. *You're insane, you need help*, but she said none of those things. Her next words were much, much worse.

"The police are here."

hen
Sarah

"YOU HAVE A TWIN?" the woman asked Sarah, eyes huge as if she'd just admitted to having a tail. "Are you identical?" she asked honestly, gazing with round blue eyes from a face heavy with powder and rouge.

Sammy leaned in, "In every way, except I have a penis," he whispered, a gleam in his eye.

Sarah elbowed him.

"Not identical. I got the looks and the brains in this duo."

"Ha," Sammy bent over and guffawed. "And also, the modesty."

The woman looked uneasily between them, her smile forced.

"Well, nice to meet you," she said before turning and hurrying back down the aisle.

"That was a prospective client, you shit," Sarah told him, snatching the bottle of pineapple juice from his hand and plunking it in the cart.

"Client, schmient," he said. "She had no sense of humor. I just saved you months of design hell. I can tell you right now, she's one of those ladies who wants marble floors and knotty pine in the same room."

Sarah cringed and shook her head. She too had the impression the woman would have been a high-maintenance client, but a paying client nevertheless.

"On to the vodka," Sammy announced.

"Let's get rum this year. I swear the vodka hangover wipes me out for days."

"If you drink three cocktails instead of eight, that'd probably help too," Sammy laughed.

"This coming from the guy who I saw bong tequila last year," she reminded him, swerving the cart at his feet.

"Hey," he jumped back. "No carticular homicide, please. You'll have to run me over like eighty times to get the job done."

"No death for you, brother. I'm just trying to maim you, so I can take my rightful place as the superior twin."

"What are you two laughing about?" Corrie asked, carrying several cans of pumpkin as Isis toddled behind her with a bag of tortilla chips half her size.

"Oh, the usual twin stuff. I imagine a color, she tells me what it is," Sammy said, grabbing Corrie around the waist and nearly sending her cans crashing to the floor.

He leaned Corrie low, kissing her.

Sarah made a gagging noise and relieved Isis of her chips.

"Mommy's crips," Isis said proudly.

"Yes, you carried the chips, didn't you?" Sarah said, picking up her niece and swinging her around.

Isis squealed and yelled more, which sounded like mo.

"Toothpaste," Corrie added, pointing toward the aisle marked toiletries.

"Umm... Corrie, my queen," Sammy said cocking an eyebrow. "I swear you came home with three tubes of toothpaste last week."

"I know," she said, frowning and making a face as if she tasted something sour. "I can't seem to get this metallic taste out of my mouth. Like pennies. Ever heard of that?" She directed the question at Sarah.

Sarah shook her head.

"Maybe you have a filling coming loose?"

Corrie shifted her jaw from side to side.

"I don't think so."

"Perhaps a visit to the doctor's in order," Sammy said, grabbing Corrie's hand and kissing her palm. "You could ask him about the sleepwalking."

Corrie nodded dismissively and ducked down the aisle.

Sarah saw Sammy's face darken. He grinned and shrugged.

"A stubborn mule, that one. But she's all unicorn to me."

CORRIE

"CORRIE, pop the champagne, I'm hanging the last of the cobwebs in three, two, one. Done!"

I heard Sammy jump from a ladder and land on the wood floor. He let out a loud moan, and I knew he was likely bending to-and-fro, trying to release the tension in his back.

"On no, you're not," Sarah called.

I peeked into the great room, where she arrived with another package of the gauzy webs.

"No, she-devil." He held his fingers in a cross and hissed at his sister.

She laughed and threw the package at him.

"Corrie, where are those dancing skeletons?" she asked, joining me in the kitchen where the counters and kitchen island were loaded with Halloween-inspired treats including spiked punch with floating jelly eyeballs, cookies shaped like bats, eclairs that looked like bloody fingers, and an array of less creepy appetizers like trail mix and bruschetta.

"Are we feeding the entire Leelanau Peninsula?" Sarah asked, plucking an olive from a tray.

"According to Sammy we are. Instead of creating a guest list this year, he told everyone with a pulse about our party and told them to bring their friends. We may need to run to the grocery for bags of popcorn if half the people he invited show up.

"Don't forget the people without a pulse," Sammy called. "Fear not, damsels. There are fishing poles in the shed if we run out of sustenance. And squirrels in the trees, ripe for picking."

"Yum," Sarah grinned. "I love a good fish-squirrel pie."

I smiled and wrinkled my nose.

"I think I'd rather go hungry."

"Speaking of hunger, did you bring the singing jack-o'-lantern in from the car?" Sammy asked me.

"I'm sorry, how does that relate to hunger?" Sarah asked.

"What do you think pumpkin spice is made from?" Sammy demanded, hands on his hips.

"Not a plastic jack-o-lantern that sings *I like big butts*," Sarah retorted.

"I'll grab it," I told him.

The sky, sunny and clear in the morning, had grown cloudy as the day progressed. I shivered and realized I should have put on a coat. I grabbed the plastic pumpkin, a last-minute impulse buy Sammy had insisted we needed for the dining room table, and returned to the house. Sammy and Sarah were talking when I slipped through the front door.

"I'm going to tell her tomorrow," Sammy said.

"Why are you waiting?" Sarah asked.

"I didn't want to upset her before the party."

"Well, I'm happy you'll be back in Traverse City. This house is too isolated to begin with. I'm not saying it was a bad idea, but seriously Sammy, it was a terrible idea."

He chuckled.

"Well, don't expect me to admit you're right, but I'm relieved too. The other day when I couldn't find her, I almost called the police."

I considered listening a moment longer. Instead, I slammed the door hard. I had heard Sammy talking on the phone about a rental property. I knew he intended for us to move out of Kerry Manor.

But I couldn't understand why he wasn't being honest with me about it. I thought about storming into the room, confronting him. To hell with his stupid Halloween party.

"Gorey, my love?" Sammy called.

"Coming," I murmured, stepping into the room.

He smiled, holding up an owl with glowing red eyes.

"I thought we'd name him Igor?"

I sighed and nodded. I couldn't ruin Sammy's favorite night. Tomorrow we'd talk and settle all the secrets, once and for all.

ow
Corrie

"START AT THE BEGINNING," Detective Collins said.

I stared at him. The first time I'd met him, his blond hair had been messy, hanging on his forehead. He had since sheared it off, giving him a hardened military look. Blond hair sprouted from his upper lip, revealing he'd skipped a shave for a day or two.

Sammy couldn't miss a day shaving unless he wanted a full beard in three.

"How many times can I start at the beginning, Detective?" I asked. "You think if I tell the story enough times, some new piece of information will suddenly pop out of my mouth?"

"You'd be amazed how stories change with several re-tellings."

"Yeah, because the witness is exhausted, confused, and likely questioning their own version of events after three hours in this fucking room with fluorescent lights that make my brains feel like they're sizzling in a frying pan."

"One more time, and then you're free to go."

"I know my rights," I grumbled. "I'm already free to go." But to appease the man who I believed was hunting me, I talked.

"On Halloween day, I woke up at six a.m., a typical time for me. Sammy was already in the kitchen making coffee and breakfast for Isis. He made her pancakes and fruit. We sat in the great room and drank our coffee. Around nine a.m., Sammy drove Isis to his mom's house and dropped her off while I started making food for the party. He got home around ten a.m. Sarah showed up a few minutes later. We decorated for the party until five."

"That's a lot of decorating."

"Is that a question?"

The detective shrugged, and I tried not to grab the edge of the table and shake it. I wanted out of there, but I hated to face Sarah.

How had the bird gotten onto the counter beneath my knife? A long sweater concealed the bandaged gashes on my hands and arms. I had been lucky the police had not handcuffed me, because they would surely have seen them.

"We decorated until five. The house is huge, it took a long time. I went upstairs to get dressed, and Sammy came in before I finished." I paused, hating to recount this again, missing Sammy with each retelling. "We made love and then we both got into our costumes."

The detective said nothing, and I hurried on.

"At six, guests arrived. We all started to drink pretty heavily."

"And it was typical for you and Sammy to indulge in so much alcohol?"

"On Halloween it was."

The detective nodded.

"I started off drinking zombie cocktails, switched to rum and Coke. At some point Sammy gave me a few jello shots a guest had brought. We danced. I talked to a lot of people, some of which I remember, but some I'm sure I don't. After dark I wandered upstairs and sat in the bathroom. I was dizzy and thought I might get sick. The feeling passed." Corrie replayed the night's events, her voice flat. She refused to reveal even a hint of emotion to the detective. "I returned to the party. I saw Sammy talking with Jack

Williams, another comic book artist, on the porch. After that, everything gets grainy. I think he and I danced again. I vaguely remember hugging Sarah goodbye. And then... nothing."

The detective put his large hands, knuckles scabbed as if he'd recently punched someone, on the table.

"And after you woke up?"

I rubbed my eyes, careful to keep my sleeves pulled over my hands, and leaned back in my chair.

"I woke up on the couch. I was dizzy and nauseous. I went into the kitchen and saw the rags by the sink. I looked out the window and saw Sammy in the yard beneath the oak tree. I knew..."

"That he was dead?"

"That something was wrong."

"How?"

I stared at the cheap particle-board table, the little black specks swimming in my gaze.

I didn't have to imagine Sammy's crumpled body every time I told the story, and yet I did.

"I just knew. I ran out of the house. He was covered in blood. His body was cool to the touch and not soft, not like him at all. I..." In my mind he was there again, those empty staring eyes. "I pulled his head into my lap and cried. I couldn't bear it. I lost connection with reality, I guess. I was still drunk, and I was so overwhelmed. After a few minutes, I just stood up and walked into the lake. It was so cold, and my dress was heavy and I walked out. And then Sarah found me."

"Why didn't you call the police? An ambulance to help Sammy."

I stared into the detective's eyes, cold and hard. He did not care that I died with Sammy that night. He had one goal in this room: to get me to slip up, to incriminate myself.

"He was dead. Maybe you can't understand the feeling of a moment like that. It was like I woke up and everyone in the world had died, and I was left here alone without an identity, without an anchor to this place. I couldn't call anyone. I couldn't breathe, think. I still can't most days. Do you know what happens every morning when I wake up? I forget he's dead. Just for a few seconds, as I'm coming back into the world, I wake up as the same old Corrie. Corrie and Sammy. And then like a tidal wave it rolls over me, pushes me under. I lay there struggling to breathe. After I finally calm down, I have to will myself out of bed. It's almost impossible. If it weren't for Isis, I doubt I'd get up at all."

"Then why did you kill him, Corrie?"

The detective's question hung in the air between us, the accusation he'd wanted to make for weeks, perhaps since the first moment we met.

"I think it's time I speak with my lawyer."

~

Sarah

"THEY'RE NOT CHARGING HER," the lawyer explained, adjusting his round spectacles on his long, narrow face.

"They put her in the police car, they read her the Miranda rights," Sarah rushed. "Doesn't that mean...?

He shook his head.

"A misunderstanding by the deputies sent to pick her up. At least they're calling it that, but I've seen some shady dealings in my time, and nothing breaks a person like getting shoved into the back of a squad car."

"But she's not arrested?" Sarah asked again, leaning back relieved.

"No. Not today, anyway."

"What does that mean?"

The lawyer, Doug Fenton of Fenton, Williams and Associates, planted both palms on the table and looked Sarah square in the face.

"They want her for this, Sarah. I saw the look in that detective's eye when I walked into the interrogation room. Let's just say, if they found so much as Corrie's broken fingernail by Sammy's body, they'll use it."

"Corrie found him, for Christ's sakes!" Sarah bellowed. "Of course they'll find a fingernail and hair and skin and whatever other evidence they were collecting for two days, but-"

"The detective mentioned Corrie's dress from that night. He said you burned it."

Sarah felt her cheeks flush red, and the mere sensation made her want to pound her fists on the table.

"I did it because I knew it would break her heart to see it again. I..."

The lawyer held up his hand.

"I'm not the cops. I'm not accusing you. I am here to protect Corrie and her family. Sammy was my friend, and I've known you guys for a long time. I believe in Corrie's innocence. That being said, if there's anything I should know - the sooner the better, so I can jump ahead of their accusations. Do you understand?"

Sarah nodded, a jumble of images flashing through her mind - the most recent of Corrie holding a butcher knife and mindlessly slashing into her own skin.

"I didn't hide the dress. Corrie assumed they took it, she told me so herself. They asked her for her clothing from that night and she told them I hung it in the laundry room."

"Did you?"

"No, it was so wet I dropped it in the bathtub. Corrie said they must have taken a black evening dress she had hanging in there. It was a mistake. We weren't misleading them."

"I understand that, I do. These situations are messy. The police know that. It's never black and white."

"Corrie's a wreck, Doug. Since Sammy's death, she's barely keeping it together. I'm afraid they'll twist her reactions into guilt when it's actually grief."

"Sometimes they do," he admitted.

Sarah stared through the window at the gray day beyond. Heavy clouds and a spattering of rain pulled the color from the city. The trees, rather than gold and vibrant, looked heavy and forlorn.

"What do they have? I mean, evidence-wise?"

The lawyer took out a legal pad and flipped several pages.

"No murder weapon, no DNA other than Sammy and Corrie's. A handful of hairs and fibers that may or may not be linked to the killer. One helpful bit is that the murderer seemed to be right-handed."

"And Corrie's a leftie."

"Yep. The attack also appeared to come from above, which would imply-"

"Someone taller than Sammy. And he was over six feet."

"Maybe," the lawyer paused. "They think he was kneeling. There was no blood spatter from the knees down, and his pants were grass-stained."

"Kneeling?"

The lawyer shrugged.

"Possibly, which implies he was being threatened. Someone told him to get on his knees - that kind of thing. Though I tend to picture a gun in that scenario, not a knife."

"And Sammy would fight," Sarah said. "He wouldn't just get on his knees."

"Which is also troubling," the lawyer said. "He had zero defensive wounds. None. Almost as if he let it happen."

"That's crazy. He'd never-"

"I know, and I agree, but the forensics don't lie. Maybe he was so intoxicated he couldn't fight back. His blood alcohol was high."

"I'm sure it was." Sarah remembered her last moment with Sammy. He'd kissed her goodbye as she left the party, his mouth sloppy and his eyes glazed. He'd reeked of alcohol. "What about the bloody rags by the sink? Was there DNA or whatever?"

The lawyer smiled.

"Corn syrup, fake blood. Sammy's fingerprints were on the rags. Maybe he spilled some and cleaned it up."

"Sammy and his fucking fake blood," Sarah muttered, grimacing at the memory of the buckets of overturned fake blood near the back porch dripping a line of red onto crumpled white sheets below.

"I would like to ask you if you have any intuition about this, Sarah, about who murdered Sammy and why."

Sarah drew her mouth into a grim line and shook her head.

"I don't know, Doug, I don't. But it wasn't Corrie. I would bet my life on it."

"As would I," the lawyer said, following Sarah's gaze to the window. "Whoever did this is out there. That's a terrifying thought."

ow
Sarah

"MAMA?" Isis called, dropping her stuffed Gizmo and running into the living room at Helen's house.

"She's not here, Icy," Sarah told her, petting her soft blonde head.

"Come here, baby girl," Helen said, leaning down and lifting Isis into her arms. "Grandma made banana muffins. Want one?"

"Muffnins!" Isis repeated. "Nana made muffnins."

Sarah followed her mother and niece into the kitchen. Like her last visit, baked goods coated every surface - this time muffins instead of cookies.

"I can call Corrie's sister, Mom," Sarah started, but Helen shushed her.

"No. I want Isis here with me. She gives me a purpose. Plus, I feel like I've got a little piece of Sammy when she's here. Is Corrie okay?"

"Yeah, they released her after questioning. I took her home and met Micah in Northport to pick up Isis."

"Do they know-"

"That she was arrested? No, and technically she wasn't. I guess that's one thing we can be grateful for about Kerry Manor. There's no prying eyes."

Helen nodded but her lower lip trembled.

Isis sat in a kitchen chair, legs dangling far above the floor, as muffin crumbs dropped around her.

"Why?" Helen asked but Sarah shook her head.

"We'll talk about it later. I have to run, but if you need help, call me, okay? I mean it. I told Corrie you'd hold on to Isis for a few days. It's better that way."

SARAH FOLLOWED Will down a steep hill into a park. Most of the leaves had fallen, and they created a wet sheath of slippery madness. Sarah wiped out and slid the rest of the way down, cringing as her coat pulled up and soggy leaves sponged across her back.

"Graceful as a gazelle," Will chided, offering her a hand.

"I might take you down with me," she muttered, scrambling back to her feet and pulling the sodden leaves off her skin. "Another white t-shirt ruined."

"Have you considered switching to black?" he asked, grinning.

"We couldn't meet this guy in a coffee shop?" she grumbled, pulling her coat around her body as she followed him.

Will looked back with a smirk.

"Not likely."

He walked a paved path to a bridge that hung over the Boardman River. As they drew closer, Sarah heard voices and slowed. She saw no one, and yet the voices drifted down as if...

"Is he up there?" She pointed at the dark underbelly of the bridge, where long shadows hid the alcoves beneath.

"Home sweet home," Will murmured. He stopped beneath the bridge and called up. "Maurice Paul? He here tonight?"

"I'll Maurice your Paul," a woman called, followed by a shrill cackle and another man's hoot of laughter.

"Stuff it, Spider Lady," a male voice snapped.

Sarah watched a shape disembark from the darkness. A man layered in sweaters and a grimy pair of corduroy pants shimmied down the concrete embankment. His hair was a long gray tangle over his shoulders. Sarah tried not to twitch her nose at the smell of whiskey and something pungent.

"What kin I do ya fer, Will the Potato Handler?"

"We need a good, long chat," Will told the man. "Buy ya a pack of smokes?"

"And a sandwich?" Maurice asked. "And a duce of Bud?" The man cast soft gray eyes from Will to Sarah, who he understood would pay for his requests.

He had kind eyes. Nothing sinister about him, other than his smell. Sarah wondered if her instincts were true or if she, like many others, simply couldn't sense bad from good.

"Sure, yeah." Sarah nodded.

"Why are you a potato handler?" Sarah asked as they trudged up the hill.

"I met Maurice when I was juggling potatoes," Will admitted.

Sarah lifted an eyebrow.

"I was working as a prep cook on Union Street, juggling potatoes by the dumpster."

"And Will the magnificent, juggling potato man gifted me this lifetime's most scrum-diddly-umptious pasty. Sixty-seventy some odd years now, but who's keeping count," Maurice said, breathing heavily as he struggled to keep up.

"You sit in the back," Sarah whispered through the side of her mouth when they approached her car.

She might not have a dark sense of the guy, but she didn't want him sitting behind her if he had a switchblade tucked in his back pocket.

Will winked and nodded. They stopped at a convenience store, where Will and Maurice ran in to fulfill the man's request.

"What cat crawled up your bum, you dragged me out of my

abode on this cold, windy night?" Maurice asked after he closed the
car door. He lit a cigarette that Sarah wanted to extinguish and
throw out the window. The smell of cigarette smoke reminded her
of her ex-girlfriend, Heather. Heather with the long blonde
eyelashes and the silky laugh.

"We have questions about the asylum," Will told him, shuffling
in a paper bag for the man's sandwich and beer. He handed Sarah a
Coke and kept a water for himself.

The man leaned his head back and took a long drag, sighing.

"Man, that's good." He turned to Sarah and held up his cigarette.
"I only smoke Lucky Strikes on special occasions. Takes me straight
back to the Vietnam War. Now a'days I roll my own, but once,
maybe twice a year, I pick up a pack of these, and it's like a little
time machine for my lungs."

"Interesting," Sarah murmured with a glance at Will, who
shrugged back at her.

"Maurice, I want to know about the rumors surrounding the
hippie tree. No, I take that back, I want the truth. The real story,"
Will said, leaning forward between the seats.

The man snorted and finished his cigarette, flicking the butt out
the window.

Sarah considered scolding him for littering but realized it
would be a wasted effort. The man was well into his seventies and
lived on the streets. He couldn't care less for her middle-class
judgments.

"The Wicked Willow," the man said in a sing-songy voice,
unwrapping his sandwich and taking a huge bite. He chewed
thoughtfully, and then returned to his song. "We lay my love and I,
beneath the weeping willow, but now alone I lie, beneath the
weeping willow." His voice had taken on a low, haunted quality, and
he stared out the window.

Sarah glanced at Will in the rearview mirror, but he held a
finger to his lips.

"Singing oh willow waly by the tree that weeps with me." When
he finished, he picked up his beer and cracked the top.

Again, Sarah opened her mouth and closed it, grinding her teeth together to keep from mentioning it was illegal to have alcohol open in a moving vehicle.

"Know that song? The Kingston Trio - mighty fine, mighty fine musicians." He drank in loud gulps, and then wiped his mouth with his sleeve.

"The Hippie Tree is not at fault. She was a beauty in her prime, a magnificent willow nestled there in the magical asylum forest. But you see, she was a beacon for a secret chamber hidden in the trees."

He turned his gaze on Sarah, but she stared forward, ignoring the intensity of his gaze.

"The lightning took her - BAM!" He clapped his hands together. Both Sarah and Will jumped.

"Shit, man. You made me spill my water," Will grumbled.

Maurice grinned and twisted in his seat.

"A story like this will make you spill your bladder." He turned back and took another bite of his sandwich. "I went there once. Few patients did, but you see, I was special. They called me Time Traveler. I could tell them what had been and what would be. My doctor wasn't in the brotherhood, the secret-keepers, the brain drainers. So, they waited until my doc took a holiday, and then they snatched me in the dead of night. Through the forest we wound, up the hills and down. I might never have known the place but for that willow, rising high into a moon-shone sky. Vines this thick buried the door." He held his hands apart. "Down a long, slick tunnel into a cold stone room. Torches on every wall, and benches, old wood benches, like you'd see in Greece at the Coliseum. I always wanted to go there, stand in the pits, watch the gladiators face off against the beasts sent in to destroy them."

"What was the brotherhood?" Sarah asked, turning down a road that led beneath towering oak trees.

"A secret society," Maurice said conspiratorially, quivering as he drew another cigarette from the pack.

"Of doctors?" Will asked.

Maurice nodded.

"I liked livin' there," Maurice murmured, rubbing his hand back and forth across his bearded face. "Nice bed, and a piano, and the canteen had a burger for a quarter. Real nice folks, except the bad ones, course." He snorted.

"Who was in the brotherhood?" Will asked.

Maurice frowned and cocked his head. After several seconds, he held up his empty palms.

"Don't know. There were so many of 'em, white faces starin' out from the dark, watching me. They were like a room full of lions, and I was their prey, strapped to a table, waiting to get eaten."

ow
Sarah

SARAH GLANCED AT WILL, who didn't look remotely suspicious of the man's story.

"But the takers get taken," he whispered, licking his lips. "One of them doctors went nutty as an acorn. He still haunts that place, like he's waitin' for his old life to be restored, to return to his post as Doctor Evil."

"He's still alive?" Sarah asked. "A doctor in the secret society?"

"Oh sure, lots of 'em prolly are. I am." Maurice tapped on his forehead.

"How do we find him?" Will asked.

Maurice picked up a chapstick from Sarah's cup holder and popped off the top. She snatched it out of his hand. He widened his eyes and leaned his head back with a sigh.

"Lips're mighty wind-burnt this time of year."

Give him the chapstick," Will said exasperated, as if he were mediating a fight between two children.

She handed it back, rolling her eyes.

"Lookin' fer your brains in there?" Maurice asked with a grin before slathering the chapstick on his scaly lips. He replaced the cap and dangled it above the cup holder.

"It's yours," Sarah mumbled.

He stuffed it into his pocket.

"I can set a meeting. 'Course, I'll need a few bucks. Bus fare, a sandwich, pack of slims."

"Done," Will said.

Sarah glanced at him, and he glared back at her as if daring her to disagree.

It wasn't the cost so much as the concern that Maurice would take the money and vanish into the cracks.

"The Doc's real particular, and a strange one too. I'll send word with a time and place."

Sarah pulled twenty dollars from her purse, and Maurice snatched it from her hand, opened the door, and hopped out.

"Wait," Sarah called, but he'd already vanished into the shadows beyond the streetlights.

Will opened the back door and climbed into the passenger seat.

"A secret society of doctors," he murmured, gazing into the darkness where Maurice had disappeared.

"Do you believe him?" Sarah asked, dubious.

"Sure, why would he lie?"

"To get twenty bucks."

"Nah. Maurice is good people. He's never steered me wrong."

"You've gotten information from him before?"

"Yep, he told me about the restoration of Kerry Manor. He knew the history of the house, heard about it during his asylum days. He knew of Delila; that's how I found her. I cross-checked his stories with newspapers when the house originally burned, and it was spot-on. He's an odd one, but not a liar."

"Do you think he knows an exorcist?"

Will gazed at her. She expected him to laugh. He didn't.

"If not, I can find someone who does. One thing at a time, though. Let's meet Doctor Evil."

~

CORRIE

"CORRIE, I'M SO SORRY."

Jillian grabbed me and pulled me close. I smelled perfume mixed with almond lotion. Her heavy black hair pressed into my cheek and reminded me of an animal pelt, a black bear perhaps.

I had not spoken with Jillian since I took a leave of absence from my therapy practice. We shared an office space, but rarely socialized outside of occasional encounters between clients.

"Thank you," I said, echoing the words I'd become so accustomed to offering.

"Are you coming back?" Jillian gestured at the two doors that opened from our little waiting room.

She meant was I coming back to practice.

I nodded.

"Do you have a few minutes?"

Jillian wrinkled her brow, and then understood.

"Oh my, yes. I'm not seeing another patient for two hours. I'd love for you – not love. I'd be honored. Yes."

She opened the door, and I followed her into her office.

Like our waiting room, which she'd decorated, a small, bubbling fountain stood on a table near her desk. Two soft club chairs, patterned in black suede, faced her desk. She sat in an ergonomic rolling chair decorated with a brightly colored afghan.

On the floor next to her desk, I saw a dog bed and a small basket of chew toys for her Welsh corgi, Sigmund, who we called Siggy. He often joined her on therapy days, but today his bed lay empty.

"No Siggy?" I asked, wishing he'd been there. It would have been nice to run my hands over Siggy's amber fur to avoid fiddling with them as I talked.

"Jackson and Cherie are taking him to the groomer," she explained. Jackson was Jillian's husband and Cherie their eight-year-old daughter. Sammy used to jokingly ask me 'when are Jillian and Jackson starting their stand-up comedy routine?' Jackson was, in fact, a dry, humorless man who talked about nothing but politics and the trouble with youth today. The one time we'd all gone to dinner together, Sammy had feigned an allergic reaction to his dessert to end the meal early. I smiled, remembering him scratching his face and saying, 'Huh, there must be nuts in the pecan pie.'

Under normal circumstances I would seek a therapist who didn't know me, but the events of the day propelled me to the first person who came to mind.

Jillian sat back in her chair and waited.

"I, umm, I'd just like your thoughts, I guess." I smiled awkwardly. "I didn't realize how hard it was to sit in the other chair."

She smiled and nodded.

"Forget that we know each other, Corrie. I'm just a mirror to reflect back answers already within you."

I swallowed and looked at my lap, frowning and trying to find the right words.

"Since Sammy died, I've been... lost. I always knew we were connected. I mean really connected, soul-level connected. I'm sure that sounds ridiculous."

"Not at all."

"It's almost like his death has proved it. I feel him everywhere, I see him, I hear his voice, and it's not just in my head. Sometimes it is." I laughed and pulled a string loose from my sweater, wrapping it around my index finger. "I'm trying to be strong for Isis, but..." My lip quivered, and the flood of tears would soon follow. If I focused on this tiny red string wrapped around my finger, I wouldn't cry.

"It's okay to let it out, Corrie. It's more than okay. Grief is energy stuck in your body. You have to release it somehow. Grief is a wave of energy. Let it roll through you, so you can rest in the space between the waves. Don't hold it in."

I took a long, shuddering breath and allowed my tears to rush over my cheeks. They snaked along my chin and beneath the collar of my sweater.

Jillian handed me a box of tissue.

"Other things are happening," I continued, returning to the string, winding it so tight the flesh of my finger bulged between the tiny strand. "I keep... blacking out or something."

I glanced up at Jillian, who watched me impassively.

"Describe blacking out."

I bit my lip.

"I'm not sure I can. I'll fall asleep in my bed and wake up in the great room or the study. I have no recollection of moving and time has passed, sometimes hours, when I feel like I've only just laid down."

Jillian nodded.

"Is anyone around? Has anyone seen you sleepwalking?"

I shook my head, thinking of the conversation I'd overheard between Sammy and Sarah. I didn't want to share it.

"No, only me. The other night I put furniture in front of my bedroom door and a hung a bell from the doorknob. I figured I would at least wake up if I tried to get out."

"And?"

"And I woke up in the study. When I went upstairs, the bell was gone. I haven't found it, and the furniture was all put back in place."

"You're still living in the house? Kerry Manor?"

I nodded.

"Have you considered the trauma of what happened to Sammy is causing these spells? The house is a stranger to you. Maybe you're trying to get out of the house and away from the place where you lost him."

"Then shouldn't I be waking up in my car with the engine running?"

Jillian smiled.

"The subconscious mind is mysterious. It has its own ideas about where freedom lies. Have you considered leaving the house, Corrie?"

I stared at her hard. It wasn't the first time someone had asked, and the familiar flicker of rage arose within me at her words.

"No."

"Can I ask why not?"

"Because we belong there. Because it's my home now, and..."

Jillian held up her hand.

"But it's not your home, Corrie. You and Sammy rented it for the winter. You're moving out in May."

I shook my head and wound the string tighter. The irrational anger bubbled like a steam kettle, ready to blow.

"Corrie," Jillian's voice dropped and she leaned toward me. "Are you hurting yourself?"

I followed her gaze to my exposed hand, where blood showed through the white gauze.

"I have to go," I said, jumping to my feet. "Thanks, Jillian."

I hurried from the office and let the door swing shut a little too hard behind me.

28

 ow
    Sarah

"WAIT, WHERE ARE YOU GOING?"

Sarah looked up at the sound of her receptionist Lorna's voice.

"Out," she said, turning away.

"You're meeting with Paul Hudson in twenty minutes. The New York developer."

"Fuck." Sarah looked at her watch. How did she forget? She'd set the meeting months ago.

"At Top of the Park?"

"Yep, so he can check out the gorgeous views of Traverse City," Lorna reminded her, grinning.

"I'll be there. I'm going to run a quick errand, and then I'll be there."

Lorna frowned but didn't say more. Sarah got it. Her receptionist couldn't understand why Sarah wasn't going early to survey the room, drink a vodka on the rocks, and settle in before the man arrived. It was a ritual Sarah did before meeting any big client, and Paul was by the far the biggest she'd ever had.

She skipped the elevator and ran down the stairs three at a time, jumping four to reach the landing before running full speed to her car.

"Come on, come on," she grumbled, sitting behind a woman in a Buick who struggled to slide her credit card into the payment slot. Sarah bit her lip and tried not to jump out and do it for her. Once on the street, she squealed down back roads, pulling to a stop in front of the arcade and barreling through the doors, nearly knocking over an acne-covered teenager playing Area 51.

"Sorry," she called, bursting into the sticky back room that Will often called home.

The room was empty.

"No," she muttered, scanning the room and then jogging back to find an unfamiliar face at the desk. "Where's Will?" she asked the tall, skinny boy-man who sported a thin line of splotchy red hair on his upper lip.

He looked up and shrank away, as if she might reach under the window and throttle him.

"I don't know, lady. He comes and goes."

Sarah sighed and kicked the cement wall, which sent a vibrating beam into her hip.

In the parking lot, she pulled out her phone and called the number of his friend, Melanie for Emergencies Only. It went to voicemail. Will didn't own a cell phone, and she chastised herself for not forcing one on him.

She was supposed to meet Maurice at two-fifteen, with directions to Doctor Evil for a three o'clock meeting. Her meeting with Paul was at two p.m. sharp.

When Paul Hudson arrived at the cocktail lounge, Sarah was downing her vodka and tapping her foot furiously beneath the table. She had intended to change before the meeting, but instead wore her usual jeans and white shirt. At least she'd opted for a white button-down shirt that morning.

A tall, broad-shouldered man in an expensive navy suit walked into the little restaurant. His hair was streaked in silver, and his face was tanned, as if he lived in California rather than New York.

"Sarah Flynn?" he asked, gazing at her. She noticed his eyes flick over her casual attire and fought the urge to apologize for her outfit.

"Paul Hudson," Sarah said, standing and extending her hand. She shook his hand hard and led him back to her table.

"I didn't expect you to be so lovely, Sarah," he said, sitting across from her. "A woman of your accomplishments should be homely, I'm sure."

She offered the customary laugh and searched within herself for the cool Sarah who met with men such as this all the time. Instead, she found a niggling sense of dread. It was five minutes after two. Time was running out.

"I see you've started without me," he said with a wink. He ordered a scotch on the rocks and leaned back in his chair, surveying her.

Sarah tried to sit up taller, but her legs had taken on a life of their own and bounced rhythmically beneath the table.

Paul leaned over the side and looked down.

"I think you're jiggling the whole building." He smirked.

Sarah took a deep breath, reached into her folder, and pulled out a stack of prints.

"Paul, I'm sorry to do this, but an emergency came up right before I walked in this door. As you can see," she gestured at her clothes and shaking legs. "I'm not prepared for our meeting. I'm going to have to reschedule."

He frowned and tilted his head to the side.

"You have something more important than this meeting?" he asked.

"Yep." She stood and handed him the file, wondering if she'd be leaving behind a dream when she walked from the building. "This is an overview of what I hoped to speak with you about. If you're not too insulted to see me again, give my secretary a call. It's been a pleasure."

She turned before he could speak and ran from the room. The lounge was on the tenth floor, and she had no choice but to the take the elevator. The seconds dragged like hours, and when she reached the first floor, she dashed out, narrowly missed two old ladies clutching their purses and staring at her in alarm.

CORRIE

I WATCHED the man leave the little table stacked with books. He meandered through shelves to the coffee bar at the back of the bookstore. After they handed him his paper cup decorated with dancing coffee beans, I hurried out from between the shelves.

He looked up, startled, but smiled. I rarely made men uneasy. On the contrary, they liked me on sight, for which I could thank my looks entirely.

"I read your book," I blurted.

"The Owl Tree?" he asked. "It was a fun one to write. Would you like me to sign your copy?" He looked at my empty hands and back at my face.

"Not *The Owl Tree*. Your other book, *The Summoning*."

His face darkened, but he masked it with a larger smile.

"Well, now I can thank you and my mother for the two copies I sold. Wherever did you find it?"

"In a used bookstore. I think it found me."

Before I could go on, a young woman with bright red spectacles perched on her freckled nose bustled over to us.

"You're on in fifteen minutes, Mr. Wolfe." The girl glanced at me before turning back the way she'd come. I had the distinct impression she was sizing up her competition.

"Speaking of summoning, I'm being summoned right now. It was a brief pleasure, Mrs....?"

"Flynn," I told him, but caught his sleeve before he turned away.

"I'd like to speak with you about the book. Please?" I had a momentary terror that if he said no, I'd collapse screaming to the floor.

Perhaps he saw something similar in my eyes. He sighed and nodded.

"After my reading, I intend to visit Seven Monks. It's a taproom here in town. I fancy myself something of a beer connoisseur, though I can seldom tell an ale from a lager."

I forced a smile and nodded.

"I know the place. I'll get us a booth."

"MRS. FLYNN, you realize *The Summoning* was a work of fiction, right? I see a certain look in your eye, one I've unfortunately encountered before, and I want to get that part over straightaway. I made the book up."

"Call me Corrie," I told him, sipping the hard cider the waitress had delivered. It tasted good, but the sweetness made my stomach churn. "I know it's labeled fiction, but…"

"But nothing," he said. He took a drink and nodded. "I love a good sour. Care to try?"

I shook my head.

"I don't believe you, Mr. Wolfe."

"Please call me Fletcher. If you're going to insult me, you should at least use my first name."

"I'm not insulting you. I understand you might have stretched the truth, changed names, but I feel the truth in that book. I know it, Fletcher. I know it."

He took another drink and stared away from me, his eyes flitting over pictures on the wall, patrons sitting at the bar, landing everywhere except my face.

"Let's have a hypothetical conversation, shall we?" he asked. "Let's say, hypothetically, when I was a young man, I became interested in the occult. While immersed in such things, I experienced a great tragedy."

"The death of your girlfriend," I murmured.

"Yes, in the book her name was Ann. Ann," he did air quotes as he spoke her name, "drowned one summer while we were boating

177

with friends. My fictional self became obsessed with the notion I could bring her back from the dead."

"And you did," I finished, remembering the final pages of the book when he awoke in the night to see Ann crossing his yard in the rain, moving toward his front door.

"In the book, yes, I summoned Ann back. In real life, no. She stayed buried. Because that is the truth of life, Corrie."

"I don't believe you," I told him, studying the way his eyes avoided mine.

He smiled.

"Of course, you don't. But that's not because I'm lying. It's because you want to believe the alternative. But where is she, Corrie? Where is my beloved Ann? Search my life. You will find no trace of her after July 7th, 1991, when she drowned in Moosehead Lake."

29

Now
Corrie

"I know it's real, Fletcher. I can feel it in here," I touched my chest, "in my blood, in the marrow of my bones. Maybe not everyone qualifies, but Sammy-"

"Who's Sammy?" Fletcher interrupted.

"My husband," I whispered, feeling the tears rising. Strange how they seemed to start deep in the stomach, the far-off rumble of a storm, then passed into your lungs, contracting up to your throat, and finally hovered at the back of your eyes with the same energy of an oncoming squall.

"And he died?" Fletcher dropped his voice and offered me the sympathetic smile I saw everywhere I turned.

"He was murdered."

Fletcher opened his eyes wide and gave me a pained expression.

"I'm terribly sorry for your loss, Corrie. I truly am. I get it, not your exact feelings, but my own horrid version of them. I wish I could offer words to help, but we both know words are useless in cases such as these."

"But words are magic too," I murmured, quoting his book - a particular section when he wrote of the summoning spells spoken when drawing someone back from the other side.

He sighed and rubbed the bridge of his nose.

"Corrie..."

"I'll do anything, Fletcher."

"So much for a relaxing drink with a beautiful woman," he complained, draining his beer. He signaled for a second.

I waited, holding my breath, knowing in the stretch of his silence something had shifted, a sliver of consideration.

"My book tour ends this weekend. I can't dredge all this up while I'm working. It's too distracting. When it's over, I'll tell you a story."

"Does your tour end in Michigan?"

He nodded.

"Petoskey tomorrow, then Harbor Springs, with the grand finale of a lecture in..." he trailed off, pulling a little notebook from his leather bag. "A signing in Marquette. Then, *voila*, another six months travel-free. I'll come back here to Traverse City on Sunday, and we can have a proper conversation about this."

"After that you'll return to Maine?"

"The one and only."

I stared at him another moment, searching his eyes for any clue he was lying. What if he finished his tour and hopped a plane back home? What if he would say anything in this moment to get rid of me?

He cocked his head to the side and smiled.

"You wear your every thought, Corrie. You must be a terrible poker player. I won't ditch you. You have my word. May I ask what happened to your hands?"

I looked down. I'd forgotten to keep my sweater pulled over my hands, and the bandages showed.

"An accident in the kitchen," I murmured, the crow's black eye rising in my memory.

He stared at my hands for another moment and nodded.

"A dangerous place, the kitchen."

~

Sarah

SARAH TURNED DOWN THE LONG, empty road that led to the Northern Michigan Asylum, once a hub of activity, now a sprawling reminder of the withering effects of time. The asylum occupied more than one hundred acres of lawn and forest.

Sarah had never explored the asylum. Growing up south of Traverse City, in a rural town with a population of less than five hundred, meant that instead of vandalizing the asylum as teenagers, she and Sammy threw rocks at old barns. When their parents relocated to Traverse City, Sammy and Sarah had passed the age of sneaking into the abandoned asylum with a can of spray paint and a bottle of Boone's Farm strawberry wine.

The asylum carved a foreboding chunk out of the blue sky. It was an architectural marvel in the Kirkbride style, which Sarah had studied briefly during her graduate program. She preferred modern - straight clean lines, minimal embellishments - but Kirkbride asylums took an opposing view. *Beauty is therapy*, they said. Pointed spires rose sharply from the highest and most elaborate building.

As she turned down a small side road, she pushed deeper into the old hospital grounds, buildings rising up decayed and crumbling, eerie in their grandeur. She parked along a dirt drive facing several smaller buildings, still large, the size of huge old plantation houses complete with balconied porches shadowed by rusted metal screens.

Sarah stepped from her car, unable to draw her eyes from the crumbing edifice, where brown vines and overgrown bushes clawed up the side of the brick face.

"Hey."

The voice startled Sarah, and she dropped her keys.

"Jesus, Will." She braced a hand on the hood of her car. "You scared the crap out of me. Where have you been? I looked everywhere this morning."

"I told you I'd meet you here."

"I know, but I had a meeting I'd forgotten about, and…"

He watched her, eyebrows raised.

"Forget it," she murmured, looking beyond him to the soaring limestone buildings, their paint yellowed and grimy.

"Welcome to the Northern Michigan Asylum for the Insane," Will said as he followed her gaze.

"Are they doing construction here?" In the distance, Sarah heard the sounds of an active construction site with heavy equipment and the voices of men.

Will nodded.

"The city sold the institution to a restoration company. In a few years, you'll be sitting here sipping a latte."

Sarah grimaced.

"Unlikely."

"They're working on Building Fifty," Will said, pointing toward the spires she'd passed. "The cottage we want is this way."

"These look awfully large for cottages."

"They called them that, probably to make them seem quaint and homey when obviously they were anything but."

"Where's Maurice?" Sarah asked, looking at her watch.

"Come and gone about ten minutes before you arrived."

"What?"

"Don't worry, he pulled through. Dr. Evil, who Maurice said we should call Dr. K, is waiting for us."

"Why Dr. K?"

Will shrugged. "Maybe his name starts with K. Then again, maybe Maurice pulled it out of thin air."

Sarah stuffed her hands in her pockets and gazed at the buildings left so long in abandon, they'd taken on a mythical, spooky quality.

"PLEASE TELL me this isn't our entrance," Sarah muttered, pausing at the overgrowth that mostly blocked a smashed-out basement window in one of the decayed buildings.

"Unless you know how to jimmy a deadbolt." Will squatted down and kicked the remaining glass from the frame. It rained onto the cement floor and shattered.

Sarah leaned down and peeked inside. A mass of dirty blankets lay in a corner. Graffiti covered one entire wall. Will moved her aside and climbed in, laying his jacket over the frame to shield against glass shards. His feet hit the floor, crunching into the broken glass. Sarah stood and glanced behind her.

What if Maurice had set them up? Inside they'd find a few of his friends carrying steel pipes, looking to score cash, sex, whatever they could get high on.

"You coming?" Will asked, peering up at her.

She marveled at his young face, unblemished, clear sparkling eyes - and yet he stood comfortably in the basement of an abandoned asylum, anxious to meet a man they knew only as Dr. Evil.

Reluctantly, she dropped in.

"Katie sucks cumquats," Sarah read aloud, studying the graffitied walls.

"This one's original," Will said, pointing to scrawled red writing. "Sumwun was heer."

"That kid better quit skipping school," Sarah said, following Will into a dark hall.

As they walked, Sarah felt equal parts dread and a morbid curiosity that had her imagining life in such a place. They shuffled down dark corridors littered with debris and leftovers from the building's asylum years. A steel table, missing one leg, lay crippled in the hall. Dredges of sunlight filtered through smashed windows that had been partially covered with boards or plastic.

They found Doctor Evil sitting in a battered wooden chair, gazing at a peeling wall.

"You're Dr. K?" Sarah asked, glancing at Will. How could they possibly know if he'd once been a doctor? Today, he looked like he lived under the bridge with Maurice.

"Out of practice, but yes," he hissed, casting dark eyes on Sarah and Will.

"We need help," Sarah said. "We heard about the brotherhood and your interest in supernatural things. Do you think we can trap an evil spirit in the asylum woods?" Sarah pushed the words out in a rush, and Will gave her a peeved look.

The man regarded her coolly.

"There's only one place where you can rid yourself of a dark spirit. The Chamber of The Brotherhood."

"Can you get us in?" Sarah asked.

"You think I have a key to the chamber?" The old man cackled, and his sour breath filled the room.

Sarah pretended to itch her nose with her arm to block out the stench.

"We assumed it would have been entrusted to someone who knew it best," Will said.

Sarah gaped at him. His prickly nature could transform in a moment.

The man's eyes sparkled as he gazed at the grimy window, one pane smashed and plastic flapping noisily in the wind.

"Dr. Coleman," the man murmured, touching his fingers to his lips. "Yes, I do believe the key lies with Markus Coleman."

"He was in the Brotherhood?"

"Is," the man hissed. "The brotherhood never dies. It is an oath for life, more sacred than blood, more valuable than gold. The knowledge - you can't begin to imagine…"

"Where is Dr. Coleman now?" Sarah asked.

The old man pulled his lips away from his teeth, as if he'd eaten something rotten.

"Nearby, I'm sure, in some uppity hellhole that God's forgot. He always put on airs, Markus." The man spit on the ground, leaving a drip of saliva clinging to his stubbly chin.

"How do you shave?" Sarah asked.

Will looked at her, surprised, but the man seemed unfazed by the question.

He grinned and lifted an eyebrow, digging into a pack around his waist. It had come from Crystal Mountain ski resort, likely a souvenir discarded by tourists and now this man's prized possession. He pulled a swatch of fabric clearly dotted with blood from the pack and opened it to reveal the lid of a can.

"You shave with that?" Will asked, grimacing.

"Used to be weak, had a sleek leather bag with a straight razor and whipped froth I put on my face. The conveniences of the modern world make you weak, boy." The man spat again, and Will took a quick step back as it landed where his feet had been.

"I don't understand the cloak-and-dagger around this chamber. It's decades old. What's there to protect?" Sarah asked.

The man shook his head, as if disgusted.

"And you are why women were not allowed in the brotherhood," he hissed. "No loyalty. Fair-weathered, self-serving lot that you are."

Sarah ignored the bubble of rage that surged in her chest. She considered giving him a lecture on feminism but bit her tongue.

"And the brotherhood never dies. Do you believe such a powerful entity could cease to exist?" The man scrubbed at a spot on his arm and smiled, his eyes gleaming. "It is eternal. We no longer reside in the asylum walls. Now we are in the world. The magic, the evil, the power is all around us."

"Did this brotherhood experiment on Ethel Kerry?" Sarah asked, suddenly wondering if the brotherhood had been alive and well a century before.

The man pulled his lips away from his teeth, surprisingly straight. He looked at her, disgusted.

"Experiment," he grumbled. "A fool's word, the fodder of small minds. Ethel was chosen. Her sacrifice brought vast knowledge."

"Can I ask how you know about Ethel?" Will interrupted. "I mean, she was dead before you were a doctor."

The man planted his good eye on Will, as if he'd forgotten him.

"The Enchiridion of Umbra," the man said proudly.

"I'm sorry, the enchirio-what?" Sarah asked.

The man spit at her feet and she jumped back.

"Enchiridion," Will said. "A text, then? Or a book of writings?"

The man nodded, appraising Will with renewed interest.

"More, so much more. Case studies, hypotheses, conclusions. The implications. It is a book of magic, a true glimpse into this world."

"How many were there?" Sarah asked.

He glared at her.

"One. There could only be one."

"Does it still exist?" Will asked, leaning forward. Sarah knew from his tone that he desperately wanted to get his hands on that book.

"Can you destroy fire? Air? It exists. It will always exist."

"Do you know who has it?" Sarah asked. She, too, wanted to see the book. Although she feared the horrors contained therein.

"There's no who," the man said. "It lives in the chamber. It belongs to the chamber, as does the brotherhood."

"The chamber?" Sarah shuddered, not sure she wanted to know more.

"How do we get to the chamber?" Will asked, bouncing on the balls of his feet.

The man watched him.

"Only a brother is allowed entrance to the chamber."

"So, you could get us in?" Sarah said.

"I would sooner cut off my own leg," he told them, staring hard at each of them.

"What if we paid you?" Sarah asked. "What if-?" but Will shushed her before she could go on.

"We need the chamber," Will said, stepping close to the man. "We have a woman filled with dark magic. How long has it been since the chamber received its due?"

Sarah glared at Will, ready to interrupt him, but he shot her a glance and she stayed quiet.

The man rubbed his hands together and blew a puff of pungent breath between them. Sarah wanted to turn her head, but knew better than to insult the man.

"Dark magic," the man murmured. "It is real, you know? More real than flesh and blood and bone. We perish, but it lives on."

"I know," Will said, and Sarah knew he meant those words.

"We need the brotherhood," Will continued. "Your knowledge is our only hope."

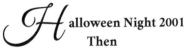

alloween Night 2001
Then

Corrie

"OH, NO YOU DON'T," Sammy murmured, surprising me in our room. I had laid the Bride of Frankenstein dress out on the bed. I stood in black fishnet nylons connected to a black lace garter I'd bought the week before.

"Sammy, this was supposed to be a surprise," I laughed, putting my hands on my hips.

He stood in the doorway, walnut eyes devouring me.

"We don't have time," I whispered.

"Bullshit," he murmured. "I'll cancel this damn party."

He hadn't put on his alien-baby shirt yet and wore a green shirt opened to reveal his smooth stomach, his chest a tangle of fine black hair.

He took three long strides across the room and picked me up.

I laughed as he threw me onto the bed.

"My God, you are beautiful," he told me, nuzzling his face into my neck, clutching one of the plastic bones sticking from my hair in his teeth and dragging it out.

I wrapped my legs around him and leaned back.

"Maybe I should switch to a Frankenstein costume, and we can ask a vampire to renew our vows tonight."

"Oh my, a second dream wedding," I murmured as he sat up and unclipped the garters at my thighs.

"I'm the luckiest man in the world," he told me, leaning down to kiss me hard on the mouth.

I opened my mouth with a sudden urge to demand he admit to renting us another house. Instead, when his lips found mine, I resisted the temptation and allowed the desires of my body to carry us away.

Sarah

SARAH HEARD Corrie's squeal of laughter and shook her head, grinning. She envied her brother's marriage. It was rare to see two people so in love after ten years of marriage, a daughter, and all the other life stuff that seemed to chip away at so many people's love.

Arranging the last tray of food on the buffet in the foyer, she slipped into the bathroom to throw on her costume.

The guests would arrive within the hour.

THE WEATHER WANTED to play too, offering an eerie mist that drifted on a cool breeze from Lake Michigan.

"Seriously, how cool is that?" Sammy nudged Sarah as they surveyed the courtyard where people had parked their cars. Sammy had turned the side yard into a cemetery, complete with plastic headstones and dangling skeletons. The fog drifted low, leaving the headstones peeking from the eerie mist.

"Isn't that a tad macabre?" she asked, gesturing at one of the headstones clearly reading 'Sammy Flynn' with that day as his day of death.

"'Tis All Hallow's Eve, Sarah-my-dear. The ghosts will run amok. I'm of an 'if you can't beat 'em, join 'em' state of mind."

Sarah shook her head, waving at Gloria, who piled from a van with a sign on the side that read TC Party Bus. Gloria had paid for a driver and bus rental for her group of ladies. They climbed out in a variety of costumes, from killer clown to mermaid. The last woman who stepped from the van, Sarah had not seen before. Her hair was long and black with bits of color woven through it. She wore a tall, pointed black hat, purple and black stockings, and a witch's dress complete with a purple lace corset.

Sarah couldn't take her eyes off her and watched the other women to see if one of them claimed her. No one seemed to.

Gloria marched up to Sarah and grabbed her in a rib-crushing hug, grabbing Sammy next.

"You've outdone yourself this year, Sam," Gloria declared.

"Thanks, Gloria. That's quite a compliment from a party planner such as yourself."

"Who's that?" Sarah asked Gloria, nodding toward the witch who had bent low to pull the laces on her black combat boots.

Gloria smiled, her mischievous eyes twinkling.

"That's Brook. Go say hi." Gloria gave Sarah a little shove and walked into the house, heading straight for the table of liquor.

CORRIE

"CORRIE, this is Gunner. The guy who does coffee shop illustrations," Sammy announced, dragging me away from the group I'd been chatting with.

A tall slender man in ragged clothes with black beneath his eyes and bits of fake flesh hanging from his face thrust out his hand.

"Corrie, you are dashing, my dear lady. Corpse bride?"

I smiled.

"The Bride of Frankenstein."

Gunner pointed to a tiny woman wearing a fairy costume. Her small, pointed face so perfect in her pixie-wear that Corrie could have believed she was the real deal.

"That's my wife, Micah. We have a two-year-old. His name's Jared."

"I said you and Micah should do a play date with Jared and Isis," Sammy told me, taking my cup and draining it. "Here, let me refill you."

I smiled, thinking I'd need another drink or two before I agreed to play dates.

Gunner winked.

"Micah's the same way, dear. Play dates are on her list next to leg waxing and drinking sour milk. But," he held up a finger. "A play date where we adults sip coffee tinged with Baileys while the kids run on the beach? I could get behind that."

Sammy returned with my drink, and I clinked it against Gunner's plastic cup.

"That's a play date I'll attend," I agreed.

"Oh look, it's Marcy," Sammy announced, grabbing my hand and pulling me toward the front door, where our neighbor from Traverse City stood wearing a Super Woman costume. Blue sparkling leggings covered her thick thighs, and her husband, half her size and a tenth of her personality, lingered behind her in a rendition of Freddie Krueger that wouldn't scare an infant.

Sarah

SARAH SAT with Brook in a dim enclave off the kitchen, what had likely once been a butler's pantry. Two smoky lanterns hung from hooks on the wall, and the pale wisps of paper ghosts floated overhead.

Brook sipped rum and pineapple and told Sarah how she first met Gloria at a gay club in Grand Rapids three years before.

"I've only hung out with her a few times," Brook admitted. "She's great, but a little too... jovial for me."

"Jovial," Sarah repeated. "That is the perfect word to describe Gloria. Oh, and tenacious."

"In the van on the way here, she held up an itinerary. Say hello to Sammy and Corrie, get a tour of Kerry Manor, sample all the Halloween-themed cocktails, convince one straight woman to question her sexual preferences, and end the night in bed with mystery lady not yet determined."

Sarah laughed.

Brook leaned forward and gazed into Sarah's eyes.

"Tell me, Sarah, what's your passion?"

"I'm an architect."

Brook studied her.

"I didn't say your job. I said your passion. Are you passionate about architecture?"

Sarah laughed, feeling buzzed not just by the alcohol, but an even deeper electricity from Brook.

"I am, actually. That probably sounds boring, but I've loved designing houses my whole life. As a kid, I used to fill notebooks with house drawings. Then Sammy would add creepy monsters climbing on the roofs and shimmying down the drain pipes."

"Sammy's your brother? The guy throwing the party?"

Sarah nodded.

"More than my brother, my twin."

"A twin. I have two sisters, but we're all three oil and water. My dad likes to call us salt, mangoes and patio furniture."

"That sucks. Sammy and I are so alike, even I confuse us sometimes. I can't imagine having a sibling that didn't get me."

"There's a lot to be learned from people who view the world differently than you."

Sarah nodded, still pretty sure she had the better deal.

"Tell me about you, Brook. What's your passion?"

"Music."

"Music?"

Brook nodded, thrumming her slender fingers up Sarah's arm.

"Piano, guitar, a little harmonica. I work at Voodoo Queen."

"The instrument place?"

"That's the one. I play in a band, teach lessons, still cling to dreams of one day making a record and hitting it big."

"Really?"

Brook shrugged.

"Maybe *si*, maybe *non*. Childhood dreams die hard, but I get to make a living doing what I love and sharing it with others. I have friends that live the real musician's life. It's a lot of travel, a lot of cheap motels and diner food. I'm rather fond of my studio apartment, my bird, Baba Yaga, and my little balcony covered in flowers. Though the flowers have been moved to my living room, where they'll live until spring."

"You're in a band?" Sarah asked, embarrassed that she found it as sexy as she did. "Is it totally cliché if I'm automatically turned on by that?"

Brook laughed.

"How can an emotion be cliché? It either exists, or it doesn't. My band is called North State of Mind."

"I like it. What kind of music do you play?"

"I call it folk meets the blues."

"Intriguing."

"You should come hear us play sometime."

"I'd like that," Sarah said. "Though I fear we're already doomed for failure."

"Why is that?" Brook asked.

"I'm a dog person."

Brook leaned forward, admiring Sarah's backside.

"I don't see a tail."

Sarah grinned.

"I seriously dig you, Brook with the bird named Baba Yaga."

∽

CORRIE

I LOOKED AT THE CHAOTIC, drunken scene. Costumed bodies writhing to the haunting music blasting from the speakers. A trash can near the door overflowing with plastic cups and paper plates. My head swam, and when I looked at the grandfather clock standing astutely in the hallway, I saw it was after midnight. People had been leaving for an hour, the group slowly thinning, cars disappearing from the crowded courtyard.

I slipped up the stairs and rested on the edge of the bathtub, staring at my dress and willing the floor to stop tilting.

SAMMY NEVER CHEATED ON ME, never. I know that. But that night, something happened. Maybe it triggered all that followed.

Her name was Chloe. I've never much cared for the name. It sounds like a fake name for a fake person. Chloe would be the name in giant starburst letters on the cardboard box of a blow-up doll with puckered lips and a rubber 'flesh-like' hole, meant to bring pleasure to some sad man whose wife had left him a decade before. Chloe might be a nickname or a puppy's name, but a grown woman?

She showed up to our Halloween party in silver tights and a tiny red velvet dress that tucked around her body like cellophane. Red pointed horns stuck from her thick black hair. She was beautiful in that terrifyingly exotic way that so many women fear. Slanted cat eyes thick with mascara, and enormous red pornographic lips that made every spoken word look like an invitation for oral sex. Worse, she worked with Sammy. She was the secretary for a comic book artist he was doing a collaboration with.

Most of the guests had gone home. I stopped in the kitchen and filled a tall glass with water, gulping it down in two long drinks.

When I saw her kissing him beneath the oak tree, I felt the weirdest sensation - as if I was tumbling down a mountain caught in avalanche, getting buried. And as the light began to disappear, I watched my life with Sammy vanish as well. I watched his sweet smile turn grotesque and angry as we fought over the custody of our love child and the stupid bullshit we'd accumulated during our marriage. I watched a real estate agent hammering a for-sale sign in front of our little bungalow, and the tire swing in the backyard getting ripped down to improve the resale value. I saw Chloe putting lipstick on the innocent face of my beautiful daughter and insisting that Sammy enroll her in jazz classes and pierce her ears.

I went crazy. I didn't know it at the time, but I did. I took a knife out of a kitchen drawer and went upstairs to lie down.

I placed the knife beneath my pillow, closed my eyes, and fell asleep.

ow
Sarah

"CRASH AT MY PLACE, if you want," Sarah told Will.

He glared at her.

"I have my own places to crash. I don't need charity."

"It's not charity. I need your help tomorrow, and I don't feel like hunting through all your little hovels in the morning."

Will looked away, and then returned a hard glare at her.

"I'm not exactly 'Leave it to Beaver' material, Sarah. What will your friends think?"

"Seriously? I'm a lesbian. I dropped the judgey friends ages ago. We marginalized folks have to stick together."

"You're gay?" He lifted an eyebrow.

"Yes, and not the merry kind. I date women."

He picked his duffel bag off the ground and slung it over his shoulder.

"All right." He plopped back into the passenger seat.

She smiled but directed her expression toward the window, lest he flee from her obvious joy at his staying the night. It wasn't the company she wanted, but an end to the niggling unease that woke her at least once every night since meeting him. Fear for his safety, for Corrie, Isis, her mother. Fear drove her out of bed to her home office, where she sketched house plans until her hands ached and her eyes grew bleary. It was ridiculous.

Will was a seventeen-year-old man, able to take care of himself, and yet... She thought of Isis, small and innocent and caught in the same cycle of loss. She wanted to believe that if Isis ever met a similar fate, there would be kind strangers who would guide her.

SARAH'S DOG turned from his spot on the sofa, where she imagined seconds before he'd been springing in the air like a dog on a trampoline. He bounded across the room and greeted Sarah with a cheerful bark.

"How's my little Archie?" Sarah knelt and scratched behind Archie's fluffy white ears.

"Hey, Archie," Will said when the dog shifted his attention to the stranger in his house. He nudged his head into Will's knee. "Did you name him after the comic strip?" Will patted the dog on the back and held out his palm while Archie licked it and barked a seeming approval at Sarah.

"After Andy Warhol, actually. Well, not him, but his dog." Sarah gestured at a half-wall painting of a vivid Marilyn Monroe set against a pale blue background.

"Is that an original?" he asked.

Sarah shook her head. "I'm doing pretty well, but not that well. Do you know his work?"

"Nah. I mean, we brushed over it one of my online classes. Apparently, he's the father of pop-culture or pop art or Pop Tarts. I can't say his stuff moved me."

Sarah surveyed the picture. "I find Andy fascinating because he rebelled against the status quo. He chose an authentic life - not easy to do, as you yourself know."

Will nodded looking at the image for another moment before taking in the rest of the house's spacious interior.

"Damn, this place is swikkety-swank. Did you design this?"

"Yep, with the help of my mentor, Richard Haller. This was my third house and my favorite for obvious reasons. I intended to sell the house plans, but after I finished, I knew it was mine. I built it instead."

"What's it called?" Will asked, gazing at the slanted ceiling strung with a jumble of hanging silver pendant lights. The ceiling ended at a high white wall that ran between two walls of corrugated metal.

"I'm not sure it has a label. If I had to, I'd call it Modern Refurbished. I took liberties when it came time to focus on aesthetics. The house itself follows the tradition of modernism. I thought a lot about Frank Lloyd Wright when I designed it. I wanted the inner and outer life of the house to flow." She gestured at the wall of windows that looked out on her backyard, where a mature cottonwood tree stood surrounded by wooden benches. "But I also love re-purposing old materials. This floor is made from palettes."

"It's cool," Will said, dropping his duffel bag behind a chair and leaning over her coffee table stacked with books on unique structures.

"Get comfortable. I'm going to walk Archie, and then I'll pop some food in the oven."

～

"WHY DID YOU BECOME AN ARCHITECT?" Will asked, eating the last egg roll and scooting closer to the fire, where he stuffed a pillow beneath his head and reclined on the floor.

Sarah took a sip of wine and pulled her legs beneath her on the couch.

"My dad spent most of our childhood sketching his dream house. He always said one day he'd find a little lake in the forest and buy a piece of land, and we'd build the house. Unfortunately, he never did. Partially because the design was a nightmare and never could have worked, but also because it was the dream more than anything else that he loved. His passion moved onto me. I drew dream houses too. When it came time to declare a major in college, I'd already known for a decade what I wanted to do."

"That's cool," Will said. "My dad was a technical writer. I almost feel like I should do it too. I don't even know why."

"Did he love it?"

"Nah, not really, but I don't know many adults who love their jobs. Do you?"

The first person who popped into her mind was Sammy. He had loved his job.

"Some of them do, the happiest ones do. I would never have become an architect if I didn't love it."

He closed his eyes and yawned.

"Why aren't you with family, Will? Not to pry. I'm just surprised."

"My dad was an only child and wasn't close with his parents. They live in Boston. My mom has a brother that lives downstate."

"And you didn't want to live with them?"

"They believe my dad is a murderer."

Sarah sighed. "That's terrible."

"Yeah, and logical too. They're not exactly open-minded. They never liked my dad to begin with. I'd rather live in a dumpster."

"Well I'm happy you've found better options than that."

He grinned.

"Yeah, the arcade is a slight upgrade. I've had friends offer, but..." He opened his eyes and looked at her. "They all sort of tiptoe around me like I'm fragile. I'm not fragile, my dad wasn't a murderer, and I prefer to be on my own. I have a job. I'm saving for my own place."

"What's your job?"

"The Computer Caper." He reached into his pocket and pulled out a stained business card, handing it over.

"There's no phone number. Your name's not even on here."

"I prefer to work incognito. My business is mostly word-of-mouth. I need that back." He plucked the card from her hand.

"Do you only have one business card?"

"I had about twenty, but I've passed them all out. I'll order more one of these days, but why bother? I've got more work than I have time for."

~

CORRIE

I LAID Isis in her crib, her lower lip trembling with breath, and kissed her forehead before returning to the great room where Fletcher sat, legs crossed, hands clasped in his lap.

"She's beautiful," Fletcher said.

"Thanks," I told him, guilt crowding my brain. "Since Sammy died, I've lost touch with being the mommy she deserves. I can't tell you the last time I got on the floor and played with her. I feel terrible."

"It's not your fault, Corrie."

I walked to the window, where mist swept off the lake and crawled over the shoreline. A mass of dark sky prowled the horizon; soon rain would drench the house and lawn.

"It is, though. Parents don't get to stop. No catastrophe justifies abandoning our children. My mother was a drinker, an alcoholic. She abandoned us, and I hated her for it. Now…" I trailed off, unable to say the words, hating myself for the comparison.

Fletcher looked uncertain, but then seemed to find the words he wanted.

"When Lauren died…" He paused. "Lauren was her real name, not Ann. When she died, I ceased. I mean it, every single routine in my life stopped. I switched from drinking soda to black coffee. I stopped sleeping. I chucked my TV out the window." He chuckled. "I couldn't tolerate any aspect of my life that reminded me of Lauren. Eventually, the new habits replaced the old, the new me was born, and that's how I survived. It may be a long time before you're on the floor again with Isis, Corrie. My advice? Let go of the mother you used to be and let a new one be born. For both of you."

I smiled, forced my feet across the room and perched on the edge of a maroon chair, planting my hands on the carved mahogany arms to stop their restlessness. "Tell me about Lauren."

He gazed at me a moment longer, and then nodded.

"I met Lauren in college. She was studying to be a teacher. I was a wayward soul, taking philosophy and psychology courses, but had a no-preference major."

He shifted in his chair and glanced around the house again.

"I must admit, Corrie, this house seems like a strange place to recover."

I stiffened, a little flare of defensiveness lighting in my head.

"It's big," I said.

He laughed.

"Big's not even the half of it. It's..." he paused and looked toward the fireplace. The black mouth yawned empty beneath the grinning pagan face. "Unsettling."

"It grows on you," I murmured.

"I'm sure it does, though I sense an invasion more than a growing."

I frowned but didn't argue. I needed this man, and I didn't want a petty squabble over the strange house to send him on his way.

"Tell me about Lauren," I prodded.

He returned his eyes to mine.

"We were oil and water in the early days. I liked to sit around chain-smoking Virginia Slims and discussing Tolstoy. She headed a bunch of activity groups - sand volleyball, ski-club, softball. She was in a sorority when I met her. I poked fun at her. She could have blown me off, should have. She smiled and said, 'Join us.' I didn't. I would not reduce myself to the sun-tanned, always smiling Phi Beta Whatta's, but then I saw her one day in this little park at the edge of campus. She was sitting alone, reading a book. Something happened. That strange magic that has people using words like 'the one' and 'love at first sight.' The words don't do the experience justice, and the hard thing is the moment is fleeting and you might only get it once in your life."

I nodded, balling my hands into fists in my lap and struggling to breathe. I knew the feeling. I'd experienced the magic.

He hesitated and looked at his feet.

"I'm sorry, Corrie. I shouldn't have gone there. This is fresh for you, and I remember those encounters of my own after she died. It was like a knife grinding in my chest every time a couple kissed or laughed or held hands. Happiness had become like poison to me."

"Don't stop, tell me the rest."

"We were on Moosehead Lake, drinking. It was close to dusk and my friend Gary was driving the boat. Lauren went up to sit in the bow seat, and Gary was driving so fast. He didn't see the waves. We hit 'em going fast. I saw her fly up into the air. Her face is frozen in my mind, that look of shock, and then she was overboard. She disappeared into the water so fast, and by the time we got the boat turned around and circled back to her, she was gone."

"Could she swim?"

"Like a seal," Fletcher said, frowning as if it still puzzled him. "But I heard something, a thud. I don't know if she hit her head, or the boat ran her over."

He stopped and closed his eyes, shook his head as if that might remove the images seared there.

"We didn't find her body for two days. The coast guard was out, helicopters, search-and-rescue teams. A tourist found her tangled in weeds on the north side of the lake along an isolated stretch of forest."

I heard a thud upstairs and jumped.

Fletcher looked toward the stairs.

"Is there someone else here?"

I shook my head.

"This house makes a lot of noise," I said. "Sammy liked to say 'it talks a lot.'"

Fletcher peered at the foyer, but when no one appeared, he continued.

"After the funeral, I dropped out of school. Like I said, I stopped functioning. I read books, a hundred at least."

"On the occult?"

He nodded.

"The one-year anniversary of her death was approaching, and I dreaded it. I decided to take my own life."

ow
Sarah

"Yeah?" Sarah called at the knock on her study door. Her study consisted of a hexagonal room perched on the top of her house. It was the only upstairs floor and allowed sunlight to stream in through six windows, one on each wall. Today, rather than sun, rain poured down the glass and occasionally Sarah glimpsed a streak of lightning in the gray sky. Her drafting table stood in the center, and waist-high file cabinets designed to look like sleek bureaus butted all but two walls. She had installed surround-sound speakers and played a variety of binaural beat tracks that helped her immerse in a new project.

The door to her study lay at the bottom of a staircase. She heard Will call up.

"You have a guest."

Sarah frowned, staring a moment longer at the drawing of the Millers' new summer cottage, over four times the size of her own house, and reluctantly set her pencil down. She trotted down the stairs to where Will stood. He grinned.

"What?" she asked, irritated at the interruption.

He stepped aside, and Sarah saw Brook standing inside the front door. She held a bottle of gin her hand.

"Isn't it a little early for gin?" Sarah asked, stopping halfway across the room.

Brook looked momentarily wounded, and then wiped the expression and smiled.

"Isn't it a little late in your life to be bisexual?" She gestured at Will, whose mouth dropped open.

"What? No," he said shaking his head and stealing a glance at Sarah, who smiled and winked at him.

"It was a joke, Will. I can't believe your humor has finally run out."

"Well, I," he sputtered. He looked between the two women, and then shrugged, returning to the couch where he had several books opened and a bowl of tortilla chips balanced precariously on a stack.

"If I find salsa on that rug, you'll be licking it up," Sarah called as she led Brook to the kitchen.

"I love wool with my salsa," he yelled back through a mouthful of chips.

"Did you adopt a son since I last saw you?" Brook asked, setting the bottle down and perching on a high-stool.

Sarah pulled a bottle of tonic from the refrigerator and poured them both a glass. She never worked buzzed but knew she wouldn't be returning to the Miller house that day.

"I'm sorry I haven't called," she told Brook, passing her the glass. Their fingers touched, and Sarah felt the stirrings of passion.

Brook took a sip, studying Sarah over the rim of the glass.

Sarah noticed her low-cut black shirt and the pale pendant wrapped in a silver moon resting on Brook's chest.

"I considered fashioning a voodoo doll and punishing you, but thought a peace offering might be a wiser choice."

Sarah twitched, imagining the leathery doll in the attic at Kerry Manor.

Brook saw the look on her face.

"I'm sorry, was that in bad taste?"

Sarah sighed and drank her gin and tonic, miserable that she'd blown off Brook and still wasn't sure why.

"I don't have an excuse," Sarah admitted. "I mean, I do, but nothing that's good enough."

"I'm not here for an excuse," Brook said. She traced her finger, the nail painted dark violet, along the rim of her glass and then slipped her finger into her mouth.

"I-" Sarah started, but Brook stood and pressed a finger against Sarah's lips. She moved closer and Sarah smelled the piney sweetness of gin on her breath. Brook leaned in, her generous mouth painted dark.

Sarah closed her eyes, and the room tilted as she pushed deeper into Brook's hungry lips. Suddenly falling, she shot her arm out and caught the edge of the counter. Brook held her firmly around the waist.

"Whew," she breathed. "Are you okay? I thought you might take us both down."

Sarah blinked and raked a hand through her blonde hair. It felt oily. When had she last washed it? As she considered the question, she realized she had eaten nothing that day, either. No wonder the kiss rendered her senseless.

"I need a shower," she murmured.

Brook's smile widened, but Sarah shook her head.

"I want to, eventually. I do, Brook. I'm into you all the way. Okay? I know you might think I've been playing games, but honestly-"

"Hey," Brook grabbed her hand and kissed it. "I meant what I said. I'm not here for excuses. You're in a strange place. I don't have a twin, but I adore my sisters. If I ever lost one..." She trailed off. "Don't feel guilty, and don't feel obligated. I'm here right now. That's enough for me."

Sarah kissed her on the lips and rested her forehead against Brook's.

"Thank you," she whispered.

After she showered, Sarah slipped into a pair of freshly laundered jeans and a crisp white t-shirt. She pulled her hair into a ponytail and returned to the living room, pausing in the hallway at Will and Brook's conversation.

"Ethel Kerry," Will explained. "That was her name."

"Wow," Brook said. "I knew I heard a little girl that night. I tried to do research on the house, but that was fifteen years ago. The Internet wasn't exactly thriving."

"I can't imagine a world without the Internet," Will said. "Here, check out this article I printed."

Sarah stepped into the room.

"Well, you guys are fast friends," she said, winking at Brook when she looked up from the article.

"We share a common interest," Will declared, tapping the pile of books.

"Ready for lunch?" Sarah asked. "We can continue our Kerry Manor discussion at North Peak."

~

CORRIE

"YOU DIDN'T WRITE that in the book," I murmured.

"The book was fiction," Fletcher said gently. "I had read about resurrections. Different texts told different stories. The dead would come back as an apparition, or in the body of another. What did I have to lose? One way or another, I would have her back. Whether she returned, or I joined her on the other side."

He stopped and gestured at my hand.

"Corrie, you're bleeding."

I looked down. I had been squeezing my hands in a fist so tightly, my nails had drawn blood from my palms. I opened them and stared at the line of red crescent moons. I started to wipe the blood on my pants, but Fletcher stood.

"I'll get a towel," he said, "and maybe this is a good time for a cup of tea?"

I nodded, trembling, most of me wanting to insist he sit back down and finish the story. Instead, I followed him into the kitchen. He doctored my hand, wiping it clean and wrapping it in a paper towel.

I started to fill the kettle, but he took it from my hands.

"Sit, I've got this."

I watched him move through the kitchen, filling the kettle, pulling packets of tea from the jar by the sink.

"Have you been with anyone else? Since Lauren?" I asked.

He paused and looked out the window, where rain had begun a soft patter against the glass.

"Yes, several. But no one has compared to her. Not to the love I shared with her." He turned back to me. "I didn't expect anything else. But you don't have to think about that yet, Corrie. My advice to you is not to rush into anything or anyone right away."

"I wouldn't," I whispered. "I couldn't. And I won't need to."

"Because you're going to bring him back from the dead?" Fletcher asked.

I looked away from him and nodded.

He sighed.

"I wanted to hold her again, so I opted for the resurrection that included another person. I needed someone who wanted to die, someone ready to leave the world, but also who resonated with Lauren. I searched for months."

"And you found her," I said. I had read the book. I knew.

"Yes, her name was Jade. She lived in New York City and she reached out to me online. She had planned a day for her death."

"And it worked…"

"No," he shook his head. "It didn't work, Corrie. I wrote the book because I needed the catharsis. I needed to follow the possibility to its end. The night of the ritual, Jade swallowed a bottle of OxyContin. I rushed her to the hospital. I couldn't go through with it. They pumped her stomach, and she survived. She hated me for a long time, and then she forgave me. We're still friends."

He took his phone from his pocket, scrolling for a moment before handing it to me.

I stared at an image of Fletcher in front of the Statue of Liberty. A small, dark-haired woman with huge brown eyes and piercings in her nose, eyebrow and cheek looked back at me.

"That's her, Corrie."

As I looked at the picture, my shoulders slumped. My head seemed to grow heavier, and I rested it on my hands.

"I'm sorry." He touched my hand, and I stared at his fingers, long and smooth with the nails clipped short.

I used to clip Sammy's fingernails. Every few seconds he'd jump and howl in pain, and Isis would giggle.

I couldn't even look at fingernails; the most neutral thing in the world reminded me of Sammy.

∾

Sarah

"FUCK," Sarah grumbled when she spotted one of the detectives she'd seen during her last trip to the police station. The detective put his menu down and glanced their way. His eyes stopped on Sarah, and then widened when he spotted Will.

Will craned around in his seat, following Sarah's gaze.

"Hey, Detective Lawson. How's it hanging? Put away any innocent men today?"

Brook had just begun to ask who they were all staring at, but closed her mouth at Will's comment.

Sarah kicked him under the table.

He jumped but continued glaring at the detective until the man lifted his menu back up, concealing his face.

A moment later, Detective Collins walked in.

Sarah dropped her head into her hands, looking up when Detective Collins cleared his throat. He stood next to their table.

"I see you've found Will Slater. Funny, you didn't get in touch with us so we could interview him."

"Obviously it wasn't that hard," Will declared, folding his arms across his chest. "Hoping to pin this one on me? Follow in your mentor's footsteps?"

Detective Collins considered Will, nodding his head as if coming to some conclusion.

He pulled a card from his pocket and planted it on the table.

"It would be great if you'd come down to the station to answer a few questions, Will. Maybe your new friend can drive you." He nodded at Sarah and turned on his heel.

"What was that all about?" Brook asked.

"Oh, they'd like to blame me for the murder," Will said nonchalantly. "And now Sarah's my accomplice."

"I don't want to talk here with those detectives in hearing distance," Sarah said. She turned to Brook. "Will and I have to meet someone this afternoon, but I promise I'll fill you in on everything soon."

ow
Corrie

I WATCHED Fletcher hurry to his car, his coat held above his head as a flimsy shield against the downpour.

I couldn't let him go. I ran into the storm. The rain had soaked me clear through before I stepped off the porch and plummeted into the muddy yard. I slipped on wet leaves and nearly fell.

"Fletcher," I called out his name, but the roar of the wind drowned my call.

He opened his car door.

I surged forward and caught his coat, yanked him around to face me.

"Tell me, damn it!" I howled, and maybe he heard, or perhaps he read the desperation in my face.

"Get in," he yelled into my ear.

I scrambled around to the passenger side of his car and climbed in, soaking his seat.

The cold seeped through my skin, slowed my blood, turned my

bones to ice. My teeth chattered as he started the car and turned on the heat.

"I met a woman," he said at last. She described a place - a dimension, if you will, where evil does not exist. And then there is earth, where everything, good and evil, manifests as matter. And then there is the space between, the place where souls and energy might linger, might get trapped."

"And you found her? You summoned Lauren's spirit?"

He closed his eyes briefly and looked back at the house. I saw the troubled way he watched it, as if were not a house at all, but a monster waiting to devour us.

"I can't explain how, but the woman-"

Something in the way he said 'the woman,' gave me a chill.

"She showed me the way. But Corrie, if you do this..."

"I don't care!" I slapped his dashboard so hard my hand stung.

"I know," he said, hanging his head. "Why is the moment of clarity always after the disaster?"

"Fletcher..." I pleaded.

"I don't know her name. She lives in our world, but she's not of it. You're fortunate - though I hesitate to use that word - because she doesn't live far from here. I drove for a day and a half to find her. She lives in a little Upper Peninsula town called Ishpeming. She may choose not to help you. For each of us the summoning is different, and somehow she sees what needs to be done."

"Ishpeming," I repeated the name and city. "Do you have a phone number?"

He smiled.

"She doesn't use a phone, or didn't then, but believe me, she'll know you're coming. When you get into Ishpeming, find Bluff Street. A stone wall runs along the front of her property. You can't miss it. Take cash, five hundred dollars."

"How did you find her?" I asked breathlessly, renewed hope making me want to bounce in my seat.

"Jade. After I saved her, she told me her life story." Fletcher put his hands on the wheel and frowned. "Horrible things had happened to her as a girl, and she'd never gotten over them. Her friend insisted Jade travel to the Upper Peninsula in Michigan, to the home of a witch who could right those wrongs, punish those who'd hurt her. Jade never went-"

"But you did."

Fletcher nodded.

I jumped from the car. I wanted to write it down before some detail slipped my mind. The rain battered me, but I paused for a moment and mouthed 'thank you.' I don't know if he saw through the rain-slicked window.

Sarah

GLEN BLACKBURN LIVED in a large Tudor-style house protected by an iron gate and rows of flat bushes.

The rain had ceased, and pockets of sun shone through openings in the cloud cover.

"I can jump that fence," Will said, sizing it up.

"No, we're not breaking into the guy's house."

"Okay, genius, tell me what your grand plan is."

"We'll ring the bell. I'm an architect, you're my pupil. We'll ask for a tour."

Will shrugged.

"Okay, yeah, that will keep us out of jail, anyway."

"Yes. If we manage nothing else today, let's at least stay out of jail."

"It's not that bad," Will said. "Unless you're in with the drunks hogging the toilet all night while they puke their guts up."

Sarah grimaced.

"Thank you for the visual."

"My pleasure," Will said, swinging his door open and jumping out.

"Let me do the talking," Sarah told him.

Sarah knocked on the door. An older gentleman, well into his seventies, with a portly belly and twinkling blue eyes answered the door. He smiled cheerfully, and Sarah had a momentary image of the man dressed as Santa Claus.

"Hi, sir," Sarah held out her hand. "My name's Sarah Flynn, I'm an architect here in Traverse City, and this is Will, an intern at my office. Today we're learning about Tudor architecture, and your home is a stunning example. Would you be open to giving us a tour?"

The man beamed, glancing from Sarah to Will.

"Oh yes, that would be lovely. You know, this house dates back to 1926? It's an absolute jewel. My father built it."

Glen led them through the house, and Sarah pointed out examples of Tudor style.

"Do you notice the irregularly shaped rooms, Will? This supports the asymmetry of the Tudor style."

Will played along, asking questions, murmuring in the right places.

"Can I use your bathroom?" Sarah asked as Glen led them through a glass door that opened on a brick patio.

"By all means, dear. Down the hall, third door on your left."

"Is that a pizza oven?" Will asked, pointing at a tall brick oven on the patio.

"Go ahead," Sarah told them. "I'll be out in a minute."

Sarah paused at the bathroom listening as Will and Glen left the house. She crept down the hallway, pushing doors open. The first room contained a front-loading washer and dryer, the second a bedroom fitting a child, most likely for a grandchild. The third was Glen's study. She closed the door behind her and hurried to his desk, pulling open drawers and rifling through paperwork, pens, and an odd array of little wooden figures. She hadn't fancied Glen a whittler, but apparently he was.

She found the bottom left drawer locked.

"Fuck all," she said.

"Hi."

Sarah jumped and let out a little squeak of surprise.

A little boy stood shirtless in the doorway, a pair of dinosaur pajama pants pooling around his Batman slippers.

"Grandpap?" he asked, though obviously she was not Grandpap.

"Oh, hi. I'm sorry. I was looking for the bathroom and stumbled in here." Her voice shook, and she was tempted to ramble further but doubted the little boy cared either way.

As she stepped into the hall, a woman peeked around the corner spotting Sarah and blinking as if she questioned her own eyesight. She looked at the little boy, alarmed.

Sarah held up a hand.

"Sorry, hi. I'm Sarah Flynn, an architect. Glen was showing me the house."

"Oh." The woman stepped into the hallway. She wore crisp white pants and a gray cashmere sweater, her long dark hair falling over her shoulders.

"I'm Diana, his daughter. I was reading to my little rugrat when he ran off."

"He's adorable," Sarah said with a gesture at the little boy, who'd stuck his thumb in his mouth and started sucking on it loudly.

"Everett, what did Mommy say about sucking your thumb?"

The boy continued, a line of drool dripping from his mouth onto the cream carpeting.

Diana sighed and took his shoulders in her hands, steering him back down the hallway.

"Nice to meet you," Sarah called as they disappeared around the corner.

"WELL, that was a blasted waste of time," Sarah declared, hitting the gas and shooting the car up the hill that led away from Glen Blackburn's house. "And I almost got caught. His daughter and grandson were in there. The kid saw me digging through his study."

"I told you to let me do the lurking, but no, you're the adult and I'm the kid."

"Well it wasn't there, so I don't see what difference it would make. Should we grab dinner?"

"Hell no. I want to get my hands on that book."

"Will, that's obviously not happening tonight. We need the key, and-"

"This key?" Will held up a long black key with a staring eye engraved in the center.

Sarah snatched it from his hand.

"Where?"

"It was in his workshop, sitting right on the window ledge with a bunch of weird little wooden figures. He turned his back, and I slipped it in my pocket."

THEY SCOURED the woods behind the Northern Michigan Asylum for two hours. Crisscrossing back and forth among the graffitied trees, pushing through thickets of dead brush. They knocked on trees, shuffled leaves, thinking perhaps the door to the chamber was beneath their feet. They found nothing.

"He said only a person in the brotherhood could find it," Will muttered.

"Which has to be bullshit, right? I mean, if it's a real place..." She stopped at the look on Will's face.

"Suspend disbelief, Sarah. Remember?"

Sarah swore and kissed a tree, wincing.

"We need Dr. Evil," Will said at last.

ow
Corrie

I KISSED Isis goodbye and hugged my sister.

"Maybe you can come stay for a few days next week?" Amy asked, balancing Isis on her hip.

"Yeah, sure." I nodded, offering a final wave before climbing into my car.

The drive to Ishpeming passed slowly. I tried the radio, but every song reminded me of Sammy. For an hour I cried, and then numbness took over and I allowed my body to slip into autopilot.

Bluff Street contained only a handful of houses. I slowed when I came to a crumbling stone wall crawling with dead vines. I turned onto the cracked pavement of a circular drive and surveyed a decrepit two-story Victorian house shuttered against the wind. Wood planks hung loose, and several shingles had slipped off the roof and lay on the weed-choked lawn.

I walked to the front door, and my breath hitched in my chest. I lifted a trembling hand. Before I knocked, the door flung open and a thin, sunken woman with white hair pulled back from her face stood surveying me.

"Are you coming in or not?" the woman asked sharply.

I followed her in, hesitating for only a moment. The door slammed behind me. I turned expecting someone standing there, but I was alone in the foyer.

The old woman shuffled along dark wood floors into a vast sitting room with furniture jumbled on threadbare rugs.

"Sit down," the woman insisted, motioning toward a stiff black chair with cracks in its leather cushion.

She sat opposite me, and I noticed her eyes had an opaque sheen. I wondered if she was blind. Though she stared at me for a long time, as if she saw me clearly.

"Tell me what you want," the woman said, her cheeks sunken so that the bones of her face cast huge shadows in the dim light.

"I want my husband back," I whispered.

"Do you?" the woman asked, her wrinkled hands hovering in the air as if she were reaching out, asking the question not of me, but the empty space between us.

She reached down. Her gnarled hands clutched a cup of bitter-smelling tea with surprising steadiness. She held me in the most intense steely gaze and I wanted to break the stare, but feared she would consider me weak and choose not to help me. "Because when you open that door, you don't get to choose what comes through," the old woman hissed.

"I'll do whatever it takes. I need guidance, that's all, a place to start."

I set the envelope of cash on the table between us. Her thin, chapped lips curved at the corners. I felt sure she knew I'd placed five hundred dollars in the envelope with no need to count it.

She stood and shuffled out of the room, and returned with a tattered, stained book as large as the old dictionaries at the public library. I was amazed that she was able to carry it. She set it on the table with a thud and nimbly flipped it open to the exact page she wanted. She pulled out a notebook of yellowing paper and scratched words on the page in tiny cursive handwriting.

As she wrote, I stayed perfectly still. I feared at any moment she would realize what a terrible mistake she was making.

Somewhere in the ancient, heavy house, a clock chimed. It reverberated along the walls and floorboards, and it reminded me of the tolling bells of an old church from my childhood. A church that always smelled of dust and the talcum powder of old skin. The church my mother insisted we attend every Sunday, when I was eight years old, during one of her rare periods of sobriety. She'd had a nightmare about the devil and suddenly believed in an angry God who punished those who did not worship.

I shivered and counted ten chimes.

Night had fallen, and I was not sure when, because I swore I'd been in the old woman's house for only a few minutes. But when I returned my gaze to the yellowing paper, her hand no longer moved across the page. Her chair sat empty. She had folded the paper in half and left it behind. The smoldering candles on the fireplace mantel had burned down and sat gooey in their waxy red bases.

I shook my head and looked around, expecting to see her, but only emptiness greeted me. I stood, and my back and legs ached as though had I been in the chair for a long time.

When I opened the front door, a violent wind pulled the door from my hand. The wind caught the folded paper and sent it, in a whoosh, back into the house. I fought the door closed and returned to the shadowy hallway. I got on my hands and knees and looked beneath a heavy buffet. Dirt and balls of cat hair greeted me, but no slip of paper.

A loud bang sent me reeling back into the room, and I whipped around. It was only the front door, slamming in the wind, but a chill streaked down my spine.

Only desperation to have that piece of paper kept me in the old woman's house. I returned to the floor and slid my hand under an ancient-looking sofa, and then continued to a cabinet filled with moth-eaten books and half-melted candles. I eyed a few of the titles, dealing with the esoteric, and noticed the spine of a withered red book.

"Calling Back the Dead," the title promised, and I eased open the cabinet door that groaned in protest but gave way beneath my insistent fingers. I pulled the book from several others and blew a layer of dust off the surface. The cover held the image of a shadowy figure with its mouth stretched wide, and as I looked into the gaping mouth, a thousand other dimensions seemed to pour forth.

In an instant, I saw the beginning of all life in an explosion of light, and then the desperate crawling from the primordial muck to become dwellers of the land. I saw men, skin and bones, and women with flesh sagging, tearing at each other with sharp, taloned fingers. I gazed at radiant beings of light fleeing from the dense, darkened earth. The cold wind of their absence numbed me, and maybe I cried out, but could not say because already the image of a mother nursing a dead child had overtaken my sight. And then she too vanished, replaced by a field, the soil freshly tilled, heaped with rotting bodies. The bodies writhed and climbed up out of their shallow graves to trek across the field toward me.

The old woman snatched the book from my hand, and with unnatural speed returned it to the cabinet and locked the glass door. Her eyes gleamed, and I recognized both anger and glee there, as if she wanted me to find that book, but also felt protective of its secrets. She thrust the paper I had been searching for into my hand and shoved me out the door.

I stood on her porch, and a gust of wind brought me back to reality or sanity or somewhere between. My knees wobbled, and I imagined sinking down and sitting on the porch, wrapping my arms tight around my legs, and willing away the horrors that had just beseeched me.

I needed to get away from her house. It rose behind me like one of the undead things crawling from the earth. I stumbled and nearly fell getting to my car, but once inside I could breathe again.

I tucked the paper in my purse. As I pulled from her driveway, I glanced in the rear-view mirror and slammed the brakes.

Sammy stood behind me. He reached toward the car, and in the taillights his eyes were two red orbs. I gasped and clutched the handle, cursing my locked car door. I hit the unlock button, thrust the door open, and stumbled into the night.

The empty driveway yawned before me. Dried leaves swirled in the crackling air.

"He's dead," I whispered, a reminder that never quite took hold. "Sammy is dead."

3 5

ow
Sarah

SARAH WATCHED the man's face twitch when Will held open his palm and revealed the key resting in its center.

The man reached out, but Will jerked his hand back.

"I'll hang onto it," Will said.

The man smirked but said nothing, and a sense of unease fell over Sarah.

Dr. K insisted they return to the forest at night, lest the curious eyes of the construction crew at Building Fifty spot them. Sarah stuffed her hands into the pockets of her brown suede jacket, pressing her chin to her chest to protect her neck against the icy wind that slithered cold beneath her collar.

As they walked through the asylum forest, the old doctor grew livelier, his pace quickening.

As they neared the hill, a three-quarters moon lighting their way, Sarah heard a voice.

"Wait," she demanded.

Dr. K and Will stopped, turning to face her.

"Did you guys hear that?"

Will looked around uncertainly, but the doctor's thin mouth turned up in a malicious smile.

"You'll hear many things in these woods at night. Best not to linger."

He turned back to the trail and hurried along.

"Please..." the voice came again, a whisper so much like the wind she couldn't separate the two. This time Will cocked his head, glancing back at her with an uneasy look in his eyes.

They walked down the small hill into the hollow of trees.

"The key, please," the man told Will, his eyes almost feverish with desire.

Will handed him the key.

Sarah and Will had searched the space for hours, coming up empty, but the doctor strode purposefully to a wall of brush, stuck his hand inside and pushed open a door.

"How?" Will asked, shaking his head. He reached his hands into the brush around the opening, patting and searching.

Sarah stared at the bushes for a long moment, committing the tangle of vines to memory, noting the angle of a young maple tree. She bent down and raked her hands through the dirt, marking the entrance to the door.

∾

CORRIE

"ARE ANY OF THE BIRDS SICK?" I asked, gazing into the glass cage where parakeets hopped from little wooden branches. They cheeped and chittered.

"I'm sorry?" the young man asked who'd walked over to help me.

"I'd like to adopt one nobody else would want. If there's a sick or injured bird..." I trailed off.

He scratched the blond stubble on his chin and shook his head.

"We don't sell 'em if they're sick."

I swallowed thickly and pointed. "I'll take that one."

"The blue with the black spots by his nose?"

I nodded and turned away.

"Do you need a cage? Food? I can get him ready while you pick out your other-"

"No," I interrupted him. "I have those things at home."

I drove to Kerry Manor, listening to the bird. He chirped for the first few minutes, and then the sounds grew quieter with long stretches of silence between. I wondered if he sensed what lay ahead.

∾

Sarah

THE ENCHIRIDION LAY heavy and neglected on a wooden pew in a dark corner of the cold chamber.

As Will crept toward the book, his eyes wide, Sarah blinked around the room, using her torch to illuminate the wooden benches, the stone floor, and rows of carefully laid bricks curving to the ceiling.

A moist, rank smell hovered in the chamber.

The old doctor walked to a bed suspended on a platform. He placed his hands on the grimy yellow sheet and closed his eyes.

Sarah preferred not to imagine the memories he savored.

"Let's get out of here," Will said, taking up the heavy book and holding it against his chest.

"Not just yet," the doctor said, and his eyes looked darker, without color, as he pulled a small pistol from beneath his layers of coats.

"No way, man. Is this a joke?" Will asked, taking a step back.

"The chamber is a special place," the doctor told them, tilting his face up as if relishing the odor of something ancient and decayed the space emanated. "It gives, and it takes. The power of this place," again he fingered the filthy hospital bed, "brought the key to me. Now payment is due."

~

CORRIE

I CARRIED the box containing the bird and set it on the kitchen counter. After grabbing the other items on the old woman's list from my car, I pulled a cast-iron pot from a cupboard and set it near the butcher block. Carefully cutting open their pouches, I dumped dried yew, thyme, and yarrow in the pot. The house creaked and groaned, growing louder as I worked. The bird cheeped, the wind whipped against the windows.

Near the lake, I scraped bark from the oak tree with a hammer's claw. I filled a plastic bag with dirt and grass from the space where Sammy's body had lain.

I added those to the pot. Next came bits of his hair from a brush, the bristles from his toothbrush, and a letter he'd written me. I grimaced and drew in a hard breath as I dropped the sheet of paper with his words, his writing, into the pot.

When I took out the bird, he squeaked and hopped away. I did not want to look at his tiny black eyes as I lay him on the block and lifted the knife.

~

Sarah

"Us?" Sarah asked. She glanced at Will, whose knuckles had gone white as he clutched the book. He wasn't looking at Dr. K. but studying the room, as if planning his attack.

"That book doesn't leave here, and neither do you," the doctor whispered.

"Why?" Sarah asked, knowing their only hope was time and mentally chastising herself for her stupidity. Who followed a deranged man into a hidden forest chamber without a weapon?

"I, better than anyone, know the score of this place. Do you think it gives freely? Don't you hear their cries?" He cocked his head, and a little smile played on his lips.

"You are completely insane," Sarah muttered.

Will had begun to edge toward the only other torch in the room that was lit when they first entered.

"I'm not a vagrant. I'm a scholar, a doctor. I've waited twenty years to come back to this place. The source of my awakening, of a power that is indescribable."

His voice had shifted. The rambling of the homeless man had given way to someone much cleverer and more controlled.

"This is an act?" she gestured at his clothes. "You're not really homeless?"

The man's eyes glittered, and Sarah suspected that no, he was not homeless.

"I have many friends in low places. Unlike my colleagues, I learned years ago your greatest assets are the people beneath you, the people who can slither and slip into the dark places where secrets live."

"Why did you need us? If you wanted the key, you could have gotten it yourself."

The doctor laughed and put his finger on his chin, as if watching them squirm delighted him.

"Time is irrelevant, but magic, synchronicity, that is where the power flows. I have known for years the key would come to me. I had to be patient and allow the forces that work tirelessly from the shadows to bring the moment into being, the perfect placement of myself, you, and this key. The chamber had chosen its sacrifice. I am merely a messenger."

"But you orchestrated the whole thing. No supreme power brought us here. You told us where to get the key, you brought us here," Sarah insisted.

The man's eyes flickered, but his smile did not shift.

"Every outcome has a series of players, of action and conse-quence. Consider this gun. When I cocked it, I prepared the gun for firing. When I pull the trigger, a tiny pin will hit the bullet encased in its primer shell. An explosion will occur and the bullet will find its target. If a single component was absent, the firing pin for instance, the outcome shifts. Death occurs when every piece plays its part. The moment Maurice contacted me, I knew the chamber had created the way. And now here we are, fates colliding. For me it is the beginning of the next journey, and for both of you, it is the end. Don't you see? A thousand choices had to occur to bring us to this instant. And here we are."

Sarah's mind reeled. If this man murdered them, they'd never be discovered.

~

CORRIE

I DROVE to the graveyard in a state of numbness. Periodically, the chirp of the bird seemed to fill my car, but then I remembered what was left of the bird lay in the pot, and it most definitely was not singing.

At the cemetery, I heaved the pot from the back seat, ignoring the dark mixture that lay within it. I dug my hands into the dirt on Sammy's grave and poured the mixture into the tilled soil. I spoke the words from the sheet, ancient-sounding foreign words I could not pronounce. As I stroked and kneaded the muddy mixture, I shut down my mind. Sense wanted to steal me from this place, demand I return home, hide the evidence and never think of it again.

I read the old woman's directions.

"The essence must ripen for thirteen hours. Do not retrieve it a second before."

~

Sarah

WILL STEPPED CLOSER to the torch.

The doctor frowned and pointed the gun at him.

"You can only shoot one of us," Will told him, the fire reflected in his green eyes. "I think this book will burn in seconds. By the time you pull the trigger, if you drop me with one bullet, a lifetime of research will be half-burned. Then you'll have a choice - to fight Sarah, who'll surely be attacking you to get the gun, or put out the book and salvage a few pages."

Will pushed the Enchiridion closer, and the fire reached toward the yellowed pages.

"Stop," the doctor barked. He shifted the gun toward Sarah, as if he'd decided shooting her would somehow serve him better.

"The outcome will be the same," Will told him, staring hard into his eyes. "You're outnumbered, man. Even with the gun, you're losing something here tonight."

And it was clear he would lose the Enchiridion, perhaps the item he wanted most of all. But Sarah sensed the doctor had gone too far. His intention to kill them both outweighed any ability to rationalize the moment. Will also seemed to recognize the direness of their situation.

Will threw the book as hard as he could at the doctor, and then lunged toward him.

The doctor fired, and Sarah felt a sting as the bullet whizzed by her shoulder.

The man jerked the gun toward Will, but Will was upon him. He shoved the doctor to the ground and slammed him into the stone floor. The doctor butted his head hard, connecting with Will's jaw. Will grunted but didn't release the man's arm. Sarah grabbed the gun and wrenched it away. The man grabbed Will around the throat, and Sarah cocked the gun.

"Let him go, now."

But the doctor gritted his teeth, stared hard into Will's eyes, and tightened his grip.

Will opened and closed his mouth, holding onto the doctor's wrists and trying to pry the man's hands away.

"Shoot him," Will croaked.

But she couldn't. She turned the gun in her hand and cracked the man on the top of his skull. The impact shook her arms, but he continued to squeeze, and then his grip loosened and went slack. His eyes remained open, but shuttered and closed before opening again and blinking into the room.

Will rolled off him, snatched the book up with one hand, massaging his throat with the other.

"Come on," Sarah said, grabbing Will's hand and dragging him to his feet.

"Wait." He dropped next to the man and scrambled to the dirty little fanny pack at the man's waist. He rifled through and grabbed the long, dark key. They stood and fled back down the dark tunnel and into the night.

ow
Sarah

"I SHOULDN'T HAVE DONE THAT," Will said, his face pale as he watched Brook bandage Sarah from across the room.

Archie lay curled in Sarah's lap, licking her hands as if he sensed something tragic had nearly befallen his owner.

"You saved us," Sarah reminded him. "That doctor would be digging our graves right now otherwise." She winced as Brook patted the wound with a peroxide-soaked cotton ball. The bullet had grazed her upper arm, tore away a bit of skin, but otherwise done little damage.

"He could have shot you in the head," Will muttered.

"He didn't."

Brook put a bandage over Sarah's shoulder and wrapped it with medical tape.

"I think you'll live," she told her, kissing her bare shoulder.

"Thanks, Brook."

Brook nodded and sat down in the chair beside Sarah. "So, where's the book?"

BY THE TIME Sarah's head hit the pillow, her eyes ached, and her mind swam with a blur of words and images so disturbing she left the light on. The three had stayed awake until nearly two in the morning, reading the stories of experiments committed on patients by asylum doctors for a century. Even after the asylum shuttered its doors in 1989, the Umbra Brotherhood continued to meet in the chamber several times a year, bringing people from all over the country to strap down to the lonely chamber bed and perform all variety of horrors.

"They were like paranormal investigators," Brook had said at one point, which elicited a snort from Will.

"More like paranormal torturers."

But it was true. The doctors devoted their studies to patients exhibiting certain abilities, ranging from communication with spirits to the ability to levitate objects. They often used drugs to enhance the subject's abilities during a presentation in the chamber. Sometimes the patients died. Several patients had additional appendices that spoke of experiences after their treatment at the asylum.

Ethel's story sat near the start of the huge text. A tiny footnote detailing how she'd burned her family alive was barely perceptible in the cramped writing.

What was clear from the story was that Ethel had gone into the chamber as a little girl, and come out possessed by evil.

CORRIE

I TOOK the chalk and drew a huge pentagram on the dark wood floor. The smell of the chalk reminded me of Isis. In our old home, Isis had a little chalkboard she and Sammy played with for hours. He would draw elaborate monsters, and Isis would promptly scribble over them with her chubby, untrained hands, frustrated when the image in her mind didn't appear on the dark surface.

In the circle's center I lay Sammy's clothes: a pair of jeans worn out at the knees; his Overlook Hotel t-shirt, based on the creepy Stephen King book *The Shining*; and of course, his fuzzy Bigfoot slippers at the bottom. If I closed my eyes, I could imagine his body filling out the clothes, his shaggy hair sliding through the neckline, his grin emerging from the fabric.

Holding a box of tall white candles, I walked around the pentagram, arranging one at each point, lighting the first and then using the candle before to light each thereafter. I suffered a strange sense of hope and hilarity. This was the kind of thing Sammy and I might have staged for a Halloween party, laughing all the while. As I arranged the items, I imagined Fletcher's face in the car. His eyes had looked haunted and also defeated. Here was the man who supposedly had done it, and yet...

It didn't matter. Fletcher's experience would not be mine. Sammy was right there, on the fringes of every moment. If anyone could come back, it was Sammy.

I took the pot I'd filled with the mixture from Sammy's grave and I dropped it in handfuls within the circle.

Sitting on my knees in the center of the circle, I held a handful of the mixture against my chest and read the final incantation three times. Closing my eyes, I shoved the dirt and blood and herbs into my mouth, choking them down, gagging but refusing to spit out even a drop.

Lifting a candle, I waited, watching the flame.

After several minutes, a shape flickered near the window.

"Sammy?" I whispered his name and then said it again, louder. "Sammy?" I had heard him, and then I saw him, there in the corner for only an instant.

I ran to the drapes and ripped them open with such force, they crashed to the wood floor. I dropped to my knees and raked my hands through the fabric.

"Sammy?" I heard the hysteria in my voice, but within seconds had lost all control. I stood and searched the room, raced to the furniture and peeked behind and underneath it. As if what? I believed Sammy were playing one of his little games of hide-n-seek with Isis, and he would be curled into a ball beneath a blanket, standing stock-still behind a coat rack?

I still held the candle in my hands, the one whose flame had flickered as if in signal, or maybe in warning. I squeezed so hard the wax collapsed. Hot wax poured over my hands and dripped on the floor. I threw the candle, the wick already devoured by wax, and raced to the stairway, taking the stairs two at a time.

"Sammy!" I shrieked, running from room to room, slamming open doors, tearing clothes from the wardrobes and comforters from the beds. I flung pillows at the walls. When I reached our room, the room we had shared, I stared at the bed and tried to will his shape to emerge.

"He has to be here," I mumbled, pulling off blankets and sheets and finally the mattress itself. I shoved it onto the floor and stared at the box springs. My hands shook, and I put them to my mouth, feeling the raw spots where the wax had burned. I wanted to chew them or slam them against the windows and break the glass. I wanted to die. Was there any better explanation than that? I wanted to be done with the charade. How could I live the next year, the next ten years, without Sammy?

I gazed around the room searching for a weapon, something sharp to slash myself with, but instead my eyes flitted over my nightstand and the little pink cup streaked with rainbow clouds that Isis had brought to bed on some earlier night.

I released a horrible gasp, a sound that seemed to come not from me, but from an ancient place - a damp, dark place that understood how love could not only bring life, but also take it away. I sank to my knees and crawled toward the bare mattress. With the last of my energy, I pushed myself onto the bed, pressed my face down in the white softness and cried.

Sarah

. . .

SARAH PUSHED OPEN her mom's door with her hip, holding a paper sack of groceries and wondering if she should have brought olive oil. Her mother usually had it, but bread and oil didn't exactly work without the olive oil, and she hadn't checked ahead of time. Her stomach turned at the thought, and she directed an irritated glare at the sensation. Nerves rarely plagued her, especially when introducing her mother to a new girlfriend, but today they seemed to gnaw a hole in her stomach.

The meeting was barely the half of it. She replayed the scene in that dark, terrifying chamber again and again, her shoulder pulsing each time. Will was at her house, poring over the Enchiridion like a man obsessed, and she had reluctantly agreed to a night of normalcy so that her mother could meet Brook.

"Mom?" Sarah called. "Please tell me you have olive oil."

"Sassy," Isis squealed, running into the foyer. She wore a pair of pink bib overalls over a gray t-shirt smeared in something blue and sticky.

"Hey there, Icicle," Sarah grinned, setting her bag on the floor and scooping up her niece. She walked into the kitchen, where her mother stood at the counter vigorously chopping vegetables. "You're watching Isis?" Sarah asked.

"Yes, yes, and sorry I haven't gotten a thing done. Isis needs a lot of attention right now," her mother explained. Her hair was sloppily pinned up, and she wore jogging pants with a sweater.

Sarah had expected her to be overdressed, candles wafting from every surface with a spotless kitchen. The opposite appeared to be true. Isis scrambled from her arms and ran to the table spread with crayons and coloring books.

"Nana and me made cookies," Isis announced, picking one up from a plate and taking a bite.

"Why's she here, Mom?" Sarah asked, growing uneasy.

She loved Isis to bits but had spoken with Corrie that morning, who insisted they were spending the night at Amy's house in Cadillac. She had called Sarah to let her know she didn't need to check on them. If Isis was with her mom, Corrie was alone at Kerry Manor.

"Corrie's sister dropped her off a few hours ago. Isis stayed with Amy last night because Corrie had errands to run. Corrie called this morning and asked if I'd keep her tonight, said she had a migraine coming on. Poor lamb." Her mother shook her head, and Sarah saw her eyes glistening.

"Corrie doesn't get migraines," Sarah murmured.

Helen looked up.

"What's wrong, honey? You're as white as a ghost."

"I have to go, Mom." She gave her mother a quick peck on the cheek. "The groceries are in the hallway."

"Wait, what do you mean go? Isn't your friend coming? Did you break up?" her mother frowned, and Sarah smiled, shaking her head.

"No, we're fine. Great, actually. But Corrie's not. I'm going to check on her."

"Maybe she needs a little time, Sarah."

"That's exactly what she doesn't need, Mom." Sarah didn't wait to hear more. She jogged out to her car, sending Brook a text as she drove.

CORRIE

"CORRIE." I heard my name not as a whisper, a sound snaking away - but solid, firm, as real as the walls surrounding me. I sat up and stared into the dark room.

"Sam?" My voice trembled. I placed a hand over my thudding heart. I had not expected to feel fear when he arrived, and yet blood roared through my ears and I found I could not swallow. I thought if I screamed, only a whimper would emerge.

"It's time, love." He spoke again, and this time I saw him, or the shape of him there by the door wearing the clothes I'd laid out.

He slipped from the bedroom door and I followed, my bare feet sticking to the floor. My body was coated in sweat. I had slept hard, and I found the dark hallway and the shape of my husband surreal and hard to focus on.

"Sammy, wait," I said, hurrying to catch him. I reached out, but he moved away down the stairs, drifting into the hallway.

I lost sight of him for a moment and my pulse quickened. What if he disappeared around the corner and I never found him? What if he was not there at all?

"Sammy, please," I called, desperate now and running. I spotted him at the door to the study. He walked inside. I saw him for an instant, illuminated by the glow of a fire in the hearth I had not built. His unkempt auburn hair glowed near red in the light. He smiled his irresistible grin, and I rushed down the hallway, skidding to a stop when another form stepped from shadows within the study. A small girl stood silhouetted in the doorway. Her eyes were black holes in her face, and her blonde hair looked sooty and stained. She smiled, a strange, unhappy smile, and slammed the door.

ow
Corrie

I RAN to the study door and turned the knob. It turned, but the door didn't move. Somehow it was sealed shut. I pounded my fists on the door.

"Sammy, Sammy," I screamed, knowing the girl inside intended to hurt him. I had only just gotten him back and feared she would send him away again.

As I pounded, the surrounding air seemed to grow hot, stifling, Sweat poured down my face. Something sharp and hot bit the back of my leg and I wheeled around. I was no longer in the hallway. I stood in the study, pounding on the door as if I wanted out. Blinking, I tried to make sense of the vision before me.

The room was on fire. Fire climbed the opposite wall, catching the drapes, melting wallpaper in bubbling waterfalls. As the curtains burned, I saw the blaze reflected in the tall windows.

"Sammy?" I tried to call but choked as smoke reached into my mouth and singed my lungs. I coughed and pulled my shirt up, stuffing it over my face.

Every tip I'd ever learned for dealing with fire popped into my mind: stop drop and roll, throw flour on it, put a wet blanket over your head. Instead I stared, transfixed. I was trapped, and Sammy was trapped too, but where had he gone?

"Sammy?" My voice dropped to a whisper. He had vanished, and the girl too.

I ran to the window and tried to unlatch the locks, antique but new. They worked. I had opened them myself during our first week at Kerry Manor, but now they stuck as if someone had glued them shut. I grabbed a chair and slammed it against the window. The glass did not break. I stared at my reflection, my face red and slick, my glassy eyes filled with terror. Smoke filled the room. Soon my reflection in the glass would be obscured by smoke and the flames would move to my pants and shirt, my hair.

I returned to the door and shook the handle, yanking with all my strength. I grabbed another chair and slammed it into the door, but the effort was feeble. My eyes watered, and breath came in ragged gasps despite the shirt covering my face. I cried and wiped at my face and turned to face the burning room. I could not escape. I would burn alive in this house.

∾

Sarah

"I HATE THIS FUCKING HOUSE," Sarah grumbled as she pulled into the drive, no longer with dense with foliage but surrounded instead by brown, crinkling bushes and trees. Wet leaves blanketed the driveway and rain fell in a steady stream, blurring the house. The windows were dark, but Corrie's car stood in the driveway.

The yard was atmospheric, the house sitting in a gray bubble of rain and wind that did not seem to move past the lines of trees that shielded it from the road.

The wind wrenched Sarah's car door from her hand and she struggled to force it closed. A twig grazed her cheek, and she fought leaves away as they blew up and swirled around her as she ran to the front door.

The door was locked. Sarah knocked and shouted for Corrie, but the driving wind muffled her call

"Corrie," she yelled a second time, slamming her fists into the door. The windows were dark except for a flickering glow. She peeked in the porch windows, but heavy drapes blocked the interior.

The smell of smoke permeated the damp air, and as the rain slowed to a drizzle, Sarah realized it was more than a fire in the hearth. Panic rising, she raced around the house toward billowing black smoke. Fire engulfed the back of the house. Plumes of black smoke billowed out, combining with the damp fog sweeping across Lake Michigan. It was an unnatural image, biblical, and for an instant Sarah could do no more than stare in petrified awe at the odd spectacle of orange flame, black smoke, and white mist colliding at the edge of the dark lake.

As the realization that Corrie was inside washed over her, Sarah willed her legs to move. She ran toward the back porch obscured by dark smoke. She glimpsed her sister-in-law peering from one of the study windows, terror etched in her face, but then she vanished.

Sarah raced back to her car and fumbled her phone from her bag.

She dialed 911, but no sound came across the line. She pulled the phone away, saw the 'no signal' in the corner of her phone.

"Fuck, no, not now. This can't be happening right now."

Running across the lawn, straining to hear Corrie within the house, she stared at her phone until she found a spot with a single blinking bar. She dialed again. At first nothing, and then finally a voice on the line.

The operator's voice cut in and out. Sarah yelled the address for Kerry Manor and screamed that a fire was consuming the house. She didn't hear the woman respond, and after a frustrating minute of silence, she threw the phone on the ground and raced back to the house.

She ran around the side of Kerry Manor, searching for another way in. As her eyes raked over the house, her breath stopped. Sammy stared down at her from a second-story veranda. The door before him swung out, caught in the wind, and slammed against the side of the house.

"Sammy?" she asked, dazed. He had been there, and yet now the doorway stood empty, a black yawning hole into the house. She climbed onto the porch rail, shimmied up the eavestrough and swung her leg up, clinging to the damp roof and knowing she might need the ambulance too, if this failed.

When she reached the little porch, she gasped for breath, clinging to the black iron rail, pausing for only a second before rushing through the doorway. The darkness consumed her, but as she fled down the hallway, she searched for her brother. He couldn't be there. He was dead. She had touched his waxen skin as he lay in the coffin, his body emptied of its humanness, replaced with chemicals to preserve him a bit longer - no longer a man, but a science project.

She slipped on the stairs and smacked her elbow on a step, wincing as pain shot up her arm and lodged in her temple. Sliding down two more stairs on her butt and cradling her arm, Sarah forced herself back up and ran toward the study. A sliver of bright orange ran beneath the door and rivulets of smoke poured out. She threw her coat over the doorknob and turned it, but the door stayed firmly closed. She yanked it a second time and then pounded.

"Corrie!" she screamed, but only silence returned her call.

She twisted the knob again, and then she spotted the nails poking along the doorframe. Someone had nailed the door closed. No, not someone - the evil that had invaded Ethel in that dark chamber a century before.

Sarah grabbed a nail, but she couldn't pull it loose. Sprinting back to the kitchen, she ripped out drawers, sending one of them sprawling across the kitchen floor, forks and spoons scattering. She found a junk drawer with a hammer and whipped it out, running back to the study.

"Hold on, Corrie. Hold on."

Prying the nails, recoiling from the heat pulsing beyond the door, Sarah tried not to imagine what lay on the other side. Would she find Corrie crumpled, burned black, only the bones of her beautiful sister-in-law left?

The last nail pulled free, and now when she turned the knob, the door swung open. Flames devoured the room; the opposite wall was a mass of burning and writhing. Sammy's monster figures had melted into pools of colored plastic on the mantel. Sarah tried to push the door in further, but something blocked it. She leaned down, struggling to see through the smoke, reaching with her hands. Her fingers found warm flesh and soft curly hair.

"Corrie," she moaned, grabbing Corrie's legs and awkwardly shoving her deeper into the room. She pushed in, grabbed Corrie beneath the arms and pulled her out. She dragged her down the hallway, pausing near the kitchen when the haunted sound of a girl's voice found her.

"One for sorrow, two for mirth, three for a funeral, four for a birth..."

Her strength faltered, and Corrie slipped down.

"No," she mumbled, and then she shouted. "No, you fucking devil. No!"

She lifted Corrie into her arms and ran. The front door was locked, but even when Sarah undid the latch, the door refused to move.

"You bastard, you goddamn fucking bastard," she screamed, kicking the door and losing her hold on Corrie a second time.

Sarah laid her down and checked her pulse, finding an almost imperceptible throb.

Upstairs she heard footsteps running along the hall, a child's footsteps.

"This isn't real, this can't be real," she whispered.

Candles flickered from every surface in the great room, and a fire spit orange embers.

She dragged Corrie into the great room and stopped, staring at the pentagram chalked on the floor, Sammy's clothes lying in the center as if he'd simply lain down to take a nap. Dark blobs of what looked like mud lay in clumps around the floor. Sarah had a momentary image of Sammy clawing his way through coffin and earth. Tracking across the wet cemetery, bound for Kerry Manor.

Footsteps pounded down the stairs and Sarah clenched her jaw, waiting for the monster to appear.

Instead, Corrie came to. Her eyes flashed open and locked on Sarah's.

"Oh, thank God," but the words died on her lips as she saw the black rage in Corrie's pupils.

Corrie reached up and locked her hands around Sarah's throat.

Sarah grabbed Corrie's hands, usually delicate, but now strong and stiff as they squeezed the tender flesh of Sarah's neck.

In the distance, sirens broke through, but closer she heard voices shouting. Suddenly there was pounding on the door, and a moment later it burst open.

Will and Brook stumbled in.

Sarah tried to call out but managed only a groan.

"Sarah," Brook yelled.

Will was there, prying Corrie's hands away.

Corrie's lips pulled back from her teeth, she snarled, and then as quickly as she'd awoken, she went limp, flopping to the ground, her head snapping back and smacking the wood floor.

Will and Brook stared at her with wide, shocked eyes.

"We have to get out," Sarah croaked, relief draining the last of her energy. She looked at Corrie, hesitating before lifting her body and struggling towards the door.

Will stopped her, pushing his arms beneath Corrie.

"I've got her. It's okay," he told Sarah.

Her arms dropped slack at her sides, and Brook put an arm around her waist, helping her outside.

"What's in there?" Brook asked, eyes huge as she glanced back at the house.

"It's on fire," Sarah shouted. "The whole place is about to…" But she stopped suddenly. The smell of burning had vanished, the billowing black smoke no longer marred the sky. "The study…"

Sarah walked around the house, dismayed, unable to believe her own eyes. No fire, no smoke. The house stood untouched in the rainy day, the study windows reflected the gray sky and nothing else.

ow
Sarah

"THE DRAPES CAUGHT FIRE," Sarah explained, holding up a pile of singed drapes. "I panicked."

The fire engine stood in the circular driveway, several men hanging off and watching as Sarah attempted to explain.

"You said the house was on fire." The fire chief looked disgusted.

"It looked really bad," Brook cut in. "The phone service isn't good. We tried to call back and say we'd put it out, but it was too late," she lied.

"What happened to your neck?" the chief asked, eyes narrowed on the red flesh encircling Sarah's throat.

"I ran into a clothesline." It was a terrible lie and the chief's face told her as much but the words tumbled out.

Brook shot her a sidelong glance, but nodded at the chief.

The fireman looked at the house, and then glared back at the two women.

Sarah glanced at her car where they had laid Corrie in the back seat. Will had slipped into the woods to wait until the men cleared out.

Beyond them Kerry Manor stood dark and foreboding against the gray sky.

CORRIE

I SAT at Sarah's table, sipping an espresso and listening to Sarah explain what she saw at Kerry Manor. Brook and Will stared, breath bated, until she finished, and then all three turned to me.

I looked at the red welt surrounding her neck and tried not to cry.

"Did you see a fire, Corrie?" Sarah asked.

I nodded, replaying in my mind the moments leading up to the fire. I couldn't possibly tell them the truth.

Will studied my face and I glanced down, unable to look him in the eyes.

"Before you tell us," he said. "I have something to show you." He went into Sarah's living room and returned with a folder stuffed with papers. "Read it."

Sarah nodded.

"Go up to my study, Corrie. Take your time."

I took the folder and lumbered up the stairs, exhausted, sad, embarrassed, but most of all confused. I thought back to Sammy's final days, the overheard conversations between him and Sarah. Something was terribly wrong with me.

"DON'T WORRY," Sarah told me as I crept into the kitchen, the folder clutched to my chest. "Everyone's gone to bed."

My eyes hurt from crying. I'd read for nearly three hours beginning with the stories of Kerry Manor, then Sarah's documentation of my behavior according to her own observations, and those relayed through Sammy. Will typed the final page verbatim from the story in the Enchiridion. It revealed a terrible experiment in a chamber behind the Northern Michigan Asylum; a night when a little girl was sacrificed to a horrific evil that would haunt the Leelanau Peninsula for a century.

"It's all true?" I asked, taking the tissue Sarah handed me and wiping my eyes. "Sammy wanted to leave. He was planning to move us out of Kerry Manor. I didn't want to. I'm responsible."

"Not you," Sarah said, taking the folder from my hand. "The spirit that took possession of Ethel in 1901. It wasn't Ethel who burned her family. The Brotherhood chose her because she was easy prey for the spirit. Those doctors deserve to burn for what they did."

I sat heavily in a chair, glancing at the refrigerator where photos and papers were tucked beneath magnets. I saw an image of Sammy and Sarah as children. Sammy pulled Sarah in a wagon across a muddy yard. Their faces and t-shirts were splattered with mud, their grins identical.

"Corrie." Sarah squatted in front of my chair, taking my hands. "We believe whatever possessed Ethel Kerry one-hundred years ago is moving into you. It's only a matter of time before something terrible happens."

I swallowed and looked away.

"Something more terrible, you mean?"

She nodded.

～

Sarah

SARAH LOOKED up when a man cleared his throat.

Glen Blackburn stood in front of her desk. He wore a red and green Christmas sweater and looked the part of the grandfather.

Sarah shifted her hands to her lap, sitting back in her chair.

"Mr. Blackburn, how can I help you?"

He smiled, studying her with bright blue eyes that looked far younger than his seventy-odd years.

"I believe you have something that belongs to me," he said, sitting in the chair opposite her desk.

"Do I?" she asked, imagining the key tucked in her purse.

He nodded and folded his hands in his lap, waiting.

"Let's say I did. Why shouldn't I take it to the police? And that sick book along with it."

Glen cast his eyes down. He reached into his pocket and Sarah tensed, ready to throw herself sideways if he pulled out a gun. Instead, he slipped a small metal box out and opened it, tilting the contents toward her.

"Butterscotch?" he asked, taking one out and popping it in his mouth.

"No, thank you."

"I understand your concerns, Miss Flynn."

"Call me Sarah."

"Sarah, then. That key offers access to a terrible place, and that book contains terrible secrets."

"That you were a part of."

The old man nodded, his eyes sad.

"I came to psychiatry late in my life. I was over forty when I finished my Ph.D. and was offered a position at the Traverse City State Hospital. I was naïve, desperate to prove myself. But I promise you, I entered the world of medicine with the best of intentions. When Dr. Knight approached me about the Brotherhood, it was tantalizing. A secret society of doctors who studied the paranormal. He gave me an initiation of sorts, a battery of questions. They checked my background, even interviewed my family, I found out later, though they used a cover. Said it was a census or some such nonsense. To feel chosen, what an odd gift."

Sarah thought of the stories in the Enchiridion and stared hard at the man before her. Whatever he looked like today, not so long ago he'd been a part of the torture and even murder of his own patients.

"I didn't know it then, but they carefully chose which meetings I attended. The cases were intriguing, and the displays mysterious, but not harmful. They gave the patients standard medicines. I watched a man who could tell you your ailments by merely staring at your body. I believe they're called medical intuitives today. I saw an old woman turn water to ice. They did not hurt the patients, they were not distressed. Some of them basked in the special attention."

Sarah snorted.

"These sound like excuses for your conscience."

"They may be that, but they are also true. It was carefully orchestrated, I understood later. The Brotherhood was dying, fewer members each year, a shift away from institutionalized care. They didn't want to risk the loss of a member, so I was not invited to the cruel and barbaric showings in the beginning.

"By the time I witnessed one, I was so entangled, I could not escape. The Brotherhood had very wealthy, influential members. In my first year, they sent me on an all-expense-paid trip to Barbados - myself and my entire family. They told me to interview a medicine man during my visit and report on my findings."

"How fascinating," Sarah said dryly.

"A month after I returned from the trip, I saw a patient die in the chamber. She couldn't perform, and her doctor was angry and embarrassed. He gave her some concoction until pink foam flowed from her lips." He closed his eyes and frowned. "I can still see her face. I left the chamber and vomited. The doctor who brought me in was cold and angry when I confronted him later. He said I had signed a blood oath, and I would pay with the lives of my family if I left the Brotherhood.

"I suffered in silence. It was wrong. I will take that guilt to my grave and atone for my sins with my God. After the asylum closed, the Brotherhood continued meetings for a period, but the key holder - Dr. Knight, my original mentor - grew ill. He had cancer. I visited him on his deathbed and demanded the key. I told him it was his final opportunity before leaving this life to end the evil he had taken part in for so long. I would protect the chamber and its secrets. In return, he would claim to have thrown the key in the ocean at the bequest of an angelic visit as he neared death."

"And he agreed?"

"He was feverish in his final days, and terrified. I told him I was being divinely guided in my requests. He obliged me."

"Why didn't you just throw the key into the ocean?"

Blackburn paused.

"A part of me feared the evil that lived in the chamber would find a way. That key would have been plucked from the sand by some wayward traveler. It would make its way into the hands of the Brotherhood once again. If I kept it, I could ensure that no one ever opened it."

"The Brotherhood didn't search for it?"

"Oh, they did. They unearthed Knight's coffin months after his death; they desecrated his grave. They attacked his eldest son one night while he was leaving his job in the city. The Brotherhood wanted the key, but they never found it."

"And yet a doctor in the Brotherhood pointed us to you."

Glen nodded.

"Which concerns me, yes. I am fortunate, perhaps, that it was Kemper who put it all together. You see, Kemper, or Dr. Frederic, believes that everything must arise on the waves of energy. He cannot seek it himself, because it must be delivered to him by forces greater than our own. If he were to steal it, he would fear the action was cursed and he would surely lose it, or perhaps fall ill. However, if he were sought out, by you for instance, and you delivered him the key-"

"Which we did," Sarah admitted grumpily.

"So, he has it then?"

Sarah shook her head.

"He had it, and honestly he might have kept it, but he decided to offer us as some kind of sick sacrifice. I smacked him on the head with his gun."

"And you now have the key?"

"Yes."

"You're not safe as long as you have it. I ask that you return it to me."

"Under one condition."

Blackburn cocked an eyebrow.

"I need you to get us in one last time." Sarah paused before her next words. But who could understand what they were facing more than this man? "My sister is possessed. I want to perform an exorcism within the chamber. That's where this evil spirit originated, and I think that's our only hope of releasing it."

Blackburn blinked at Sarah, his blue eyes watery.

"I swore I would never step foot inside again."

"Then don't go in. Take us to the door, open it. After the exorcism, I'll give you the key. Although I'm not sure you'll be safe from Kemper."

"I will. The police have arrested Dr. Frederic for first degree murder."

"What? Who did he murder?"

Glen looked at a little 3-D model of a house on Sarah's desk, his eyes troubled.

"He murdered a nurse at the asylum twenty years ago, when she threatened to expose him. During one of our meetings in the chamber, a patient saw the spirit of the dead nurse revealing how Frederic murdered her. She described where he hid the body and the murder weapon."

"And you waited twenty years to tell anyone?"

"I had a family, Sarah. We could never bring the things that occurred in that chamber into the light. I believed that for a long time. Now it's time to make amends. I know I'll pay for my silence, and for my sins."

Sarah shook her head, disgusted with the man but understanding if it ever came down to protecting those she loved or outing a murderer, she'd protect first.

"What about the rest of the Brotherhood? Won't they come after you?"

"In less than a month, I am moving with my family. We are leaving the country, and the chamber will be closed forever."

"Where are you going?"

He smiled and shook his head.

"That, I cannot disclose."

"Are you leaving out of fear?"

Blackburn shrugged.

"I've been having prophetic dreams. I feel it is time to relocate. My daughter is recently widowed. She would like to raise her son in another world."

Sarah thought of Corrie, also newly widowed and left with a child to raise alone. The exorcism would rid her of the evil spirit, but it wouldn't bring Sammy back. There would still be a long road ahead.

"Sarah, exorcisms are not to be handled lightly. The realms of spirit are as real as you and me, and if you release an energy, it seeks to go somewhere. I have seen it with my own eyes."

"I've found someone who can do it. I just have to convince him. I read the accounts in the Enchiridion. You guys wanted the spirits channeled into other patients. You did it on purpose."

He frowned and sighed.

"It was done. But I did not do it - and I promise you, if those doctors knew how vulnerable they were, they never would have attempted it."

"Vulnerable how?"

"No one controls the spirit when it's released. It finds the path of least resistance. That means a person who is compromised in some way - whether that be mental illness, grief, or a child. I'm sure you read about Ethel, the first such official experiment in the chamber."

"Yes." Sarah shook her head, fury ballooning in her chest.

"Take only those who are strong into the chamber, Sarah. Otherwise the evil will accompany you out."

ow
Corrie

"GOREY…" His voice whispered my name and like a thousand other waking moments, I returned to my body as if it were the most natural sound in the world.

It's unbelievable how sleep erases our worst fears, our worst realities. In sleep, Sammy was not dead. But every time I woke and faced the empty room, I confronted that truth as well.

Except…

"Gorey, wake up."

My eyes fluttered. I stared at the ceiling in Sarah's guest bedroom, but when my eyes shifted down, I found his face, his soft brown eyes searching mine, and I struggled to breathe.

He touched my cheek, his hands familiar as they cupped my jaw.

I tried to say his name but choked on a guttural sob that stuck in my throat. I cried, clutching him, my hands wrapped in the fabric of his t-shirt, pushing into the hardness and softness of his body.

"Shh, there, it's okay." He leaned into me, wrapping himself around me, slipping down into the bed and pulling me close so I could feel him - solid, real.

"You're..." But the words died on my lips, because whatever he was, it wasn't alive. I remembered his body on the cold pre-dawn ground, blood congealing, eyes absent of their light.

"I'm here. I'm here right now."

And he was.

I sat up, wiping at the wetness on my cheeks. I touched his face, kissed his lips and tasted the salt of my own tears in his mouth. I thrust my hands into his hair and then into his chest as I cried against him.

I had a million questions, but suddenly none of them mattered. One thing alone mattered - this second that spun into eternity. If only I could hold it, hold him. So, I did. I held him, wrapped my arms around his back and kissed his eyes and nose and mouth and neck. He kissed me back, and we rolled in the bed playfully as we'd done so many times.

He pinned me beneath him, holding my arms and sweeping his hair across my face, tickling my neck. I laughed and bucked, and when he fell to the side, I grabbed him and yanked him back.

"Make love to me," I whispered.

"There's nothing I want more in the world," he said leaning close. I smelled his breath and faltered. A dank smell poured out of him, earth and moss and decay, but I fought it away and kissed him again, pulling his shirt over his head, fumbling my pants away.

I pulled my shirt up. It stuck on my head and I laughed, fighting it off, noticing his weight had lifted, his warmth had slipped away, and in an instant the room grew bitter cold. I yanked off my shirt and thrust it to the side.

The bed before me lay empty, the sheets rumpled, my bare feet and legs stark against the white fabric.

"Sammy?"

A loneliness heavier than a thousand bags of sand poured over me. I sat and stared and wondered if he'd ever been there at all.

~

Sarah

"THIS PLACE IS TERRIBLE," Will whispered, swinging his flashlight through the stuffy, attic room at Kerry Manor.

"I know. Let's get in and get out. The last time I was in here, Corrie shut the door. I'm not trying to repeat that experience."

Will grimaced.

"After what happened in this house yesterday, I'd rather be anywhere else on earth."

Sarah touched her neck, still raw from Corrie's fingernails, and winced.

"What do you think we should take?" she asked. "Delila said they used one of Ethel's dresses to trap the spirit."

She picked up the ugly doll, created from the cat of a corpse, and held it between her thumb and forefinger.

"Not that." Will shuddered.

He grabbed a tarnished hairbrush. "How about this?"

"Yeah, that's less freaky," Sarah agreed.

Will lifted the old mattress and gave a start.

"What?" Sarah asked stepping beside him.

"It's the knife." He stared at an object resting on the plank of wood beneath the bed.

"What knife?" Sarah asked. She moved closer and looked at a long, antique knife.

"The murder weapon," Will muttered.

"How do you know?" Sarah asked. "I don't see blood on it."

"The bone handle with the jewel head," he said gesturing to the long white handle with a red jewel capping the end.

Sarah stared at it for a long time noticing the silence, how the longer it stretched the more tense it became.

Will dropped the mattress with a thud and stepped away.

"But how could you know what the handle looked like?"

She turned and sought his eyes but he looked away from her, his jaw tense and his hands suddenly fidgety. He shoved them into his pockets.

When he finally looked at her, she knew.

"You were there that night. You saw it happen. Didn't you?"

He started to shake his head but perhaps saw something in Sarah's eyes.

"Don't fucking lie to me Will, I swear to God-"

"Okay," he blurted. "I saw... I didn't know I saw it happen. I went into the house during the party. I was searching the rooms upstairs."

"For what?"

"For her, for Ethel. I wanted to find her."

"She's dead, Will. How can you find a ghost?"

He shrugged.

"I looked out the window and saw two people kissing."

"Sammy and Corrie."

"The guy was in a costume with a weird baby hanging from the stomach, which I know now was Sammy. The woman was younger, in a devil's costume."

"Wait, what? You saw Sammy kissing someone other than Corrie?"

"Yeah. I mean I didn't know what I was seeing. They stopped and Sammy looked like he was shaking his head, telling her no. I'm assuming she wanted more than a kiss but I'm not exactly an expert at these things. Maybe an hour later I heard humming in the hall outside the room. I panicked and hid behind the curtains. I looked out and saw the same guy sitting beneath the tree. A few minutes later, a figure walked across the yard. I thought it was the girl, Ethel. She wore a long antique-looking dress. And then..."

He stopped, and Sarah fought the urge to shove her hands over her ears and blot out the rest.

"Corrie," Sarah whispered.

"I saw her walk towards him. They were talking. Then she lifted her arm in the air and I saw the knife, the white handle with the red base. She stabbed him, and I panicked. I ran out of the house and into the woods. I walked for hours. I slept in an old barn in Omena, and the next morning I hitched a ride back into town."

"You saw Corrie kill my brother, and you said nothing?"

"It wasn't Corrie," he murmured, tentatively reaching for Sarah's hand. "It wasn't. And I knew it. It was this house, the evil here. If I told the police, your-sister-in-law would face life in prison. I knew what I saw, and it wasn't real. Ethel killed your brother."

Sarah took a step back and then another, clunking down the stairs to collapse on a chair in the master bedroom.

Hadn't she already known Corrie killed Sammy - Corrie's body anyhow? Why did Will's story cut so deep?

Will followed her into the room.

"Sarah, you have to make a decision. You either believe Corrie is possessed or you don't. I didn't want to tell you because you were skeptical. I understand that, but you can't be now. After everything we've learned, everything you've seen. Don't you see how close we are to ending this once and for all?"

"You should have fucking told me," she muttered.

Will hung his head. He looked troubled - guilt and defensiveness flickering across his face.

After a long silence, he nodded.

"You're right. I should have."

SARAH FOUND a seat at the back of the room. Twenty or so people occupied the other folding chairs facing the small stage where a man stood speaking, hands braced on the podium as if letting them all in on a fantastic secret.

"How can something so empty also feel owned... inhabited?" he said. "As if there are invisible beings walking among us, sitting at the cracked table, short one leg, sipping tea from the remaining half-tea cup that rests on a spider-webbed saucer. Perhaps they are trailing up and down the stairs, brushing so close. If only our senses were a shade keener, we would feel them, spin around and shout 'who's there,' only to find ourselves staring into an emptiness that is not quite empty."

The man gazed out at the small crowd of people, the dimmed overhead lights reflected in the round lenses of his glasses.

"If one opens the mind the tiniest crack, such questions may become a lifelong pursuit, a passionate investigation into the unseen world. Modern science has proved already that nothing is as it seems. I lift my finger to the light and marvel at what I see - a solid, fleshy appendage - but had I the tools to slip only the tip of a fingernail beneath a microscope, I could observe a billion cells in ecstatic dance, driven together by an energy we cannot perceive... or can we?"

He gestured toward a corner of the room.

"The rocking chair shifts of its own volition, offering a groan of protest before settling into its unnerving squeak-squeak-squeak. Somewhere in the house, laughter rings out as if a child has glimpsed a wondrous thing - their first pony, or a bubble lifting from their bath and landing on the tip of their nose. It is a sound so endearing for a moment you forget this house is empty, no rosy-cheeked toddler plays in these rooms. And with that thought, the warmth in your chest turns cold and drips like ice down your spine, pools low and deep, in your feet perhaps, because you cannot seem to move them to save your life."

Sarah held her breath, the memory of such experiences so close, she shivered.

"I have experienced true hauntings and human fabrications. Sometimes it is a vain bid for money or attention, but many times it is deeper than that. A person desperate to have their own glimpse of the unseen world validated by another. A near-impossible task, I tell you, because the energy world is ever-shifting. Rarely do you find a place where the spirits are stagnant. I might see an ethereal woman bent low in a garden, gazing into a freshly blooming daffodil, and then I might never see her again. For the rest of my life I could sit on the pavers stone, knees pulled to my chest, back aching from the effort. I could replace my vigil with another and another to ensure that eyes never left that daffodil. Time would send the flower back to her seed, but still I could sit on hardened ground, snowflakes wetting my eyelashes, and watch. Yet still I might never see her again. In all likelihood, I would not."

Somewhere near the back of the room, a small alarm tinged. The man stood up tall, squinted toward a wall clock and grinned.

"Per usual, I have gotten carried away. If you're interested to know more, you can find me online at www.mazurssecrets.com. You can also purchase my books in the store upstairs. Thank you all for attending tonight's talk. It is with gratitude, I bid you farewell."

The man offered a little bow, and the spattering of people occupying the folding chairs clapped. Sarah watched as the meager group cleared. The man stood on the little raised stage, shuffling his papers together before returning them to a brown leather case.

"Mr. Mazur?" Sarah stepped up to the stage.

The retired professor, now paranormal investigator, peered down at her.

"Good evening. I'm sorry I didn't have more time for a Q and A session. I'm on a plane in an hour and forty-five minutes."

Sarah reached out and grabbed his pant leg, as if that might prevent him leaving the room.

When he looked at her hand in alarm, she quickly pulled it away.

"Can I walk with you? Please. I drove five hours to be here."

"Interested in the paranormal, are you? Or are you a quantum physics girl? Neither here nor there." He waved a hand and winked. "Literally."

Sarah hurried to keep up. The man was tall, well over six feet, and his strides were long and purposeful. He swung his briefcase in rhythm with his step, and she quickly shifted to his other side before it bashed her in the face.

"I have a friend who's, well she's - possessed. I need your help to get rid of the spirit."

He stopped abruptly, sliding his glasses down his nose as if he expected a sardonic smile to crack her lips.

"I'm deadly serious."

She rode next to him in the cab, detailing Corrie's possession, running through the history of Kerry Manor, and concluding with the fire that wasn't there.

His eyes lit as he asked questions about the temperature of the house at various times, the sources of light, the smells.

She rushed with him into his hotel room, his suitcase open on the bed with shirts and pants and socks hanging on the backs of chairs.

"Here, grab those," he gestured at a pair of pajama pants covered in spaceships. She stuffed them into his suitcase and held it down as he forced the clasp into place.

"Grab that, will you?" he asked, gesturing at an industrial-sized black plastic toolbox with a red handle. She picked it up and nearly dropped it.

"Whoa, whoa, highly valuable, not to mention delicate equipment in there. Here, you take this." He handed her his suitcase and took the plastic box. As they hurried back down to the cab, he peppered her with questions.

"How old is Corrie? What's her body type? Is there much water near Kerry Manor?"

"Pop the trunk, will you?" Sarah called to the cab driver, carrying his suitcase to the back.

Mazur put a hand on her arm.

"No need, cabbie," Mazur called. "I'll be catching a ride with this young lady."

40

ow
Sarah

"You will?" Sarah asked Mazur, surprised. She'd been so distracted by the questions, she'd almost forgotten her original purpose.

"Yes. I am a lecturer, but first I am a scientist, an investigator, and you have laid a conundrum at my feet. I must see it through to its end."

The cab pulled away, and Sarah reached out a hand.

"Wait..." But he was gone.

"My car is still at the bookstore," she mumbled.

"Ha," Mazur laughed. "Perfect night for a walk. Brisk, yes, but my father always said to give the cold his due, or he will chase the warmth away."

As Sarah made the drive from Chicago back to Traverse City, she filled Mazur in on the complete history of Kerry Manor, as well as the mysterious chamber in the forest behind the Northern Michigan Asylum.

"It appears you live in a hotbed of paranormal activity," Mazur said, stroking his gray goatee until it formed a point. "Lots of water around there, you said?"

"Yes. Lake Michigan, and then a lot of smaller lakes as well."

"Very interesting."

"Are they aware? The person who's possessed?" Sarah asked.

Mazur looked at her sidelong and shook his head.

"I think not, not within the possession, though I have seen cases with a sort of co-mingling. I've met people possessed who had memories of what occurred during possession but no autonomy. They often described it as watching a movie or being in a dream."

Sarah nodded, a tiny bit of space forming in her clenched stomach.

Corrie didn't know she had killed Sammy.

THEY BUMPED over the pockmarked drive that cut between the asylum cottages and led to the trailhead. In the moonlight, the buildings appeared spectral, their shattered windows watchful as the car crept forward. The chatter that had been happening since they left Sarah's house abruptly ceased, and they drove through the grounds in eerie silence.

At last, Mazur broke the quiet. "They are magnificent," he murmured. "I can feel them watching us."

"Let's not go there," Will whispered. "My brain manages well enough without additional creepy commentary."

"It's all energy, young Will. Me, you, that speck of water," he pointed at the windshield. "Your fear too - it's all energy."

They hustled from the car, and Sarah let out a long, shaky breath.

"If someone sees us, we're going to get arrested," Sarah whispered, lifting Corrie's lifeless body from the backseat. An hour before, Sarah had given her a sedative in a cup of tea. She had intended to tell Corrie about the exorcism, but Mazur insisted it remain a secret. If Corrie, or more importantly Ethel, understood what they had planned, she would do anything to stop it.

Will took Corrie's legs. Mazur lifted his plastic toolbox, and they started down the wooded path.

"Here, this way," Sarah whispered. They turned and walked across a plank over a stony brook, up a hill awash in moonlight. At the top of the hill, they looked down on the strange basin of trees. Sarah saw the scrawled neon words of kids who'd visited the tree. In the darkness they looked like ancient writings, symbols and letters meant to invoke the spirits and perhaps to keep them away.

"What if he doesn't show?" Sarah asked, feeling Corrie slipping down. She huffed and readjusted her. Her sister-in-law was not a large woman, but in her unconscious state she seemed to weigh several hundred pounds.

"Have faith," Will said, though Sarah saw the trepidation reflected in his eyes.

After several more minutes, they heard something crashing through the brush. Sarah nearly dropped Corrie as she and Will backed toward a grove of trees, out of sight

Mazur stood firm, toolbox in hand, staring curiously into the darkness.

"Sarah?" The loud whisper found them.

"Ugh, thank God, it's him." She laid Corrie on the grass and hurried forward.

"Sorry to sound like an elephant pounding through the forest," Glen told her. "I got turned around back and there and had a bit of a panic. I'm not generally prone to fear, but I haven't been on these grounds in a long time."

Glen held up the key. He walked forward to a wall of brush that Sarah had not noticed moments before. She saw the puzzlement in Mazur's face as well.

The chamber door swung in. As Sarah stepped forward, Glen put a hand on her arm.

"I've got Corrie," Will said, hoisting her into his arms.

"Are you sure?"

Will nodded and huffed into the dark tunnel, Mazur following and murmuring about the energetic aliveness of the place.

"I'll stay out here until it's over," Glen told her. "Do you have everything you need?"

"Yeah, we're good. And thanks for coming, Glen. Hopefully after tonight, we won't have any reason to meet again."

Glen reached out a hand, and she shook it, walking backwards into the tunnel and offering him a final wave.

Mazur's eyes sparkled in the lamplight as he shuffled around the chamber. He touched the walls, took bits of pebbles off the floor and tucked them into a small plastic bag, which he added to his case.

Sarah pulled a clean blanket from her bag and laid it over the bed before she and Will hoisted Corrie on top.

Sarah lifted the leather straps and secured them to Corrie's legs, shaking her head as she did so.

"This feels so wrong," she murmured.

Mazur stood.

"It will be over in no time, my dear."

He placed his case on a wooden bench and removed items.

"What's that?" Will asked leaning over his shoulder.

"A diamond." Mazur held it up. "But a very special diamond, indeed. If all goes according to plan, we will summon the dark energy from Corrie's body, and we will trap it in this crystal in an endless time loop."

"How?" Will asked, stepping to the bench where Mazur had set up a variety of other instruments.

"With this," Mazur held up a laser, "I will jumble the atomic particles contained within this crystal at the exact moment the energy is slipping out of Corrie's body."

"How do we get the energy to leave Corrie's body?" Sarah asked realizing she'd never asked the most important question.

Mazur pointed to two black paddles sitting next to the toolbox.

"Defibrillators?" Will asked.

"Wait." Sarah held up her hand. "You're going to stop her heart?"

"For an instant." Mazur snapped his fingers. "The moment the heart stops, the spirit will flee, the crystal will trap it. Voila."

Sarah looked at Corrie unconscious on the bed.

~

CORRIE

I MOANED and rolled sideways but something held me firmly in place. Blinking my eyes open, I tried to make sense of the room. A stone ceiling hovered above me, orange light flickering strange shadows.

"Corrie," Sarah put a hand on my arm. Her familiar brown eyes peered down at me and I saw fear in her face.

I turned my head and noticed Will, the young man I'd met days before, and an older man with a gray beard and long gray hair secured in a ponytail. He held a large diamond in his hand.

"Am I dreaming?" I asked her. The light hurt my eyes but when I closed them, the room swam, and my stomach turned. "I might be sick."

Sarah put a cool wash cloth on my head. "If you turn your head. I've got a little container here to catch it if you throw up."

"I can't lift my arms." I told her thickly, wondering if I was strapped down or had simply lost the use of my limbs. "Am I sick?"

"Yes," Sarah murmured, smoothing my hair back. "We're here to get you better. There are leather straps on your arms and legs to keep you safe."

I gazed at her for a long time, finally craning my head down to look toward my legs. Yes, leather straps wrapped around my ankles. My head lolled to the side, and I stared at a row of funny-looking instruments on a wooden bench.

"Tell her now," Mazur said, nodding his head. "It will draw the spirit out."

"Corrie." Sarah brushed my hair off my forehead. "We're going to perform an exorcism."

I looked at their faces, the grim set of Sarah's mouth.

"This crystal has a unique ability, Corrie," the older man explained, holding up a golf-ball sized diamond. "It draws energy, in particular spirit-energy."

I blinked at the diamond, a sudden realization flooding my head.

"No, no you can't. You'll take Sammy too." I pushed against the restraints, pleading with Sarah.

"Sammy's dead, Corrie."

"No," I insisted. "I brought him back. Sammy! Sammy!" I howled his name, searching for him in the damp chamber.

~

Sarah

SARAH CLOSED HER EYES, wishing she could blot out the sound, but she couldn't. She wouldn't. She had to stay present for Corrie. Sammy would not want Sarah to abandon his wife.

"Spirit," Mazur said, stepping close to the bed. "Show yourself."

"Sarah..." She whipped around. Sammy had whispered in her ear. She'd heard it, as plain as Corrie's cries,

"Sammy?" she asked, squinting toward the dark tunnel that led out of the chamber.

Mazur snapped his fingers at Sarah. "Don't open yourself, Sarah. Stay focused, imagine a wall of impenetrable light surrounding you. You too, Will. Let nothing come through it."

Corrie's face shifted, her anguish draining out as if someone had pulled a plug in the back of her head. For several seconds she lay still, silent, eyes resting closed.

When she opened them, they looked sharp, and angry. A smile spread across her lips. She turned and locked her gaze on Sarah.

"Your brother begged for his life," she hissed, jutting her tongue between her teeth. "He stood on his knees and wept like a child."

Sarah watched Corrie and felt tears pour down her face, but she said nothing. In her mind, she imagined a bubble of light surrounding her. Let nothing in, Mazur had said.

"He suffered, it took an hour for him to die, laying there, writhing on the ground, blood seeping into the ground. 'Oh please, don't.'" Corrie spoke in a voice eerily like Sammy's. Sarah shut her eyes, unable to look a moment longer at Corrie's hateful face.

Corrie shifted her eyes away from Sarah's, locked on Will.

"When the night has come
And the land is dark
And the moon is the only light we'll see
No, I won't be afraid, no I won't be afraid
Just as long as you stand, stand by me."

Corrie sang the words, but her voice had shifted again. Sarah didn't recognize it.

She looked up to find Will, colorless, his eyes peeled open in shock.

"My little trooper," Corrie babbled. "Why did you let me die?"

Her eyes looked dark, all the color gone, huge black pupils in a sea of white.

Will shook his head.

"He held my head under," Corrie whined. "I called for you, Will. I begged for my trooper to save me."

Will clamped his hands over his ears and turned away.

"Yes," Mazur whispered. "Let it reveal itself, let it come into the light. Fear not, Will."

Will turned back to Corrie, his blotchy face wrecked with grief.

Corrie's eyes narrowed upon him.

"What do I see in those baby blue eyes? Fear? Or is it guilt?"

Corrie's words hung in the air, and then her head jerked toward Mazur.

Mazur held the diamond into the light, a dazzling prism of color.

Corrie's eyes found the diamond, studied it.

Mazur set the gem on a wooden stool. Walking back slowly, trying not to draw Corrie's eyes from the crystal. He reached over and flipped the switch on his small laser. "Avert your eyes," he shouted as a piercing red beam of light shot into the prism.

Mazur stepped up to the table, the defibrillator in his hands. "Hit it, Will."

Will flipped the switch, and Mazur pushed the paddles against Corrie's chest, shocking her.

Corrie convulsed on the bed, teeth snapping open and closed, eyes rolling back in her head. She jerked on the table so hard the leather strap on her arm broke free.

"Do it again," Sarah cried as Mazur hovered the paddles over Corrie's lifeless body.

"In three-two-one," he murmured before resting the paddles back on Corrie's chest.

Sarah looked up. Will no longer watched Corrie. His gaze had fixed on the diamond, where a swirl of black churned within the prism.

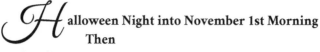

alloween Night into November 1st Morning
Then

Corrie

I HELD the knife in my hand, staring at Sammy through a pinhole. He sat beneath the oak tree, and I couldn't remember having woken up, walked outside. The moonlit lake rolled in and struck the shore.

When I opened my mouth to speak, another's voice emerged.

"I saw you," the voice hissed. The voice spoke through me and yet I had not said a word.

Sammy rubbed his bloodshot eyes, climbed up to his knees.

"Corrie? What's wrong?" he asked. He started to stand, teetered and fell back, bracing his hand against a root poking along the base of the oak tree. "I drank too much."

"I saw you," the voice snarled again through my lips, and I wanted to lift a hand to my throat, to argue with the voice, but I had no control over my arms and legs.

My body sauntered closer to Sammy, the knife slick in my wet palm.

Stop, I screamed, but no sound arose.

"You've been very bad," the voice sang, now a child's voice, a girl.

Sammy shook his head.

"That wasn't what it looked like. She was drunk. I pushed her away." He tried to stand again, but I shoved him down, hard.

I wanted to resist - force my body to obey me, but it ignored my commands.

He fell on his back, blinked through drunken eyes. For an instant, he found me, pressed within the folds of myself. He knew I was trapped.

His eyes opened wide, and then he swallowed, held up his palms.

"Ethel?"

My mouth curled upward.

"Ethel?" I crooned, mocking him. "How foolish, all of you, to believe a child holds this power."

I held up the knife, stared in horror from my place of captivity as the blade glinted in the moonlight.

"Then who?" he asked, eyes darting toward Kerry Manor.

Had everyone gone home? Would no one save us?

"Please," I groaned, and the sound slipped out.

I had regained a shred of control. I took a step away, grasping at the flimsy hold I had over my body.

"You can do it, Corrie," Sammy murmured, again pushing up onto his knees.

And then a figure, a dark blur, shot around me, whipped the knife from my hand and plunged it into Sammy's chest. The knife jerked out, slashed across his throat.

I lost the hold on my body, the scream inside me dying before it reached my lips. I struggled to reach Sammy, but my feet stood rooted in place. Shadows pulled at the edges of my vision.

Sammy fell back a final time, his words lost in the blood flooding his mouth.

The man turned, his face concealed by a black mask covering his jaw. He threw the knife at my feet, but I couldn't direct my gaze downward. His eyes looked terrified, shocked as if he hardly believed what he'd done.

He glanced at Sammy and then back at me. I wondered if he'd kill me now, but I doubted I would feel it. I had no sensation. I was merely a witness, a visitor in my own body.

The man ran into the darkness at the edge of the house.

My eyes shifted back to Sammy, to the blood pooling beneath him. I slipped deeper into myself, plunging into unfathomable darkness.

ow
Corrie

"ARE YOU GOING TO BED?" Sarah asked, flipping off the light in her kitchen, and making her way to the living room.

I sat next to the fire, Archie asleep near my feet.

"Sarah," I started, glancing toward the hall where Will slept in one of the spare rooms.

"Yeah?" Sarah sat on the rug next to me, brushing her fingers through Archie's fur. "Are you feeling okay? Mazur said you might be sick for a few days."

I searched her face, unable to shake the memory of Sammy's final moments - the memory that had emerged in the chamber as my body lay lifeless, when the dark spirit abandoned me.

"You said Will was at the Halloween party?"

She nodded.

"And he was wearing a costume?"

"A ninja costume," Sarah said slowly.

I shuddered at her confirmation though I'd already known. I

had gazed at his pale blue eyes, a lock of black hair loose across his forehead. He had believed I was possessed, would have no memory of the event. He had almost been right.

"Corrie," Sarah took my hand. "You're ice cold." She rubbed her hands on either side of my own.

"It was Will," I whispered, tears spilling over my cheeks.

"No, Corrie," Sarah shook her head. "The exorcism was my idea. It was the only way."

"Not the exorcism," I choked the words out, clutching her hands now, pleading with her to understand.

"Sarah?" his voice startled us both.

Will stood in the dark hallway.

I yanked my hand back, closed my mouth.

Sarah looked at me, frowned, and then at Will.

I saw her piecing thoughts together, beginning to understand what I had been trying to say.

"You couldn't have recognized the knife," Sarah murmured, shaking her head as if refusing to believe her own thoughts. "Not from the second floor of Kerry Manor."

Will stepped from the hall into the light of the living room. I glanced at his hand, at the switchblade emerging from his fingers.

"She was going to kill him, Sarah," he said, pointing at me. "She was standing over him with the knife."

I shook my head.

Archie woke up and lifted sleepy eyes toward Sarah. His ears spiked as if he sensed her distress.

"I wasn't, I didn't," I argued. "The spirit was controlling me, but I stopped it." My voice shook.

Will shuddered.

"So I finished it," he whispered.

"Why?" Sarah asked, her eyes a shade darker. Her hand had fallen on the heavy ceramic coffee mug I'd been drinking from.

"To prove my father's innocence." His face changed, grew defiant. "If there was another death, they'd have to question their bullshit beliefs. It was only a matter of time. Sammy was dead the day he moved his family into Kerry Manor. Don't you get that? He sacrificed his whole family for the thrill of living in a haunted house."

I touched my throat, remembered the blood pouring from the wound in Sammy's throat.

"Arghhh," I screamed, and snatched the mug from Sarah's hand chucking it across the room.

Will ducked, and the mug smashed against the wall.

He didn't fight.

As fast as he'd appeared on Halloween night, Will vanished down the dark hallway.

I raced after him, my teeth bared. A rage, previously unknown, exploded within me as I imagined ripping at his face with my fingernails.

He'd locked the bedroom door.

I shook the handle, and then reeled back, kicking the wood. The door splintered but didn't open.

"Stop," Sarah's voice rang out as I lifted a heavy planter and prepared to smash it against the door.

She looked pale, her hand held in the air, her cell phone to her ear. I listened as she rattled off her address to the police.

"Corrie, he might have a gun in there."

"Good," I shouted. "I hope you do have a gun!"

I struck the door with the planter, ignoring the splinters of wood that stabbed my knuckles. The planter cracked and smashed on the floor.

Sarah rushed down the hallway, pushing me away from the shattered ceramic.

She pinned my arms against my sides, refusing to free me as I struggled against her. My anger turned to grief. I wept, burying my face in her neck.

∾

Sarah

. . .

"I FOUND THIS IN HIS STUFF," Sarah offered, laying a shabby notebook, with a neon green skull grinning from its cover, on Detective Collins' desk.

Sarah had read the journal twice already, thumbing through the worn pages late into the night, passing it off to Corrie who cried a steady stream of tears onto the entries.

The first fifty pages of Will's journal revealed his daily activities, the money he'd spent and saved, the books he was reading. In October, the entries grew darker. He ruminated on his father's suicide, and made almost daily entries about the evil within Kerry Manor. Two days after Halloween, Will's words took a more ominous turn.

Wrong? Yes. Evil? No. In the pursuit of evil, to aid the eradication of evil, one must abandon his conscience. It's called collateral damage. I knew the day my father killed himself that I would have to take up the torch, shine a light into the shadow that looms over Kerry Manor. Now they will have to pay attention.

A more recent entry was dated only a week before he fled from Sarah's home.

Guilt follows me. I'm staying at Sarah's house - eleven days and counting. She's HIS twin. She is kind, generous, funny. She does not see me as a broken kid, a victim of his father's insanity, but as a friend, a confidante. She trusts my judgment, listens to me. I should have said NO in the arcade. I should have vanished into the world as I'd planned. Instead I'm here in their grief. It takes me back to my mother dead in the bath, my father slumped beside her, the beginning of the end of my life. She would never forgive me if she found out. But the evil is gone. I saw that black spirit trapped in the diamond. Was it worth it? Can I ever forgive myself?

"There was a time when Will had a lot of potential," Collins told Sarah flipping through the pages. "But I think Will Slater died with his parents." The detective tapped a folder with Will's name on it. "Before his mother's murder, he was an A student, a happy, inspired kid who liked to read science fiction books, and wanted to be a computer programmer. I've spoken with his friends, his teachers, people close with the family. They all said he was a different person after the murder-suicide. Not that I blame him. Tragedy shapes our lives one way or another. But no one is above the law."

"Do you think you'll find him?" Sarah asked, massaging her jaw and glancing at her watch.

She was meeting Paul Hudson, the New York Developer, to start plans on a thirty-condo ECO-community south of Traverse City.

Collins nodded.

"Eventually. He's seventeen, and he's broke. The problem will be charging him. It's Corrie's word against his, and I'm sure we both know what he'll say."

"That Corrie killed Sammy," Sarah whispered, having thought the same herself.

"Exactly. We've got the knife, but it's been wiped of prints. Theoretically, Corrie's a more reliable witness but her lack of memory would be fuel to any defense attorney's fire."

"But he's a murderer," Sarah insisted, though she heard the lack of conviction in her voice. It was true, Will had murdered her brother, but she couldn't ignore his reasons. Will was a sick kid, tormented by the murder of his mother and the suicide of his father. She considered his accusations that final night, his insistence that it was only a matter of time before Corrie - possessed by the spirit - murdered Sammy? Or perhaps it would have been Isis who died at the hands of that evil.

"He practically confesses in there," Sarah continued, nodding at the notebook.

"Practically isn't a confession."

"Yeah," Sarah sighed.

In the weeks since Will had vanished, Sarah had thought of little else. Despite her hours of contemplation, she didn't know what she wanted to become of Will Slater.

"I printed all the documents he compiled about Kerry Manor." She handed the detective the sheaf of papers. "He wasn't wrong, you know." Sarah said. "Something dark was in that house."

275

J.R. ERICKSON

"Was?" Collins cocked an eyebrow.

"Yeah. Was."

Sarah stood and cast a parting glanced at Will's name on the manila folder. She wondered if she'd ever see him again - gaze at him sitting at a defendant's table, fighting for his life.

A part of her hoped not.

EPILOGUE

*S*ix Months Later
Corrie

I STILL MISS Sammy most days, every day. It's a deep missing, in my bones, my tendons and joints. Something that ignites with strange weather - a storm is coming and then the missing rises up, an achy specter crawling inside my body, impossible to dislodge.

But I'm better, too. Better is an interesting word. It's a transitional word, a word without end, and it can reveal all manner of possibilities without promising too much.

"Mommy, look at me!" Isis waved from the beach where she'd assembled a mound of sand and stuck a plastic Frankenstein on the top. Her blonde curls had grown longer, almost to her shoulders.

I saw Sammy in her enormous smile, her twinkling brown eyes. She bit her lip and concentrated on digging a moat around the pile of sand.

"Beer for the lovely Sarah, an espresso for Corrie, and a gin and tonic for the mysterious Brook," Fletcher announced, setting all of their drinks on the glass table.

I took my espresso and sipped it, watching the ocean yawning beyond the little white fence at the edge of beach. Seagulls swooped down, calling out their angry, guttural cries, ready to fight for any food scrap they spied.

Fletcher had rented the beach house for a week and invited us down to Florida. It had been over six months since I first met him, but he'd flown to Michigan on numerous occasions for book signings. He'd helped Sarah and I do repairs on my house.

"I read your book," Brook told Fletcher, reaching into her bag to haul out a hardcover copy. "Now I need a signature."

She pushed the book to Fletcher, who smiled.

"With pleasure, though I must warn you, my signature has been compared to a toddler's. It's hardly impressive."

Brook grinned.

"It can't be any worse than my own. Plus, I'm secretly gifting these to Sarah for her birthday. Guess the jig's up."

Sarah leaned over and kissed Brook's cheek.

"Thanks, Joplin. Your bookshelves are looking rather sparse in my living room."

"Joplin?" Fletcher asked.

"Janis Joplin. Brook has that same scratchy, sexy voice. I told her she needs to sing more. The lead singer of her band is way too vanilla. She'd be better off as a pop star. I prefer Brook's grittiness."

"You've officially moved in?" I asked Brook. "I remember Sarah once claiming she would never share her bathroom. How's that working out?" I winked at Sarah.

Brook tugged on one of Sarah's blond strands of hair.

"Pretty good, actually," Sarah answered. "She buys homemade, Amish goat milk soap or some craziness, and makes her own lotion. Here, feel my hands." Sarah brushed her hand along my cheek.

"Silky smooth," I laughed.

~

I SET my glass in the sink and watched Sarah plop down next to Isis. Isis piled sand on Sarah's bare legs. Bright umbrellas and girls clad in bikinis dotted the shoreline. A couple ran into the surf, laughing and splashing each other with water.

I felt the familiar constriction in my chest at the sight of the lovers. For a moment I couldn't breathe, and I clutched the counter counting back from ten.

"Hey." Fletcher's voice startled me, and I jumped.

"I didn't mean to scare you," he said, touching my elbow.

I looked at his hand, and he abruptly took it away.

"It gets easier, Corrie," he said, gazing into my face and offering me a smile. "I know it's hard to imagine but I promise, it gets easier."

I nodded.

I wanted to believe him, and at the same time, I wanted it to never get better. When that happened, I might no longer remember Sammy's scent, or the way his voice rose several octaves when talking to Isis in his Penny the Doll voice. I couldn't bear to lose even a trace of him.

"Do you remember Lauren? I mean, really remember her?"

Fletcher leaned against the counter and looked out the window.

"My memories are different. Some of them, I think I've created. They're imaginings, but they keep me company."

I nodded.

"Thank you for inviting us, Fletcher. I had no idea how wonderful it would be to see Isis playing in the sand, not a care in the world."

"I'm grateful you came," he said, pulling two more beers from the fridge. "I've been alone for a long time. You guys are starting to feel like family."

"For me too," I murmured.

"Any luck finding Will?" Fletcher asked.

I'd told him everything days after the exorcism. Unlike most of the people in my life, I could be honest with Fletcher.

"No. The detective called me a couple weeks ago. There'd been a sighting in Utah, but who knows." I shrugged, still angry at the thought of Will. He had taken the man I'd loved most in the world. But even if he was convicted, it wouldn't bring Sammy back.

"I'm sorry, Corrie. I hope they catch him."

"I look forward to the day when I don't think about him anymore."

"How about something a little stronger than coffee?" Fletcher asked, lifting a bottle of wine.

"Sure." I took a wine glass from the cupboard and watched him pour.

"Let's go make new memories today. Yeah?" he asked. "The old will be there when the sun sets. Let your nights be for Sammy and your days for you."

I watched the red swirl in my glass, the rich, pungent aroma filling the space between us. For a second the wine looked red, bright and oozing. I closed my eyes, and when I opened them it was only wine once more.

"Yes," I said, clinking my glass against his bottle of beer. "To new memories."

~

"FLETCHER?"

He sat on the porch swing, his arm draped along the back. I swore I'd heard him talking to someone, but not only him. I'd heard a woman's voice too.

"Is someone else out here?"

He looked at me in the dark, a shaft of moonlight illuminating his startled face.

"Come and talk," he murmured at last.

When I started toward the swing, he shook his head.

"Over there."

He pointed to a chair, and I gazed for a moment longer at the empty space beside him on the swing.

"She was here," I whispered, pulling my knees to my chest and wrapping my arms around my legs. "How?"

"You know how," he said, rubbing the bridge of his nose.

"Sammy came back, but…" I thought back to the night in the chamber, the sensation of my body being ripped in two. "After the exorcism, he was gone."

Fletcher scooted to the edge of the swing.

"Lauren came back that first night. Her spirit. I saw her, felt her. I didn't see her again for months. I still don't understand it, and that's why I warned you away, Corrie. When you open this doorway, portal, whatever it is, you close the door on a new life, a new love. I didn't understand it at the time. I've never been able to get close to anyone. At any moment, Lauren might appear. I wouldn't risk her finding me in bed with someone else."

I squeezed my hands into my shins, thinking of the night Sammy had appeared at Sarah's house.

"It's not enough," Fletcher whispered. He rested his hand in the emptiness beside him. "And yet it's more than I ever hoped for. I'll never have a wife, children, a family of my own. I gave all that up the night I called her back."

"Is she here now?"

He shook his head.

"She was, just before you came out."

"I'm sorry, I didn't mean to…" I fluttered my hand in the air.

"It's okay. I can reach out for her now and she comes - not always, but most of the time. We sit and talk, mostly reminisce. I live in the past, in a tiny block of two years when we had each other and our whole lives ahead of us."

"Does she talk about death? About what comes after?"

He shook his head.

"There's no carry-over between our world and theirs. I asked once, and she said human words don't exist to explain it. I've accepted that in life, I'll never know."

I nodded and looked toward the dark beach, the silhouette of palm trees, the sparkling of the dark water lapping the shore.

"I don't want you to live the rest of your life waiting for him, Corrie."

Tears slipped over my cheeks, and I tried to agree but couldn't seem to get the words out.

"Come, sit with me now," Fletcher said, patting the space beside him. "It's nice to have a friend."

ABOUT THE AUTHOR

J.R. Erickson, also known as Jacki Riegle, is an indie author who writes stories that weave together the threads of fantasy and reality. She is the author of the Northern Michigan Asylum Series as well the urban fantasy series: Born of Shadows. The Northern Michigan Asylum Series is inspired by the real Northern Michigan Asylum, a sprawling mental institution in Traverse City, Michigan that closed in 1989. Though the setting for her novel is real, the characters and story are very much fiction.

Jacki was born and raised near Mason, Michigan, but she wandered to the north in her mid-twenties, and she has never looked back. These days, Jacki passes the time in the Traverse City area with her excavator husband, her wild little boy, and her three kitties: Floki, Beast and Mamoo.

To find out more about J.R. Erickson, visit her website at www.jrericksonauthor.com.

Read the Other Books in the Northern Michigan Asylum Series

READ MORE BY J.R. ERICKSON

The Northern Michigan Asylum Series

- Some Can See
- Calling Back the Dead
- Ashes Beneath Her
- Dead Stream Curse
- Rag Doll Bones
- Dark Omen